'This is a respectable place for a lady to be seen, is it not?

'And we are out in the open. Surely you do not require a chaperon here? I did not mean to put you to the blush.'

He sounded so concerned that Alessa laughed. 'It is a perfectly respectable place. That is entirely the problem—I am not a lady, so I should not be sitting here.'

'Nonsense!' It was said so sharply that she jumped. 'I beg your pardon, but you are quite obviously a lady. You are an officer's daughter.'

In answer Alessa swept a hand down her embroidered bodice and kicked the basket under the table. 'I do not dress like a lady, I have no pretensions to being a lady, and I work for my living. The men watching us will have come to their own conclusions about what we are discussing, and wondering about the price.'

Author Note

I have set this book on the enchanting island of Corfu. I hope that, for everyone who has visited it, reading the story will bring back as many happy memories as writing it did for me.

It is set in 1817, and for that reason you may notice that a number of major landmarks are missing. The Palace of SS Michael and George was not begun until 1819, so I have had to locate the Lord High Commissioner's Residence somewhat vaguely in Corfu Town. The fascinating Literary Society of Corfu, which preserves its intact Regency interior complete with furnishings, was not built yet.

Mon Repos, the beautiful villa begun in 1824 for the then Lord High Commissioner, Sir Frederic Adam, is also too late for this book, although my characters picnic on the beach below its location and admire the same view. I have taken one deliberate liberty with historical fact by supplying Sir Thomas Maitland, the Lord High Commissioner, with a fictitious female relative to act as his hostess. Otherwise I have done my best to stick to the facts, including the introduction by the English of cricket, which is still played on the Spianadha.

A MOST UNCONVENTIONAL COURTSHIP

Louise Allen

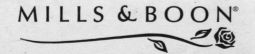

MILLS & BOON®

First published in Great Britain 2007
Harlequin Mills & Boon Limited,
Eton House, 18-24 Paradise Road, Richmond, Surrey TW9 1SR

© Melanie Hilton 2007

ISBN-13: 978 0 263 85167 0
ISBN-10:   0 263 85167 2

Set in Times Roman 10½ on 12¼ pt.
04-0407-86097

Printed and bound in Spain
by Litografia Rosés S.A., Barcelona

Louise Allen has been immersing herself in history, real and fictional, for as long as she can remember, and finds landscapes and places evoke powerful images of the past. Louise lives in Bedfordshire and works as a property manager, but spends as much time as possible with her husband at the cottage they are renovating on the north Norfolk coast, or travelling abroad. Venice, Burgundy and the Greek islands are favourite atmospheric destinations. Please visit Louise's website— www.louiseallenregency.co.uk—for the latest news!

Recent novels by the same author:

ONE NIGHT WITH A RAKE
THE EARL'S INTENDED WIFE
THE SOCIETY CATCH
A MODEL DEBUTANTE
THE MARRIAGE DEBT
MOONLIGHT AND MISTLETOE
  (in *Christmas Brides*)
THE VISCOUNT'S BETROTHAL
THE BRIDE'S SEDUCTION
NOT QUITE A LADY

Chapter One

⟨flourish⟩

Corfu Town—April 1817

Someone was trying to commit murder, and apparently they were doing it on her front step. The sounds were unmistakable. The scrape of boot leather on cobbles, the soft thud of wood on flesh, the clink of metal, the desperate, panting breaths.

Alessa sighed wearily, hefted the wicker basket up on her hip and retraced her steps around the corner to a spot where the shadows were deep and she could hide her burden out of the way of prying eyes. At eleven o'clock at night the familiar alleyways of Corfu Town were quiet, and apparently deserted, but she did not make the mistake of thinking that predators were not on the prowl.

One, at least, was in the tiny square formed by the back of the church of Saint Stefanos, Spiro's bakery and two houses, their storeys rising high so that light rarely penetrated for more than a few hours a day. Alessa stooped to slide the knife from its sheath in her short calfskin boot and melted back into the shadows.

As she slid around the corner, through the narrow passage

that opened out into the courtyard, she instinctively checked behind herself for light that might cast a shadow and betray her presence. But she was coming from darkness, and the scene before her was well lit by the lantern over Spiro's door, the dim glow from the church windows and the oil lamp Kate had set by their shared entrance as dusk began to fall.

Her view, and much of the passage, was blocked by a pair of heavy shoulders. Their owner was propped against the wall, picking his teeth. A thick aroma of fish, garlic and unwashed man floated back to Alessa, so familiar that it provoked hardly a wrinkle of her nose. Georgi, the squid fisherman, of course, always to be found on the outskirts of anything in the neighbourhood where he might profit with little risk or effort to himself.

Alessa crept soundlessly up behind him and pressed the point of the knife into the unsavoury gap between his leather waistcoat and his belt. He stiffened, jerked, then was still.

'*Hérete*, Georgi,' Alessa murmured in Greek, forcing herself to stand close enough to whisper in his ear. 'I think you need to be somewhere else just now.' She winced at the coarseness of his hissed response, pressing the flat of the blade just a fraction further into the roll of fat. 'Do you want the Lord High Commissioner's men to know exactly what you are doing when you take your *kaïki* out on a moonless night, Georgi? I think they would be very interested if someone were to tell them.'

With another muttered oath he turned and pushed past her, back into the darkness. Alessa waited a moment for the sound of his boots on the cobbles to fade, then took his place.

There were two men fighting in the tiny space. One she recognised: Big Petro, a criminal bully who made no pretence of any other occupation, was wielding a cudgel in one hand and a long-bladed knife in the other. Facing him, dodging the alternating crude blows and vicious lunges, was a complete stranger. For a moment Alessa thought he was armed with a rapier, then she realised his only weapon was a slender cane that he was using to parry the knife, while keeping it out of the way of the cudgel that would surely shatter it.

He can certainly fence, she thought critically, watching the flickering cane and the man's rapidly shifting feet, while part of her brain wrestled with the problem of what to do now she had shortened the odds for him. This was an elegant gentleman in suave evening dress. Only his discarded hat and disordered hair betrayed any loss of poise. His focus on his opponent was unwavering and, if it had been anyone else but Petro, she might have thought he had a reasonable chance of escape and could be left to his own devices. But the stocky man was a killer, and some foppish English gentleman new to the island would be no match for him.

Alessa edged round the wall towards her own front steps, her irritation at this eruption of violence on her territory, under her children's window, growing. The stranger was forcing Petro back now—or, more likely, the wily Corfiot was tactically giving ground. Then she saw why: concealed in the shadows at the foot of the central fountain the drain gaped dark, like a trap waiting for an unwary foot. She bit back her instinctive cry of warning; that was likely to trip him as surely as anything. He was going to miss it—no, she saw the edge of his foot turn wrenchingly on the stone lip and he fell to one knee. Even as he did so he raised the cane defensively, but Petro smashed down on it with the cudgel, sweeping the weapon up again to catch the falling man on the side of his head. He went down with a thud, hard against the fountain base, and Petro stepped forward with a mutter of satisfaction, the long knife gleaming in his hand.

No, this was too much. Murder, even of inconvenient and

reckless English tourists, could not be tolerated on her doorstep. Alessa reversed the knife in her hand, stepped out from the wall and brought the pommel down hard in the angle of Petro's neck and shoulder, just as she had been taught. The blow jarred up her arm like a hammer blow, but the stocky figure collapsed with a grunt, sprawled across his victim's legs—which meant that she now had *two* unconscious men cluttering up her courtyard. One of them was as likely as not to be in a killing frenzy of rage when he came to. The other one would probably yell for the Lord High Commissioner, the army, the navy and his valet—all of whose presence would be nothing but a thoroughgoing nuisance—or he would be murdered before dawn by some passing thief before he regained consciousness. And in common humanity, she could not leave him there, however much work he made.

With a sigh that reached down to her aching soles, Alessa climbed the steps, unlocked the battered wooden door and shouted up the stairs, '*Éla*, Kate! Kate, are you there?'

There was the sound of footsteps high above and a woman leaned over the banisters, her hair a tumbled red mop, her ample bosom challenging her bodice to constrain it at this angle. 'Aye, I'm here, love. Do you need a hand with the basket?'

'No, I need a hand with a man,' Alessa replied, her head cricked back to look upwards. 'Is Fred with you?'

'He is that, just finishing his supper. Is someone giving you trouble? I thought I heard a scuffle. Fred!'

'Yes, love?' A dark cropped head topping a white shirt appeared next to Kate's. 'Evening, Alessa.'

They made their way down and joined her on the step. 'Well, what have you got here?' Sergeant Fred Court walked warily out to eye the tangled heap of limbs with professional detachment.

Kate, the love of his life and Alessa's friend and neighbour, scratched her head, disturbing her coiffure even more than usual. 'Who are they Alessa? Are they dead?'

'One's an English milord, some stupid tourist who wandered in here and got set upon by Big Petro and his friend Georgi. Goodness knows whether he is dead; Petro hit him on the head hard enough. Petro will have nothing worse than a stiff neck and a headache.'

'I'd better get the Englishman back to the Lord High Commissioner's residence.' Sergeant Court scrubbed a hand over his stubbled chin. 'Let me get my jacket and I'll carry him.'

'I don't doubt you could,' Alessa said, eyeing Fred's well-displayed muscles, 'but it'll take you half an hour and it won't do him any good, being dangled upside down. Best if we bring him in, I suppose.'

'Do you want me to take a message to His Nib's place anyway?' Fred rolled Petro's limp body away with a shove from one booted foot and stooped to lift the victim.

'No, don't trouble, it will make you late. I will send Demetri in the morning. I'll just go and get the laundry basket.'

Fred was already inside and mounting the stairs with his burden slung over his shoulder by the time she got back with the basket. Kate swung it out of her hands, then grimaced at the weight. 'I thought this was the fine stuff! Are they wearing lace by the pound these days? Go and catch his head, Alessa, Fred's not being any too careful.'

Alessa climbed behind the trudging sergeant, fending the lolling head off the walls and grumbling under her breath at the spots of blood disfiguring the wooden treads that she and Kate kept scrubbed white. Fred was displaying the silent contempt most soldiers felt for their lords and masters in his handling of this one, and she could not say she blamed him. *What was the reckless idiot doing, wandering round the streets and alleyways at this time of night anyway? Getting himself into trouble and causing a nuisance for hardworking people, that's what.*

'You had better put him on the couch.' She darted forward and swept an armful of mending and a rag doll off the battered leather. 'Are the children asleep, Kate?'

'Like logs, bless them. I looked in not ten minutes ago, checked the fire's safe under the cover.' She nodded towards the dome of discoloured iron that protected the embers on the brick hearth in one corner.

Alessa rummaged in a painted chest, found a pillow and a rug and eyed the now-prone stranger. His head had stopped bleeding, but he showed no sign of recovering consciousness. 'I suppose I had better check him over, he went down with a wallop and twisted his ankle into the bargain. And, of course, Petro administered a light clubbing, just to put him to sleep before he slipped the knife in.'

'Right. Let's get on with it.' Kate rolled up her sleeves, revealing brawny forearms. 'What are you looking at, Fred?'

Her lover ducked back from the window where he had been leaning out. 'Big Petro's just staggered off, rubbing his head. I doubt he'll have a clue what happened, come tomorrow. Do you lasses need a hand? Only I need to be back at the fort soon.'

'We'll manage, thank you, love.' Kate followed him out on to the landing to make her farewells, leaving Alessa to study her involuntary guest. What made him so obviously English? His skin, for one thing—he was tanned, presumably after weeks at sea, but the colour was the gold of a fair skin, not the olive of the Mediterranean. His hair was brown, which she presumed meant he was not a Scot, whom she understood were all redheads, or Welsh, who were all dark if the regiment stationed at the Old Fort were anything to go by. His hair had streaked in the sun from its natural mid-brown to honey and toffee and autumn leaves. The tips of his improbably long lashes were gilt as they lay on his cheeks.

'Good English suit,' Kate observed, coming back into the room and fingering the cloth of the midnight-blue coat. 'He's a pretty lad.'

'Not such a lad.' Very late twenties, she supposed, probably thirty. Old enough to know better. And *pretty* was not the word either. He was too masculine for that, despite even features and an elegant frame that contrasted sharply with Fred's sturdy bulk.

'He is to me; don't forget I can give you a few years. Do you want to bandage his head or shall we get his clothes off first? I've brought one of Fred's old shirts up, it'll do as a nightshirt.'

'Thank you. Let's see the damage.' Between them the two women lifted and tugged and finally managed to reduce the stranger to his shirt and a pair of short drawers. Alessa tossed neckcloth and stockings to one side and hung the fine swallowtail coat and satin knee breeches over a chair. 'He must have been at the Lord High Commissioner's tonight.' She gestured towards the splendour of evening dress and patent leather pumps. 'Just what you want to be wearing for wandering around the back alleys.'

Kate was eyeing the long legs sprawled over the worn leather. 'I don't like the look of that ankle, and is that blood on his hip?'

'It is,' Alessa said grimly, eying the sinister stain showing through the thicknesses of both shirt and drawers on the man's left side. 'He went down against the fountain base; I just hope he hasn't broken anything. I suppose we had better get the rest of his clothes off and see.'

They eased off the drawers with more care than they had

the satin knee breeches and fine silk stockings. Alessa got the shirt over his head and caught her breath at the ugly contusion that discoloured his hip. There was a purpling bruise the size of a dinner plate, a jagged cut in its centre oozing blood.

'Hell.' Alessa went to kneel at the foot of the couch and began to manipulate his leg. The ankle was definitely sprained—it was darkening and swelling already—but the bones felt safe as she ran the ball of her thumb up the elegant length of them. There was nothing wrong with the well-shaped calf, nor the muscular thigh. Alessa began to move the leg, one hand pressed to the hip joint, feeling for any clue that a bone might be damaged.

'Very pretty.' Kate sounded as though she was contemplating a fine roast dinner. 'I don't think I've seen the like since—'

'Kate! For heaven's sake! You are virtually a married woman, I am bringing up a boy, neither of us should be carrying on over the sight of a man in the nude...' Alessa stopped focusing on his injuries and followed Kate's appreciative stare. Yes, well, perhaps a naked, fully grown stranger was a different matter to a skinny eight-year-old after all. Come to that, he was a very different matter to the numerous marble statues of classical male nudes that littered the Lord High Commissioner's residence. This was not a pre-pubescent boy. This was not even chilly white stone equipped with a fig leaf. This was a long-limbed, well-muscled, completely adult male with curling dark hair on his chest and—

'He's certainly well—'

'Don't you dare say it, Kate Street! You should be ashamed of yourself. You are a respectable woman now and I...I am attending to him purely in a medical capacity.' Alessa snatched up the discarded neckcloth and dropped it strategically over the focus of Kate's admiring scrutiny. Conscious that her cheeks were flaming, she finished her examination.

'Nothing is broken, I am sure of it, although he probably shouldn't try and stand up tomorrow. I'll put a poultice on that hip.'

Kate, who had finally finished her unabashed inspection, began to pick up the discarded linen and took it to drop into one of the pails of water that stood against the wall. 'Shall I put the other stuff to soak too?'

'Please.' Alessa kept half an eye on the delicate lingerie from the ladies of the High Commission as it dropped into the soaking-pails. It was a valuable source of income and she could not risk any damage; but Kate, despite her rough hands, was treating it with suitable care.

She fetched salves and bandages and a pad of old shirting from the cupboard and set them on the floor. The wound in itself was easy enough to dress, but wrapping a securing bandage around the slim hips was nothing short of disturbing and Alessa knew she was pink-faced before she had finished. *Get a grip on yourself, girl!* she scolded mentally, gratefully shuffling down on her knees to strap up the twisted ankle. The head wound, although angrily bruised, did not seem to call for a bandage, so she was ready by the time Kate had finished dunking the lawns and laces for their overnight soak.

It was no easier to wrestle the limp body of an unconscious man into a shirt than it was to get one off him, they discovered, and both women were panting with effort by the time the Englishman was decently covered, his head on the pillow, a rug pulled up to his chin.

'You going to be all right with him here?' Kate asked, taking a grateful gulp from the cup of watered wine that Alessa held out to her. 'I can come up and spend the night, if you like.'

'Thank you, but, no. He can't give me any trouble—not

with that ankle.' Alessa regarded the silent figure resentfully. 'He is just a thoroughgoing nuisance, and another mouth to feed for breakfast.'

'Sir Thomas will have him fetched before the day is out,' Kate forecast confidently. 'Whoever he is, the Lord High Commissioner won't want English nobs cast adrift in the back streets, that's for sure. Good night!'

Alessa slipped the peg into the door latch to secure it behind her friend and started on the evening's chores. Clean clothes for tomorrow, Demetri's slate to find, Dora's piece of lumpy sewing to flatten out so that it would not scandalise the nuns too much when they came to assess it, check there was enough wood by the hearth…

She realised she was achieving little, almost too tired to go to sleep, too restless to try. A deep sigh from the couch— which she had been carefully avoiding—made her start, but the man was still profoundly unconscious. Alessa hesitated, looking down at him. Why was he disturbing her so? He was nothing but extra work, her actions in helping him could lead her into all sorts of difficulties with some very unsavoury characters, and he combined the three things she distrusted most in the world: he was English, he was an aristocrat and he was male.

Trying to be fair, Alessa sat down and studied him. He *might* not be English, he *might* not be an aristocrat—although she doubted that, he had all the trappings of the upper classes—and not all men were bad. Just an awful lot of them. It was, taken all round, much the safest course to treat him with the deepest mistrust and to get rid of him as soon as possible.

If only she did not have this urge to touch him, to run her fingers through that intriguing tortoiseshell hair, to enjoy the feel of clean, faintly scented, healthily muscled skin under her palms. To touch those sharply sculpted lips with hers, to— Alessa clasped her hands together in her lap and stared aghast at the stranger. *Witchcraft*. Not that she believed in it, whatever old Agatha, their neighbour in the country, had told her on countless occasions. No, the only sorcery here was the effect of a handsome and mysterious stranger on a tired and bad-tempered woman who had long since given up any hope that there was a man somewhere for her.

'And even if there was, it certainly is not you,' she informed him crisply, getting to her feet and picking up the ewer of water that had been keeping warm on the hearth.

In the bedroom she stood for a moment with her back to the door, surveying the scene. At least here was normality, a very temporary peace, and her only sure source of contentment. Behind a screen Demetri lay sprawled face down on sheets rumpled as only an eight-year-old boy fighting pirates could make them. Across the room on one side of the big bed Dora was curled up with only the tip of her nose showing, her tousle of black curls spilling over the pillow.

Alessa went to touch the back of her hand to the warm cheeks of the sleeping children, beginning to loosen ties and hooks on her clothes as she did so. Undress, a lick and a promise with soap and water, then bed. Heaven. She slid in, careful not to wake Dora, and settled down to sleep, the sound of the children's breathing a soothing backdrop to her own dreamless slumber.

It must have been hours later when the yowls and shrieks of a catfight on the roof of the bakery roused her. Alessa opened one eye, listened for any sign the children had woken, and then jerked into full consciousness. She was curled around the bolster, holding it in her arms like a lover, her cheek pressed against it. She snatched it up, dealt it a firm thump with her fist and settled it back at the head of the bed where it belonged. Goodness knows what she had been dreaming about. The sooner that man was delivered back to the Residency where he belonged, the better.

Chapter Two

The bed was not moving, which meant he was on land, which was fine. That was where he was supposed to be: in bed, on land. The only problem was, he could not recall getting into his bed—or anyone else's, come to that. Chance lay very still. The thunderous headache might be one explanation for why his memories of last night were very hazy, although it argued a powerful amount of strong liquor, which he definitely could not remember. But there was someone else in the room. He had not yet engaged a servant; he was quite positive he would have had some memory of it if he had found himself female companionship; the only possibility left was a sneak thief.

Only…they were a very noisy sneak thief. There was the pad of soft leather soles on the boards, the occasional rattle of what sounded like pots, and someone—or something—was breathing like a grampus just inches from his face.

And the smell—that could not be right either. Wood smoke, herbs, soap, food. A kitchen? Chance cracked open his eyes and found himself almost nose to nose with a child. She jumped back and he realised there were two of them, brown eyed, olive skinned, with identical mops of black curls and identical expressions of intent curiosity.

'He is awake!' The small girl was squeaking with excitement.

'Shh! What did I tell you about standing so close? Now you have woken the gentleman up.' The voice from behind him was clear, flexible, and, although it was uttering a reproof, neither Chance nor the child made the mistake of thinking the speaker was angry with her. Then his befuddled brain started to work and he realised that both were speaking English. It seemed only courteous to make a corresponding effort.

'*Kaliméra,*' he offered.

It provoked an outburst of giggles from the small girl. 'He speaks Greek!'

The boy, who had been regarding him closely, produced a rapid burst of what were obviously questions.

Lord! Now what? 'Um…*Parakaló, miláte pio sigá…*'

'He doesn't speak it very well,' the boy said critically, in accented English, to the unseen woman. 'I speak English, Italian, French and Greek, all perfectly.' There was a soft laugh from the watcher. 'So, my French is not so perfect, but I am only eight and he is a man.'

Goaded, Chance retorted, 'I speak English, French, Italian, Latin and *Classical* Greek. All perfectly.' Then he smiled ruefully. *What am I doing, entering into a bragging contest with an eight-year-old?*

'Aiee! Greek like the heroes spoke it?'

'Yes. Like Paris and Hector and Achilles spoke it.' Silenced, the boy stared at him, mouth open. 'I am afraid I do not know where I am or how I got here.' *Or why I do not get up and find out, come to that. I cannot be that hung over, but nothing seems to want to work.* Chance levered himself upright on the coach and fell back gasping. 'Bloody hell!'

'Not in front of the children!' Now that *was* a reproof if ever he had heard one.

'Sorry.' He twisted round, trying to ignore the flame of pain in his hip and side and the sickening ache in his ankle. 'I was not expecting anything to hurt.'

'Do you not recall last night?' The hidden speaker came into view at last. There was a moment of crowded thought and he realised his mouth was hanging open, just like the lad's, but for a quite different reason. Chance shut it with a snap and made an effort to appear less half-witted.

'I recall nothing of it at all, and I am sure I would remember you.' He would have to be dead not to, he thought, studying the tall, slender figure standing in front of him, hands on her hips and an expression of exasperated disapproval on her oval, golden-skinned face.

A veritable Greek beauty, he thought hazily, seeing how the weight of black hair at her nape balanced the imperious carriage of her head and how the traditional island costume with its flaring black skirt and embroidered bodice showed off curves that a fashionable gown would have hidden.

Then the impact of her eyes, her quite extraordinary eyes, struck him. Greek? Surely not, not with those clear green cat's eyes, slanting under angled brows. And her accent was clear and pure. 'You are English.'

She did not answer him, but the expression that passed over her face, fleetingly, was one of barely suppressed anger. 'Children, introduce yourselves, then leave the gentleman in peace.'

'I am Dora and this is Demetri.' The little girl nudged her brother with a sharp elbow. 'Stop staring, Demi. He said he can speak like the heroes, not that he is one.' She followed this comprehensive feminine put-down with a sweet smile and skipped off, pulling the boy behind her.

'Stir the pot, Dora, please,' the tall woman called after her. 'And, Demetri, more wood. I do not think you brought much up last night, *óhi?*'

The cool green eyes turned back to regard Chance. 'You may call me *Kyria* Alessa.' He was left with the distinct feeling that, whatever *his* chores might have been on the previous evening, he had failed in them also. 'You were attacked in the courtyard below last night by two men, wrenched your ankle in the drain, fell against the fountain base and were hit on the head. Do you remember nothing of it?'

Chance levered himself up his elbows again and she pushed the pillow down behind his back, stepping back sharply the moment she had done so, as though he had an infectious disease. 'I can recall playing cards at the Residency—the Lord High Commissioner's residence,' he explained. From the impatience on her face she knew what he was talking about. 'It was my first night on the island, Sir Thomas had introduced me to various gentlemen, his usher had found me lodgings. I discovered I was more tired than I thought, so I made my excuses and started back—' He broke off, trying to recall. 'I think they offered me a footman with a torch, but the night was clear, there seemed to be lights everywhere, so I refused.'

'A foolish decision, in a strange town,' she observed crisply. 'Where are you lodging?'

'In the fort—the Paleó Frourio.'

'Then what on earth were you doing here, in the middle of the town, at almost midnight?'

The chilly criticism was beginning to penetrate both his headache and the general sense of dislocation. Chance began to feel an answering anger, and some other emotion he was too irritated to analyse, tightening inside him. 'The night air

woke me up, I thought I would explore—what is there in that
to displease you?'

Any other woman of his acquaintance would have blushed
and backed down in the face of a firm masculine reproof. Not
this one. Her eyebrows slanted up and she smiled as though
humouring a rather backward child. 'Other than the fact that
you were set upon by a pair of murderous no-goods on my
doorstep? That you blunder about a strange town flashing
your silver-headed cane and your shiny fobs and your pockets
full of coin to attract them? That this happens under my
children's window and I have to deal with the consequences?'

Chance could feel the heat over his cheekbones. 'I gather
I have your husband to thank for my rescue, *Kyria.*'

'I have no husband.'

A widow then, and a very young one. What was she?
Twenty-four? 'I am sorry for your loss. Who, then, rescued
me from these two assassins?'

'No loss.' She said it so baldly that he was shocked. It
probably showed—he was still too dazed to manage much
finesse. 'And I dealt with them.'

'You?' He felt incredulous and made no effort to hide it.

In answer the widow stooped and drew a knife from her
boot. She held it as though she knew exactly how to use it.

Chance eyed it with horrified fascination. 'You knifed
them?'

'Of course not, *I* am not a murderer. I suggested to one that
it would be better if I did not tell the Lord High Commissioner
about his smuggling, and I hit the other one.' She reversed the
knife in her hand, displaying the rounded knob of the pommel.
'He left when he regained consciousness. I thought about
having you taken back to the Residency, but it was late, I did
not know how badly you were hurt, I was tired and it was inconvenient. Demetri will take a message on his way to school.'

'Thank you.' There did not seem to be much else to say, given the turmoil of emotions that were churning around in his aching head. He felt humiliated that he had had to be rescued by a woman, angered at her attitude, physically in pain and, regrettably and damnably inconveniently, thoroughly aroused.

Angry, green-eyed witches were not within his experience; if he had been asked, he would not have thought it likely that he would find one attractive. This one, this Alessa, was reaching him at a level he did not understand. It was not just her looks, which were remarkable. There was some quality in her that made him want to say *mine*, drag her into his arms and wipe that cold, disdainful look off her face with his passion.

Which was impossible to contemplate. Chance had a strict code when dealing with women: professionals or experienced society ladies only, and this young widow with her children was quite obviously neither.

'Breakfast is ready.' It was little Dora, working away in the far reaches of the room behind him where he could not see. Chance tried again to twist round and was brought up short by the pain in his hip.

'Is anything broken?' He kept the anxiety out of his voice, but it struck cold in his belly. What were the doctors like on this island? How likely was he to end up with a limp for life, or something worse?

'Nothing.' She turned away with a swish of black skirts that gave him a glimpse of petticoats and of white stockings over the cuffs of the short leather boots. The costume was exotic and alluring, yet at the same time practical.

There was a brisk discussion in Greek going on. He gave up trying to follow it and made himself relax back against the hard pillow. Then the boy reappeared, dragging a screen, which he arranged around the couch. 'This is mine, but you can borrow it,' he announced importantly, stomping off, only to reappear with a bowl of water, towel and soap, which he set down on a chair by Chance. 'You must wash your face and hands before breakfast. Oh, yes, I almost forgot.' He thrust an earthenware vessel with a cloth over it into Chance's hands and grinned. 'You are to push it under the couch when you have finished with it.'

So, her anger with him did not extend to humiliating him by making him ask about basic needs. That was something to be thankful for. Flipping back the blanket, Chance made the discovery that perhaps he was not so grateful after all. The shirt he was wearing was not his. All his own clothes had gone, down to, and including, his drawers, and someone had bandaged his hip very professionally. Somehow he doubted that this was Demetri's work.

He made himself decent again and waited, expecting the boy to come back with some food. Instead, Alessa pushed aside the screen and put down a beaker and plate on the chair, shifting the basin on to the floor.

'Did you undress me and bandage my wounds?'

'Yes.' She smiled, laughter glimmering in her eyes. He must be showing his embarrassment. How damnably unsophisticated. 'Mrs Street, my neighbour, helped me. An unconscious man is not easy to handle.'

I will wager I was not—and aren't you finding this amusing? 'Thank you, *Kyria* Alessa. You must allow me to recompense you for your trouble,' he said smoothly. He saw from the flash of her eyes that he had succeeded in angering her. She regained her poise with the agility of a cat.

'That is not necessary. Greeks regard it as a sacred duty to care for strangers.' She stood there calmly, her hands with their long, slender fingers folded demurely across the front of her apron.

'But then…you are not Greek, are you?'

Again, she dealt with the direct question by ignoring it. 'You should tell me your name so Demetri can tell Mr Harrison where you are.'

'Harrison?' The name was vaguely familiar, then he remembered. The events of the previous twenty-four hours were beginning to come back in hazy detail. 'Oh, yes, Sir Thomas's secretary. How do you know him?'

'I know everyone at the Residency,' she replied, without explanation. 'Your name, sir? Or have you forgotten it?'

'Benedict Casper Chancellor. My friends call me Chance.'

Alessa ignored the implied invitation. 'And your title?'

'What makes you think I have one?' *And what makes her ask it as though she is suggesting I have a social disease?*

'Your clothes, your style, the way you move. You have money, you have been educated in these things. You have been bred to it in a way that simply shouts *English aristocrat.*'

'Shouts?' He was affronted, then amused, despite himself, at his own reaction.

'I should have said *whispers.* Shouting would, of course, be ungentlemanly and vulgar. So unEnglish,' she corrected herself with spurious meekness 'Am I right?'

'I am the Earl of Blakeney.'

'Well, my lord, I suggest you eat your breakfast and then rest. Demetri will ask Mr Harrison to send a carrying chair for you this afternoon.'

'I can leave on my own two feet just as soon as I have eaten and got dressed, I thank you.'

'You can try to see if you can stand, let alone walk, of course,' Alessa conceded with infuriating politeness. 'And if you can, you can hobble through the streets in satin knee breeches, a sergeant at arm's third-best shirt and no stockings and neckcloth. But I imagine Sir Thomas will have something to say about the impression of their English masters that would create with the local populace.' She picked up the washing bowl and tidied the screen away. 'I will be back when I have taken Dora to the nuns.'

There was a skirmish over a missing slate pencil, the whereabouts of Demetri's jacket, the finding of Dora's bag, and then the room was silent. The absence of all that vibrancy left an almost tangible gap.

Chance tossed back the blanket again, reached out to grip the back of the chair, and tried to get up. The effort brought the sweat out on his brow and a stream of highly coloured language from his lips. He hauled himself to his feet and found he could hop, very painfully. But that little witch was quite right; he could not get back to the Residency, nor to the Old Fort, under his own power.

He could see his evening suit neatly arrayed on a chair, the shoes tucked underneath. Sweating and swearing, he hopped across the room in search of his stockings, using the sparse pieces of furniture as crutches. She was right about that as well—he might get away with this worn old shirt, but he would be a laughing stock with bare legs under satin knee breeches.

Wooden pails were ranked against the wall, each full of water and white cloth. He fished in one, hoping to find his stockings; he could dry them at the fire. The garment he came up with was unidentifiable, but certainly not his. He hastily dropped the confection of fine lawn and thread-lace back into the water and fished in the next pail, coming up with a delightful chemise. It reminded him forcibly of a garment he had seen on his last mistress the night he had said goodbye to her.

Now there was a *proper* woman, he thought wistfully. Feminine, attentive, sweetly yielding to his every desire, and flatteringly regretful to be paid off before he set out on his Mediterranean journey. Why, then, he brooded as he straightened up painfully and scanned the rest of the room with narrowed eyes, why did *this* one arouse him far more than the very explicit memory of Jenny did?

The drip of cold water on his bare foot reminded him that he was standing, as near naked as made no difference, clutching intimate feminine apparel, in the middle of some Corfiot tenement and at the mercy of an icy and mysterious widow who might be back at any moment. Chance dropped the chemise into the pail and groped his way back to his bed. It chafed to admit it, but she was probably correct—he should rest if he wanted to escape from this nightmare.

Alessa climbed the stairs, noting gratefully that Kate had already been and scrubbed the bloodstains off the whitened wood. They took it in turns to look after the communal areas, long resigned to the feckless family on the ground floor ignoring their own obligations.

There were the muffled sounds of an altercation from behind the ground floor door. Sandro was no doubt being taken to task for lying abed instead of taking his boat out. Amid the hard-working fishermen he was a notable exception. There was silence from Kate's rooms: she would doubtless be out marketing.

Alessa counted the chimes from the church bell as she climbed. Nine o'clock. So, his lordship had not put her behind so very much. Two hours to deal with the laundry and set it to dry, then there would be her usual visitors before the town settled down to its afternoon somnolence. His lordship would probably have to contain himself in patience until three o'clock when the Residency would send servants to collect him. It often took the visiting English a while to accustom themselves to the sensible Mediterranean practise of a rest in the heat of the day, although Sir Thomas, with his experience on Malta, and in the even greater heat of Ceylon, accepted it without question.

Alessa stopped outside her own door, conscious of her heart beating faster than the climb should account for. What was she apprehensive about? He was only a man, when all was said and done. However careless he had been the night before, he had behaved with remarkable forbearance on waking up to find himself in a strange place, in considerable pain and confronted by a hostile woman and two children.

She had overreacted, she admitted to herself painfully, and she supposed she had better apologise. She laid her hand on the catch and reviewed her excuses. He had brought violence and two unsavoury characters to her front door, she had been very tired, he was an outstandingly attractive man. *Yes, well, Alessa my girl,* that *is not something you are going to explain to him, even if you could explain to yourself why that should discompose you so much.* She took a deep breath and pushed open the door.

Chapter Three

Lord Blakeney was sitting up, only now the pillows were at the other end of the couch from the way she had left him. Now he faced the body of the room. 'Have you been out of bed?' Alessa asked sharply, good intentions forgotten, her eyes skimming round the room to see what else he had been up to.

'Of course,' he drawled, watching her face. 'I read your diary, I found your money hidden behind the loose brick in the hearth and I left dirty fingerprints all over the pretty bits of nonsense in the soaking pails.'

Ignoring the first part of his sarcastic retort—she kept no diary and her savings were woven into strings of garlic hanging from the ceiling beams—Alessa latched on to the final remark. 'And what were you doing with the laundry?' she demanded.

'Looking for my stockings.'

'You can have them when they are clean and not before,' she said briskly, in much the same tone as she would use to Demetri when he tried to wheedle something from her. 'And how did you get as far as that across the room?'

'I hopped.'

It must have hurt. Alessa felt a grudging flicker of admiration at his single-mindedness. 'Is there anything you need?' She set down her marketing basket and remembered she should be making her peace with him, not lecturing. 'I am sorry if I was…short this morning, my lord. I was angry that you had led such men to my doorstep.'

'I am sorry too. You were quite correct to scold me for it. I should have known better, as you said. My only excuse is tiredness, the pleasure of being on land again after several days at sea and, ridiculous as it probably seems, the warmth of the evening.'

'Warmth, my lord?' Alessa untied her flat straw hat and hung it behind the door before reaching for her apron.

'I wish you would call me Chance.' Dark brown eyes watched her, a smile lurking behind apparent seriousness.

You, my lord, are a charmer and you know it. I should refuse. 'Very well, Chance.' She reached behind her to tie the apron strings and saw his glance flick to her breasts as the movement strained them against her embroidered lawn shirt. The glance was momentary and not accompanied by the knowing leer that she had come to expect from so many of the Englishmen who had passed through the town in the wake of the French retreat. She poured a little of the heavily resinated red wine from the north of the island into two beakers, watered both generously, then passed him one. 'You were explaining how the warm evening made you careless?'

He took the beaker with a murmur of thanks and sipped. To her secret amusement his eyebrows shot up as he tasted it, but he made no comment. His second sip was far more circumspect. 'I was behaving like a tourist,' he admitted. 'A picturesque scene, friendly, smiling faces, intriguing little streets, a balmy evening made for strolling, the stars like diamonds on black velvet. Who could have expected danger?'

Alessa raised a quizzical eyebrow and was rewarded by a self-mocking grin.

'Any idiot, of course, as you are obviously too polite to remind me. If it had been Marseilles or Naples, I would have been on my guard. As it was, I took a risk and paid for it, but not as much as I deserved, thanks to you.'

Alessa hefted the cauldron on to the fire and poured in water. Then she began to lift the individual items from the soaking pails, checking each for marks that would require further treatment. 'Is your nickname because you take risks? Or gamble, perhaps?'

'Chance?' He smiled. 'No, just a convenient shortening from when I was a child. I am really quite painfully respectable and sensible.'

Alessa felt her eyebrows rising again and hastily straightened her face. He was too good to be true: handsome, nice to children and respectable to boot.

'I can see you do not believe me.'

'If that is so, you most certainly do not fit into the mould of most of the English gentlemen of my experience.' Alessa reached down a bottle of liquefied soap and measured some out into the cauldron. He was very easy to talk to. 'No gambling?'

'Well, merely to be sociable.' That sounded almost convincing.

'No carousing late into the night?'

'I do not carouse, merely enjoy fine wines and spirits in moderation.' That was positively sanctimonious, if difficult to believe.

'No ladies of the night, glamorous mistresses, orgies?' *Aha*, that had produced a faint flush of colour on Chance's admirably sculpted cheekbones.

'Absolutely no orgies.'

Alessa shot him a slanting look, but did not comment.

After all, one did not expect a man to be a saint—or one would be severely disappointed for most, if not all, of the time, in her opinion. A gentleman who did not squander all his money at play, drink himself into a stupor and pursue the female servants with lecherous intent was, as Chance said, positively respectable.

Was he also very conventional? He was standing up surprisingly well to her frank interrogation. What would he make of her story, if she were rash enough to tell him? She took a paring knife and began to flake off slivers from a block of greenish-grey olive oil soap; the last bottle she had prepared was almost empty.

'Is there nothing useful I can do? I cannot feel comfortable lying here while you are working so hard.'

Alessa shook her head, then realised that he might as well carry on with the soap so that she could be dealing with the more soiled items while the water heated. 'Thank you. Perhaps you can do this.' She perched on the edge of the couch and handed Chance a bowl, the knife and the soap. 'I need fine slivers so it will dissolve well in water, then I bottle it up concentrated and use it with the washing. It is better with the fine fabrics than scrubbing the soap directly into them.' She realised she was explaining, as though to the children. 'I am sorry, you could not possibly want to know all that. I get into the habit of teaching.'

He took the knife and began to whittle at the block. 'Like this?'

'Perfect.' She smiled stiffly at him, suddenly self-conscious at their close proximity. She could feel the firm length of his thigh against her hip and made rather a business of standing up and twitching the cover straight. It did not help that she knew precisely what lay under that blanket.

He was so approachable that it was almost like chatting with

Fred Court, or Spiro the baker, and she had fallen into the Greek habit of openly expressed curiosity about strangers. Her neighbours would think nothing of a close interrogation about family, occupation, views, interests and wealth, but she must not allow herself to fall into the trap of undue familiarity with someone from the Lord High Commissioner's circles.

As she massaged soap directly into the dirty marks on Chance's stockings, Alessa reflected that she had allowed herself to swing from irritable suspicion to liking, and, if she was honest, attraction, in the space of barely twelve hours. And all because of a handsome profile, a pair of thoughtful brown eyes and an open manner. *Careful*, she admonished herself, tossing the stockings into the cauldron, *this man is serious temptation.*

It did not matter in the least that a man in his position was obviously not going to be interested in a laundress for anything other than dalliance. Her instincts told her he would not take advantage of her in that way; she was quite safe from Lord Blakeney. But was she safe from herself? She needed to guard her heart as carefully as she hoarded her money, if she were to remain strong and single-minded for herself and the children.

They worked in companionable silence. As the bowl of shavings grew fuller and the items of clothing followed each other into the hot water, Alessa pushed the damp hair back from her forehead and forgot to worry about her involuntary guest.

The church clock striking eleven brought her back to herself. She straightened up and looked across at Chance. There was a full bowl of soap shavings on the floor beside him and he was intently whittling the remains of the soap into some kind of animal. He looked up, caught her eye and grinned. 'Pathetic, is it not?'

Alessa scrutinised the stunted creature, called on all her

tact learned from praising juvenile attempts at art, and said encouragingly, 'It is a very nice pig.' Probably it should have one more leg, but one should not be over-critical.

'Thank you. Honesty, however, leads me to confess it is supposed to be a horse.'

'Oh, dear!' His rueful laughter was infectious and Alessa was still chuckling as she pulled out the screen from the wall and arranged it around the couch. 'I am expecting…clients. Your presence might embarrass them. Would you mind…?'

'Pretending I am not here? No, not at all.'

Alessa smiled her gratitude and hurried to set the bedroom to rights. It had only just occurred to her that, as the couch which she normally used was occupied, she would have to retreat to the rather more intimate setting of the bedroom. All her visitors would be known to her, but even so, it felt like an intrusion, and she wanted to make certain no personal items were visible.

Chance lay back against the pillows, tried to get comfortable and contemplated taking a nap. That felt like a good idea—unless he snored, which would most certainly draw attention to his presence. Presumably Alessa was expecting ladies with intimate items of apparel for laundering, or perhaps she did dressmaking alterations. A strange man would most definitely not be welcome in the midst of that feminine activity.

No one had ever complained about him snoring; perhaps he could risk dropping off. The knock at the door cut across that train of thought and he listened to Alessa's hurrying feet as she went to open it.

'*Kaliméra*, Alessa.'

'*Kaliméra*, Spiro. *Ti kánis?*'

Chance sat up abruptly. *A man?* He made himself lie back, wondering at his own reaction; presumably there were men without wives or servants who needed laundry and mending services. Alessa was speaking in rapid, colloquial Greek that he could not follow beyond the initial greeting, but something about the tone, intimate and concerned, disturbed him. And they were going towards the bedroom. The door opened, shut, and the sound of their voices became a murmur.

Chance sat up again, now unashamedly listening. The conversation had stopped and all he could hear from the bedroom was a sort of rhythmic thumping. Visions of bed heads knocking against walls, and what might cause that, came to mind only too vividly. *She is...no!* His instinctive revulsion startled him. What was the matter with him? She had every right to earn her living as she pleased. Who was he to judge? And yet he was. Which made him a hypocrite.

Perhaps he was wrong. Perhaps this Spiro had come to mend a broken bed frame. *And perhaps I'm the Duke of York*, Chance thought grimly, waiting for the thumping to stop, which it did after a few minutes. The murmur of voices reached him again and after an interval the bedroom door opened.

By twisting painfully Chance could catch a glimpse of the room through the join in the screen. Spiro was a stocky middle-aged man, just now rather flushed in the face. No tool bag. Whatever he had been doing in there, he had not been mending the furniture.

Alessa was a trifle pink in the face as well. He watched grimly through his spy hole as she smoothed back her hair. There was another knock at the door. This time it was a younger man, favouring his left leg with a slight limp. Again the greeting, the rapid flow of conversation, the firm click of the bedroom door latch.

This time there was silence from the room. Chance realised he was straining to hear and shook his head sharply in self-condemnation. He was furious with himself for listening, furious with Alessa for putting him in this position—furious that she had shattered his illusion of the hard-working, virtuous young widow.

A tap on the door was followed by it opening. Chance missed being able to see who had entered beyond a glimpse of a man's coat, but the creak of a chair seat told him that the new visitor was waiting.

How many more, for heaven's sake? The sound of a man's voice raised in a gasping cry penetrated from the bedroom. Chance lay down, put a pillow over his head and waited grimly for it all to be over.

He was roused from his uncomfortable doze by the sound of the screen being pulled back. Alessa was regarding him, hands on hips, an expression of amusement on her face. 'Whatever are you doing?'

'Attempting not to eavesdrop.' Chance hauled himself up into a sitting position.

'Eavesdrop?' Now she looked thoroughly confused. Just how brazen was this woman?

'Yes, on your business transactions.'

They stared at each other for a long moment, then Alessa asked slowly, 'Just what, *exactly*, do you think I was doing in there?'

Chance said nothing, but she could read the message in those expressive brown eyes as though he had written her a placard. He thought she was prostituting herself and he was struggling to find a way to avoid answering her direct challenge.

Alessa felt sick. Then angry, both with herself and with him. She should have realised how it would look and said something first. *But why should I have to explain myself in my own home? I did not invite him here.*

'You think I was having sex with them? For money?'

Silence. Her frank speaking must have shocked him even

more. The gentry did not like to call things by their true, ugly, names. Then something seemed to change in the atmosphere of the room.

'No. I do not think that. I do not know why I do not, in the face of what I have just seen and heard. I would be a hypocrite to condemn you for it in any case. But I do not believe it, and I am glad.' Chance's mouth twisted. 'There's a jumble of muddled thinking for you.'

'Indeed.' She stared at him, fighting her way through her own muddle of emotions. What did she feel? Embarrassment, anger, disappointment that he should have thought such a thing of her, pleasure that he rejected the evidence, complete confusion over why his opinion should matter. 'Why?' she demanded, before she could stop herself. '*Why* do you not believe it?'

That direct question had taken him aback. What were the women of his acquaintance like, that he was so surprised by direct questions, a willingness to argue? 'Because I think I know you, even after so short a time. Because I do not think you would use your own children's bedroom. Because, if it were so, I would be jealous.'

The last words were soft, as though he was speaking only to himself. Her eyes, which had been watching his hands, powerful and elegant on the homespun blanket, flew to his face. He had taken himself by surprise as much as he had her.

'*Jealous—?*'

The knock on the door cut off what would have been an impossible question. Alessa tore her eyes from Chance's and went to open it. 'Mr Williams! Please come in. I had not expected you until this afternoon, but Lord Blakeney will be delighted to see you so early, I am sure.'

The Lord High Commissioner's steward stepped into the room with the polite half-bow he always favoured Alessa with. It amused her, and puzzled her too, that he should treat one of the Commission tradespeople with such courtesy, but he was unfailingly punctilious where she was concerned. She managed an answering smile and bobbed a curtsy.

'Sir Thomas was most concerned when he received the message, *Kyria* Alessa. Although, with your skills, we knew his lordship could not be in better hands.' Alessa could almost feel the waves of curiosity emanating from the couch as the steward turned towards it. 'How do you find yourself, my lord? We are all appalled that you should have encountered such violence and criminality in a town under English governance.'

'I am justly punished for my recklessness in wandering around alone at night in an unknown town, Mr Williams, but I will recover soon enough, thanks to *Kyria* Alessa.' His smile was warm, even though she was conscious of a certain constraint in it. The things that had passed between them were too recent and too strangely intimate to leave either of them comfortable.

The two stalwart footmen who had followed Mr Williams were waiting just inside the door. 'Have you brought a change of linen for his lordship?'

Roberts, the one she knew best, hefted a portmanteau. 'All in here, *Kyria,* just like young Demetri said.'

'Perhaps you can assist his lordship to dress, in that case.' Alessa indicated the screen and drew the steward to the other end of the room, leaving Chance to the mercy of his helpers. She caught Mr Williams's eye with a smile as a grunt of pain and a hasty apology from one of the men marked his lordship's progress with his clothes. 'He is not seriously hurt,' she assured the steward. 'But I imagine both his hip and ankle are extremely painful and it would be best if you can see that he rests for several days. He will be guided by Sir Thomas's own doctor, of course.'

'Doctor Pyke will not venture to contradict your diagnosis in such matters.' Mr Williams took out his pocket book and handed Alessa a list. 'He asked if you had any of these salves in stock. If not, he would like to order them.'

Alessa opened the big press and began to lift pots down. 'All except the lemon balm ointment, which I am potting up today, and the sage wash. I will have some of that ready by the end of the week—it is still infusing. Here, it will all go in this rush bag with his lordship's clothes. His linen is still in the wash; I will bring it with the rest of the Residency laundry.'

Further muffled curses heralded Chance's emergence from behind the screen. He was hopping on one foot, the other unshod, his hand gripping Robert's shoulder. 'We can carry you, my lord,' the footman was protesting. 'Make a seat with our hands. You'll not manage the stairs otherwise.'

'I am not drunk and I am not dead,' Chance retorted grimly. 'I can manage a flight of stairs.' The look he shot Alessa was defiant, but she refused to gratify him with feminine flutterings and protestations that he take care, despite the fact that his lips were set in a thin line and he had gone white under his tan. He was a grown man, and he could take the consequences of being too proud to be carried in front of a woman.

'*Kyria*, I cannot thank you enough for what you have done for me. I apologise that you have been put to such inconvenience by my actions, and, if in my…confusion, I blundered.'

Do not go, not until you explain what you meant… The words were so clear in her mind that for one awful moment Alessa thought she had spoken them out loud. 'There is nothing to apologise for, my lord,' she said calmly. '*Xenia*, hospitality to strangers, is important to us. You may best repay it by taking care of yourself. And, Roberts…' the footman turned '…be careful with that arm.'

'I will, *Kyria*.' The man grinned. 'But it's all healed up now.'

Alessa let them all out on to the landing, but went straight back inside, leaving the door a little ajar, and waited, braced for a crash. None came, but the muttered curses rising up the stairwell added a little to her vocabulary. With a smile she closed the door and went to look out of the window down into the courtyard below. Chance was resting, one hip hitched on the edge of the fountain, apparently engaged in questioning Roberts. The footman, who was wearing a sleeveless waist-coat, unbuttoned the cuff of his shirt and began to roll up the sleeve, just as Spiro wandered out of the bakery door to see what was going on. Alessa's eyebrows rose—this was going to be interesting.

'*Kyria* Alessa's a wonder with salves,' Roberts explained in answer to Chance's enquiry as they had hopped slowly down the stairs. He bared a forearm for inspection. In the bright sunlight the tanned skin was puckered with a pink scar. 'The cook splashed me with boiling water three weeks ago—and look how she's got it to heal. Hey, Spiro, you see *Kyria* Alessa for your back, don't you?'

'*Ne.*' The stocky man nodded politely to Chance, subjecting him to the intense stare he was beginning to expect from the local people. He had seen him somewhere before. 'She fixes it good now.' The man rolled a shoulder experimentally, sending flour off his coat like snow. 'She is a tough one, Alessa. She bangs my back hard where it is all knotted and she rubs in the ointment that stings, and she tells me not to be a baby when I shout. It makes it much better.' Of course—this was Spiro of the thumping bed head.

Chance regarded his clasped hands thoughtfully. He had managed to put his foot in it comprehensively. Both feet, in fact. Alessa had probably saved his life, she had dressed his wounds with a skill that ought to have told him something, if only he'd stopped to think beyond embarrassment at the knowledge that she had stripped him to do it—and what had he done? Leapt to the worst possible conclusion about her.

And why did you do that, you bloody fool? he asked himself savagely as the footman and the baker topped each other's stories of how wonderful the *Kyria* was. *Because you want her, that's why. The first thing that enters your head when you think of her is sex.*

Mr Williams strode back into the courtyard. 'The carriage has managed to get through to the next street. Just a few more yards, my lord, if you are rested.'

'Of course, thank you.' Chance got upright, his hand on Roberts' shoulder, and looked up. Far above them Alessa was leaning out of the window, framed with scarlet flowers in pots. She was watching them, her weight on her crossed arms. He thought she was smiling. Chance lifted a hand in salute and wondered if he was going to receive a plant pot in return. Instead she lifted a hand in response and he thought he glimpsed a flash of white teeth.

A forgiving woman then, or perhaps she was just enjoying the sight of his undignified exit from the courtyard and out of her life.

Chapter Four

Alessa turned from the window, the smile still playing about her lips. A stubborn man that, but one who was at least ready to admit his faults. Even from her lofty viewpoint she could read the mingled chagrin and regret on his face.

How could she blame him for the conclusion he had jumped to? And how could she explain that leap of faith, which had led him to deny what common sense told him was the disreputable truth about her?

She pulled the cauldron well clear of the fire on its hanging bracket and began to lift out the clothes and drop them into the rinsing water. She squeezed and wrung and worked her way down the mass of flimsy feminine items until she found a pair of uncompromisingly male stockings and Chance's shirt. Her hands stilled on the fine cloth, then, with a shake of her head, she wrung them out vigorously and tossed them in with the rinsing.

When the whole lot was done and the laundry basket full, she dragged it to the foot of the stepladder that rose to a trap in the ceiling, tied the handles to the dangling rope and began to climb. As she emerged on to the flat roof high above the town she looped the rope around the pulley fixed to the parapet and hauled it up. The basket landed with a wet thump and she dragged it to the washing lines strung across the roof between the chimney stacks and the rickety vine arbour.

Doing washing was so much better in the summer, when there was hardly any smoke from the chimneys and the sun shone hot, drying and bleaching the white linens and lawns in a fraction of the time they took in the winter, dripping all over the living room.

Alessa hung out the load, then went down the ladder again for some bread and cheese and a jug of watered wine. She could spare time to rest up here in the shade and eat her luncheon. There was a shirt of Demetri's with yet another missing button she should be mending and there was her accounts book to check through. The clock chimed, the bells only just above her level up here on the roof. Yes, she could spare an hour, then perhaps she would not feel quite so much on edge.

The sound of puffing and complaining jerked her out of her reverie. Kate Street emerged on to the roof, red-cheeked from negotiating the steep ladder. 'Here you are! I met your two little ones on their way home and thought I'd drop in and see what you'd done with your handsome patient.' The sound of the children drifted up from below. They were squabbling mildly over whose fault it was that there were none of the yeast buns left from yesterday.

'Whatever time is it?' Alessa jumped to her feet and looked round. 'It must be past three!'

'Half past,' Kate confirmed, perching on the edge of the crumbling parapet with blithe unconcern for the drop beneath her. 'And you've been sitting up here daydreaming for how long exactly?'

'I haven't been daydreaming—I've been eating and mending and doing my accounts.' Alessa followed her friend's gaze to take in the full mug with the fly floating on the surface, the cheese sweating in the sun, the shirt with the thread and loose button lying on top of it, the closed ledger. *What* have *I been doing?* 'I must have dozed off, I've had a busy morning,' she amended defensively.

Kate's lips twitched, but all she said was, 'His lordship's been removed, then?'

'Yes. The Residency staff collected him. And he *is* a lord, in fact—Lord Blakeney.'

'All the better. You charged him plenty for the trouble, I hope.'

'Certainly not! How could I? One does not charge guests, however unwitting they may be.'

'Honestly, Alessa, sometimes I think you are more Greek than the Greeks.'

'I am Corfiot. What else is there for me to be?' Affronted, Alessa stalked over to peer down into the room below. 'Dora, Demetri! Have you had a good day? I will be down in a minute.'

Two round faces appeared, tipped up to smile at her. 'Very good,' Demetri announced. 'Doctor Theo says my French story was incredible.' Alessa kept her face straight.

'And your English spelling?'

'Not so incredible,' the boy admitted.

'And, Dora—are you coming up here?'

'I had a good day too. The nuns have got new kittens. May we go and play?'

'If you like. Take your hats—and stay in the courtyard.'

The thunder of feet heading for the door was all the answer she got. Kate watched over the parapet. 'No hats—but then, they are born to it.'

'Mmm,' Alessa agreed absently. Getting either of the children to wear a sunhat was a lost cause. There was so much she should be getting on with—why did she feel at such a loose end?

'So,' Kate settled herself, 'tell me all about him.'

He helped me with the soap, I asked him any number of impertinent questions, he thought I was selling myself, I can't stop thinking about him, and now I do not know what he thinks about me. And that matters somehow.

'Nothing to tell,' she responded with shrug. 'He rested, I worked on all the usual things, Mr Williams came with two footmen. His lordship was too proud to be carried downstairs and had to hop, so he is probably feeling very sore and sorry for himself as a result. But he is Dr Pyke's problem now—I do not imagine he will be finding his way back here for some arnica lotion for his bruises.'

By the afternoon of the next day Chance was feeling not the slightest inclination to go anywhere. The Lord High Commissioner had announced that he must be accommodated within the Residency so that his personal physician could attend upon him, and as a result Roberts the footman had assisted him to a comfortable wicker chair in the shaded cloister of the inner courtyard.

With a footrest, a pile of cushions, a table at his side for journals and refreshments, a walking stick and a bell, Chance allowed himself to sink into unfamiliar indolence. He lazily considered that he probably resembled nothing so much as a valetudinarian colonel taking the spa waters at some resort, but really could not summon the energy to care.

Doctor Pyke assured him it was simply the after-effects of a blow to the head. Chance thought it more likely to be the reaction to a halt to his travels for the first time in months. His every need was being taken care of, there were no decisions to be made, no unfamiliar cities or uncertain modes of transport to be negotiated, no servants to hire.

He had set out four months previously, suddenly restless at the realisation that, with the war with France at last over, this was the moment to travel before doing his duty, finding a suitable wife and settling down. Not that he had been leading a life of irresponsibility and excess. Chance was used to hearing himself described by his various fond female relatives as a paragon of domestic virtues, an ideal son and a wonderful brother.

The praise amused him, but he would have thought less of himself if he led them to believe anything different. A gentleman could manage his private life discreetly, and he had a duty to his womenfolk to care for them. He turned over the closely crossed page of one of the letters that had been awaiting him when he arrived.

Mr Tarleton is proving ideal, as I knew he would, you having chosen him. Such a tower of strength over every matter small or large! And he has explained the correspondence from the estates and sat with me when Mr Crisp came with those papers about the sale of the pasture… His mother continued with her praises of the secretary he had appointed before he set out on his tour, in addition to the battery of advisors and agents at her beck and call.

Chance did not expect Lady Blakeney to concern herself with, let alone understand, the business of the estate, nor that she, or his three sisters, should have to trouble themselves with anything beyond their domestic sphere. That was as it should be and he would never have left if he had any doubts about the arrangements.

I do hope that you are looking after yourself (three times underlined) *and wearing wool next to the skin at all times. Also that you are avoiding foreign food*—he was not quite sure how she expected him to accomplish that—*and the dreadful temptations and lures that one hears these foreign cities place before English travellers*. Chance grinned. He could recognise a sharp wherever he met one—and between Paris, Marseilles, Rome and Naples he had met plenty—and he had admired, but resisted, the lures thrown out to him by an exotic assortment of barques of frailty.

He was well aware that his family regarded him as immune from the dreadful things they heard about in London society: and that too was right and proper. It simply meant that one enjoyed oneself with discretion and without excess; ladies did not have to know about such matters.

He read to the end, noted that his own letters were reaching home in an order wildly different from that he had sent them in, and lay back, brooding on the news that Lucinda, his middle sister, aged seventeen, was apparently becoming attached to young Lakenheath. His mother found that worrying. Chance, beyond wondering why Lucy inevitably fell in love with unsuitable young men who fancied themselves as poets, was less concerned. It wouldn't last, not beyond Lucy encountering the formidable Dowager Lady Lakenheath. He decided against offering any advice to his mother on the subject.

Which left him with nothing to think about but his own affairs, which honesty forced him to acknowledge he had been avoiding doing for twenty-four hours. Specifically Alessa. Not that anyone would consider that she *was* his affair. Thank goodness. He tried to put some feeling into that pious conclusion and failed. But to his mind she was very much unfinished business, and he was damned if he knew what to do about her.

She had saved him from the consequences of his own recklessness, looked after him—and in return he had insulted her about as badly as it was possible to insult a lady. But she presented herself not as a lady, but as an herb woman who took in washing. Which meant she should be treated with the courtesy due to all her sex and recompensed financially.

Chance shifted without thinking, swore at the pain, and forced himself to confront the problem. Alessa was a mystery, and, whoever she was, she was certainly not simply a Corfiot widow running a couple of business ventures to support her children. She was English. Put her into a fashionable gown, suppress her independence of speech and she could pass, very convincingly, in society. However, she had ended up in the back streets of this town, she did not belong here and something ought to be done about it.

He shifted position again, almost welcoming the warning stab from his ankle as an antidote to the almost equally uncomfortable stab of lust that thinking about Alessa provoked. Lust and liking. The soft pad of footsteps approaching the courtyard came as a timely distraction, then he saw the sway of black skirts in the shade of the arcade opposite the one under which he was sitting, the crisp white of a full-sleeved blouse catching the sunlight, the tall, graceful figure carrying a laden basket. 'Alessa.'

He spoke as she vanished through a door without glancing in his direction, and he realised he had pitched his voice as though speaking to himself, as though she was a dream.

Alessa found the steward without difficulty. As usual at this time of day he was in his cool office facing into the courtyard. 'Good morning, *Kyria* Alessa. I have your money here for last month's laundry. Are the children well?' He counted out the coins, the familiar muddle of Venetian and French currencies, and handed her his quill with a smile. As always, Alessa made the point of producing a careful squiggle, which could be taken as a signature or a mark.

'Very well, thank you, Mr Williams. Shall I leave the salve that Dr Pyke ordered with you?'

'Certainly.' He helped her unpack the pots from under the piles of ironed laundry. 'Would you care to leave that washing with me as well?'

'Thank you, but I will take it up to the housekeeper. There are one or two things I would like to draw to her attention.'

She left him with a smile, hefting the basket that was considerably lighter now the jars had been removed. The household was quiet, only the subdued bustle of servants going about their business disturbing the calm that Sir Thomas insisted upon when he was working in his study. He did not always get it, of course, not when his widowed relative, Lady Trevick, and her two daughters were entertaining.

They must all be out, she mused. They had probably taken their new guest with them in the landau to show him the sights, and to allow him to admire the Misses Trevick to their best advantage under pretty new sunbonnets. As she rounded one corner of the cloister, making for the stairs to the housekeeper's room, she was congratulating herself upon taking such a detached, ironic, view of his lordship.

'Alessa.' It could not be anyone else. Even the one word was distinctive in that pleasant, lazily deep voice that seemed to her fancy to be the same brown as his eyes. She dropped the basket. By some miracle it landed squarely on its base and none of the pristine items fell out.

Chance was half-sitting, half-leaning, on the low inner wall that separated the shaded cloister walk from the open garden in the centre. 'I am sorry, I did not mean to startle you.'

'My lord.' He stood up, taking all the weight on his uninjured leg, and she realised he was dressed like the sailors on the English ships that crowded the harbour under the walls of the Paleó Frourio. Only none of the sailors would be dressed in loose cotton trousers and linen shirt of quite such fine cloth and pristine white finish. He was hatless, that intriguing tortoiseshell hair glinting in the sunlight.

'No harm done, my lord.' To pick up the basket and bolt, as her nerves were screaming at her to do, seemed gauche, so she left it and stood waiting, feeling at a disadvantage. Who would he be today? The man who talked so easily with her while he whittled ridiculous animals out of soap? The intense, almost angry man who had spoken of jealousy? Or was he, on his own ground, going to prove to be one of those English aristocrats she had learned to despise—cool, remote, arrogant? 'Are your injuries less painful today?'

Her eyes were regaining their focus. He did look better. The lines of strain around his eyes had gone and his colour was healthier. 'They are much improved. The hip joint is much more comfortable, although the bruise is spectacular. My ankle is still painful, but Dr Pyke promises me rapid improvement if I will only rest it.'

'Good, I am sure he is right.' His feet were bare, she realised with a shock—long-boned and elegant like his hands. It was the most sensible thing, of course, with one ankle bandaged, but somehow it seemed shockingly intimate. Alessa dragged her eyes away, trying to forget the feel of his unconscious, naked body under her hands. The look of his body... Then, until Kate had commented, she had thought of nothing but his injuries, now she could no longer maintain that indifference.

She began to back away.

'No, please do not go. Have you brought me my clothes back?'

'Yes.' Alessa nodded to the basket. 'They are in there. I should—'

'Please sit down.' He patted the wall beside him. 'Have a glass of lemonade, if you would be so kind as to fetch it.'

'It would not be proper.'

'Why ever not? I am not inviting you back to my bedroom, for goodness' sake.' His shirt was open at the neck, showing just a hint of dark hair. His trousers were belted tight, emphasising narrow hips and taut waist. Alessa was certain she was blushing.

'Because of my position here,' she said stiffly. Any minute now Mr Williams might come out of his office.

'You are not a servant. Why act like one?' The deep brown eyes were amused. It was all very well for him—he did not have to tread a careful line between familiarity and subservience in the most important household on the island.

'I provide a service here. I am expected to know my place.' She said it without rancour; she did not envy them their lives, their position.

'And I am asking you to sit down, drink lemonade with me and keep me company for a few minutes. That too would be a service. If you wish, I will pay for your time. You are not in your own home, so I can offer remuneration without risking your wrath, can I not?'

Defeated, Alessa went to fetch the tray, set it on the wall and sat down. Beside her an orange tree in a pot gave out its sweet fragrance and she bent her head to inhale.

'They flower at the same time as they fruit—I had not realised that.' Chance was twisting to reach the jug of lemonade. Alessa jumped to her feet and stretched across him to take it before he hurt his hip, realising too late that it brought them almost face to face.

She could smell the tang of limes, not from any tree, but from the cologne he was using. Seizing the jug in both hands, she moved round to pour it at a safe distance. 'Limes are the same,' she blurted out. 'And lemons. Grapefruit as well, I believe.' *I'm prattling.* She stopped talking and handed

Chance his glass carefully by the base so there was no opportunity for their fingers to touch.

Back on her perch, she raised her glass to her lips. The sweet-sharp shock of the drink jerked her back from the turmoil that his closeness and the scent of him had stirred up. It was ridiculous. She was among men every day. With some of them she massaged their naked shoulders, or dressed injuries on their bare limbs. None of them made her feel like this, as though one word would tumble her into his arms…

'Alessa, what is your real name?' He said it in so conversational a tone that she responded before she could think.

'Alexandra—' She caught herself just in time.

'And you are English? You would not answer me before.'

'My father was English.' She took another mouthful of lemonade. No one in Corfu Town except Kate knew the truth. *Why am I telling him?*

'And your mother? Was she Greek?' She found she was watching the firm, expressive lips as he spoke.

'French.' His lips parted fractionally in surprise. *He did not expect that.* 'My father met her long before he came to Greece or the islands. She died when I was very young.'

'It cannot have been easy for them, with England at war with France. But of course, she was a Royalist sympathiser, a refugee in England, I presume.'

'Oh, no. Papa picked her up—quite literally—in France in '93. Her husband had been killed in the revolt in the Vendée; Papa found her near Niort.'

'Good God, that must have caused difficulties!'

'Not really. The General was dubious, but *Maman* was so very charming and Papa was always extremely unconventional, so he shrugged and did nothing. She followed the drum, even after I was born. I have been to England a few times, but I hardly recall it. Then, when she died when I was twelve, I just stayed with him. It made his disguise more convincing. He changed my name to Alessa then.'

Alessa came out of the haze of memories conjured up by telling the story to find Chance staring at her with dawning comprehension. 'There were no British troops involved in the Vendée—not regular British troops, in any event. You are an *officer*'s daughter. An intelligence officer's daughter.'

'Yes.' There was no point in denying it now. 'We'd been in and out of the Ionian islands for years on missions, but we settled on Corfu in 1807 when the French regained it. Papa would use his boat at night to rendezvous with English agents. He had a reputation locally as a smuggler, which helped.'

'But he could have been shot! Is that what happened in the end?'

'No.' Alessa shook her head, giving herself a little time to steady her voice. Even now, it was hard to speak of. 'He took the boat out one night, out towards Albania for a meeting. A storm blew up, as they do hereabouts, very sudden, very fierce. He never came home.'

Chapter Five

She had done it now, told Chance almost everything, as much as she had confided to Kate. *Madness.*

'Alessa—' She threw up a hand as if to ward off his sympathy and he caught it in his. 'Alessa, why are you still here? Where are your family?'

'Here. Dora and Demetri are all my family now,' she said doggedly, her eyes fixed on the orange tree. It was the truth in every way that mattered.

Chance had trapped her hand, palm down between his. 'But you must have relatives in England! Aunts, uncles, cousins—*someone*, for heaven's sake. They cannot know that you are alone like this, surely?'

'Papa did not wish…after Mama died… They did not want me,' she burst out hotly. 'I do not want them.'

'And so you married a local man,' he stated. 'Was it for love or for security?' His voice was oddly flat.

Alessa turned her head away, avoiding answering. He still thought her a widow and it seemed safer that way, although she was not sure why. But she did not want to lie to him.

'Well, you are not married now,' Chance said briskly. 'Tell

me your maiden name and we will make enquiries. Sir
Thomas will have all the right reference books, we will soon
see who to contact in England.'

'No.' She made herself meet his eyes. *'No.'* The idea horrified her—could she ever make him understand? No, of
course she could not. The Earl of Blakeney would be no more
capable of that than he was of flying. He was English, an aristocrat, a man. To him home and family meant wealth,
position, security, independence. For her it meant a kind of
imprisonment in a foreign country, and the aching fear that
they—whoever *they* were—would take the children away.

To Alessa's surprise he did not persist, instead looking
down at her hand as it lay trapped between his. Chance's skin
was as tanned as hers, his fingers long and somehow expressive, even though they were still. On one hand there was a
signet ring with a dark intaglio stone.

'How soft your hand is,' he commented. 'I would have
expected all that washing to take its toll.'

'You forget, I make salves for a living. I use olive oil soap
too.' She tried to match his light tone. Anything, to keep his
mind off the subject of her parentage and her English relatives.

Chance lifted her hand. For a moment Alessa thought he
was simply going to look at it, then he raised it to his lips,
fingertips to his mouth. Startled, she did not draw back until
it was too late, and the tip of her index finger was touching
his lips. The sensation froze her where she was. It could not
be called a caress—could it? He did not move his mouth, just
held her finger against it.

Wide-eyed, Alessa stared back at him, and then he parted
his lips and bit down, so very, very gently, on the pad of her
fingertip. The effect was shocking. Not the painless pressure
of his teeth, but the effect on her body. Heat pooled in her

belly, her breath shortened, she could feel her own lips parting, but there were no words.

Then she felt the touch of his tongue against the tiny nub of flesh and she thought she would swoon. Nothing in her life had prepared her for the effect of such a simple thing. How could it be so intense? He was hardly touching her and yet she was drowning in those dark eyes. Her breasts felt heavy, aching as though they, and not a fingertip, were being ravished by the brush of his tongue. His hot, moist tongue.

What would have happened next, and how she would have reacted to it, she had no idea. The shrill yapping of Lady Trevick's lapdog startled them both out of their wordless trance. Chance released Alessa's hand and she snatched it back, jumping to her feet in the same movement, her skirts sending the beaker of lemonade to splash on the flagstones.

'Alessa.' Chance was on his feet, but she caught up the basket and ran, around the angle of the cloister, through the low arch and up two full flights of stairs before she collapsed, panting, against the housekeeper's door. Safe. She was safe, but from whom? Herself or Lord Blakeney?

'Hell and damnation.' Chance sank back onto the ledge and cursed himself for a fool, fluently, and at length, and in five languages. It did not help. He had almost got the truth from her, the full story. Then he had yielded to whatever enchantment she spun around him and touched her. And not just touched her. The feel of her hand in his, so soft and slender and strangely fragile, despite the strong tendons, had completely undone him. Instinct had made him raise it to his lips, and sheer aching desire had made him open his mouth and take her in, between his teeth, against his tongue. The images that had conjured up had aroused him almost beyond bearing—were still arousing him, come to that. When he closed his eyes all he could see were Alessa's green eyes, the winged black brows, the look of smoky passion, so responsive to him.

The sound of feminine laughter brought him to his feet. Lady Trevick and her daughters must be back, and here he was, bare-footed, dressed like a deckhand and in a state thoroughly unsuitable for conversation with well-bred virgins. Abandoning his possessions, Chance hobbled, wincing, towards the cover of one of the staircases, reaching it just in time as a party of ladies entered the courtyard from the opposite corner.

He leaned back against the wall, too shaken to attempt the stairs—wherever they led—praying that no one would come exploring. He closed his eyes and got his ragged breathing under control.

'My dear Lady Blackstone, this is delightful! I am so sorry we were out when you arrived.' It was Lady Trevick, apparently greeting a newcomer. 'We had your letter, of course, but one never knows how long the sea passage will take. Now, do come and make yourselves comfortable in the shade. It looks as though Lord Blakeney has not long gone—he had a most unfortunate accident, poor man, no doubt he is resting in his room. You will both meet him at dinner.'

Chance grimaced. If they would only settle down, he could risk tackling these stairs and make his escape.

'I will just run and get my reticule, Mama.' That sounded uncomfortably like a young, unmarried daughter to Chance. He was already having to exercise considerable caution in dealing with the Misses Trevick. They were delighted to have an eligible, single, gentleman staying and Chance had no intention of being lured on to balconies after dinner or finding himself in compromising *tête-à-têtes*. Marriage was the last thing in his plans just now. When he returned to England he would look for a wife, a nice conventional, well-trained young lady who would understand her duties and who would please his mama.

'Very well, Frances.' There was the sound of chairs being moved and the creaking of wickerwork as the ladies sat. Hurrying feet scuffed lightly along the flagstones and Chance flattened himself back into the shadows of the archway at the foot of the steps.

'Oh!' The young woman who whirled round the corner collided with Chance, took a hasty step backwards and fluttered her eyelashes. 'I am so sorry, sir.'

Chance closed his mouth, which was hanging open unflatteringly, and found his voice. 'Ma'am. The fault was entirely mine. I was catching my breath before tackling these stairs.'

Big green eyes gazed back at him from under winged dark brows. He flattened his palm against the comforting solidity of the wall and made himself focus. It was not Alessa, of course. This young woman was perhaps nineteen, her hair was brown and she was shorter, and rather plumper, than Alessa. But the eyes, the shape of her chin, those eyebrows— she could have been her sister.

'You must be Lord Blakeney,' the girl said, dimpling at him. 'May I help you? Lady Trevick said you have had an accident.'

'Frances?' The woman who swept into the now-crowded lobby could only be this girl's mother—or Alessa's. And the resemblance to Alessa was even more pronounced than with the younger girl. Chance shook his head to clear it, but he was not hallucinating. Lady Blackstone was tall and elegant. Her black hair, with sweeps of white at the temples, was dressed simply and did nothing to detract from the winged black eyebrows slanting over deep green eyes.

'This is Lord Blakeney, Mama,' Frances said, before he could speak.

'Ma'am. I am Benedict Chancellor.' Chance got his face under control and managed a reasonable sketch of a bow. 'Am I addressing Lady Blackstone?'

'You are, my lord.' The cool look swept down past his open-necked shirt and loose trousers to his bare feet. Chance decided that convoluted explanations were pointless—if she decided he was a dangerous eccentric, not to be allowed near her daughter, so much the better in his current mood. Her ladyship deigned to smile. 'I understand you are convalescing, Lord Blakeney. Perhaps we will see you at dinner. Come along, Frances.'

Left alone, Chance negotiated the stone stairs with gritted teeth, but his mind was only vaguely aware of the pain. It was surely impossible that Lady Blackstone was not related to Alessa. Which left one glaring question—what was she doing on Corfu? Could her presence there possibly be coincidence?

He found his room. Alfred, the valet put at his disposal by Sir Thomas, was folding away something in the chest of drawers. 'Your clothing has been returned by *Kyria* Alessa, my lord.'

'Let me see.' He lifted the neckcloth off the top of the pile. It smelt of rosemary and some herb he could not identify. The valet waited patiently for it to be returned. Reluctantly Chance laid it back with the stockings. 'Will you ask Sir Thomas's secretary if he could lend me a *Peerage*, Alfred?'

'Of course, my lord.' The man shut the drawer and hurried out. Chance opened it again and lifted out the neckcloth, letting the soft fabric drape over the back of his hand. *Soft, like her skin.* Fragrant. Somehow he imagined her hair would smell like this, of sunshine and herbs and the sea air.

Alessa had been snatched out of her rightful place by a father who, however courageous, seemed to have been unconventional to a fault, and now she was being kept there by her own stubbornness. He could not believe that her English relatives would not want her. There must have been some falling-out over the French wife and Alessa was refining too much on the stories her father would have told her of that.

He folded the neckcloth and was standing holding it, deep in thought, when Alfred came back into the room. Hastily, Chance stuffed it into his pocket. Carrying a lady's handkerchief around was one thing, one's own neckcloth quite another.

'The *Peerage*, my lord.' Alfred laid it on the desk. 'Dinner is at eight. Shall I have your bath fetched at seven?'

'Yes, thank you.' Chance was already thumbing through the thick, red book. He found Henry, Lord Blackstone. The name rang a faint bell: someone in the diplomatic service possibly. He ran his finger down the entry: *Married to Honoria Louisa Emily Meredith, only daughter of the late Charles Meredith, 3rd Earl Hambledon and his wife the late...*

Impatient, he flicked forward to the entry for Hambledon. Edward Charles Meredith was the fourth Earl, married and with a large family. His father had been less prolific: one daughter—Lady Blackstone, his heir Edward and one other son.

'The Honourable Alexander William Langley Meredith,' Chance read out loud. '*Alexander.*' And Alessa had said that her real name was Alexandra. He studied the entry, but it showed no marriage, no date of death. It was as though the Honourable Alexander had vanished into thin air. 'Or into the Ionian islands with his scandalous French wife and his daughter.'

Chance dressed for dinner with care. He had not got off to the best of starts with Lady Blackstone and now much depended on the degree of diplomacy he could exert.

Sir Thomas had loaned him an elegant silver-topped ebony cane and Chance considered that with its aid he managed to cut not too ridiculous a figure as he limped out on to the broad terrace overlooking the bay. It made a charming setting for the Residency dinner-party guests to assemble.

Sir Thomas, easily distinguishable amongst the gentlemen with his bald head fringed with pure white, came over to greet him. 'My dear fellow! Do you find yourself in less pain this evening? Yes? Excellent, excellent! Now, I think you have met everyone except Lady Blackstone and Miss Blackstone.'

Her ladyship acknowledged the introduction with an inclination of her head and a gracious smile. It appeared she was going to pretend that she had not already met the Earl in bare feet and shirt sleeves. Miss Blackstone giggled and blushed. Chance, who would have expected nothing else from a young lady at a fashionable London dinner party and thought nothing of it, now found himself making unfavourable comparisons with another young woman altogether.

'Are you taking a Greek tour, Lady Blackstone?' Chance enquired once Sir Thomas had taken himself off.

'My husband is on a mission in Venice—he is with the Foreign Office, you understand. Frances and I are joining him for the last few months of his time there.'

Corfu was certainly not on the obvious route from England to Venice. Chance risked some further fishing. 'How imaginative of you to take this route,' he observed. 'So many people would have gone direct to Venice—from Milan, perhaps.'

Lady Blackstone smiled tightly and Chance recognised discomfort, for all her poise. *Oh, yes, she is hiding something. Just so long as it is not a flaming affair with the Lord High Commissioner...*

'It seemed such a good opportunity. I am sure Frances will never have the chance to see the classical sights again.'

Not that there were any classical ruins to be seen on

Corfu—Chance knew that perfectly well, and so would any educated English traveller. 'Will you be staying long, Lady Blackstone?'

Again, a hesitation. 'I am not entirely certain; it seems such a charming island, and Lord Blackstone is most anxious that Frances gains the most benefit from the tour.'

Chance was saved from comment by the butler announcing dinner and the polite scrimmage while partners sorted themselves out. Charming Corfu might be, but surely Lord Blackstone would consider the artistic merits of Venice of more educational value to his daughter, and she would most certainly find far more in the way of balls and company to entertain her there.

He offered his arm to Lady Trevick. 'I was just speaking with Lady Blackstone, your daughters must be delighted to have a houseguest of their own age.'

'Indeed, yes.' Lady Trevick took the seat at the foot of the table and waited while Chance sat at her right hand. 'Although I am not sure how long they will be staying. Lady Blackstone has some family connection with the island, I believe.'

'Indeed?' Chance put polite indifference into his tone and began to discuss the plans for the new Residency that Sir Thomas had mentioned. At the other end of the table, Lady Blackstone sat next to her host, his secretary, Mr Harrison, on her left. She appeared to be asking him questions. Chance accepted a dish of salmon and tried not to think about Alessa, but the name *Alexandra Meredith* kept running through his mind.

He looked up and saw Frances Blackstone looking at him. Her hair was up in a fashionable style, her gown was silk, a pearl necklace and pearl earbobs glowed against her pale skin. What would Alessa look like in that gown, her hair coiffed, her throat circled with jewels?

He smiled at the thought and Frances blushed rosily as

she dimpled back, thinking the smile was for her. *Careful,* Chance admonished himself, *or you'll find yourself with the wrong cousin.*

It was only much later that evening, as Alfred eased the tight swallowtailed coat off his shoulders, that the import of that thought struck him and he swore softly under his breath.

'My lord?'

'Sorry, Alfred. I was thinking about women.'

'Indeed, my lord? An endlessly fascinating subject, if I might be so bold.'

'Endlessly.' One could puzzle for hours over why one was attracted to a green-eyed, mercurial widow who was anything but encouraging.

'The island is famous for its handsome women,' Alfred persisted, shaking out the coat. 'And they are most…hospitable.'

'I have encountered island hospitality.' Chance limped over to the bed and allowed the valet to gently remove his shoes.

'And, of course, there are a number of eligible young ladies, if your thoughts are turning to less er…*recreational* relationships.'

'I am not looking for a mistress on Corfu, nor for a wife, Alfred,' Chance said repressively. 'I was just thinking about women in the abstract.'

'Of course, my lord, forgive me. Does your lordship require assistance with the rest of your clothing?'

Damn his tact. Chance had no intention of confiding in his valet. 'Thank you, no. Just pass me my dressing gown.' He was not at all sure there was anything to confide about, come to that. Only Alessa was beginning to preoccupy him, and he was uncomfortably aware that he was feeling proprietorial towards her.

The solution was to solve the riddle of her birth and restore her to the bosom of the woman he was increasingly certain was her aunt. Then he would not have to think about her at all, he would have done his duty and he would have restored things to the state they should be in. As this would normally have gratified him greatly, it was a puzzle why it now seemed to give him very little peace of mind.

Chapter Six

$\infty\!\!\sim\!\!\infty$

The morning sun was warm, the sky was blue, she had no visitors for medical attention that morning, and no pile of dirty laundry waiting either. Alessa sighed happily at the prospect of an almost lazy day. There was some marketing to be done, certainly, and the basket on her arm was for that. But there was no hurry. She could stroll, chat, or find a bench in the shade of the young lime trees the French had planted to fringe the Spianadha. From that vantage point one could find endless, idle, amusement, watching the English residents as they went about their business or drank coffee in the Italian coffee shop under the arcades of the Liston.

She narrowed her eyes against the brightness as she looked at the dazzling white of the line of apartments and shops that the French had newly built. No sooner had they completed them then they had to abandon the island. There were jewellers in the shade of the arcades, a silk shop, another shop selling luxurious little trifles of no purpose at all other than to amuse the wealthy and to enchant little girls, whose noses would be pressed up against the window if they were allowed. Dora loved it, but she understood that these shops were not for people like them, people who dwelt in the back streets.

Alessa knew Signor Luigi, who kept the coffee shop. He came to her with his sore knee sometimes. He had set up shop under the French and found no problem in continuing business under the English. 'They all drink coffee, they all pay me,' he would observe with a shrug.

A number of people were already seated at the tables, men mostly, singly or in pairs, reading the newspaper or talking. Alessa kept her eyes on the road as she passed, unwilling to be ogled.

'*Signora!* Signora Alessa! *Mi scuzi...*' It was one of the waiters, running down the steps. Puzzled, Alessa turned, and the man stopped. '*Scuzi, signora, ma il signore...*'

'*Questo signore?*' But she knew. Alessa looked and saw Chance half-rising from his seat, his wide-brimmed straw hat politely doffed.

She could turn her back and walk on. Or return a stiff bow and still walk away. He could hardly hobble after her down the street. But the waiter would probably give chase in the hope of a good tip, and that would create a scene.

Conscious that she was the focus of several pairs of interested male eyes, Alessa walked back to the table. 'Good morning, my lord. Is there something I can do for you?'

'Good morning, *Kyria* Alessa. I would be glad it if you will take coffee with me.' He put the hat down on the chair beside him and waited, head slightly on one side, watching her. Alessa swallowed. There was nothing she would like more, just at this moment, than to sit and talk to Chance, she realised. And nothing could be more indiscreet than to be seen talking to one of the English gentlemen in public like this.

'I can't sit down until you do.' His smile was charming, although she suspected mischief behind it. 'I am sure it is not good for my leg, standing about,' he added, with a faint implication of pain bravely borne. Yes, definitely mischief.

Alessa perched on the edge of the chair, then, suddenly defiant, sat right back and pushed her basket under the table. *'Un succo di arancia, per favore.'* That disposed of the hovering waiter. She folded her hands in her lap and watched Chance warily from under the brim of her wide hat while he sat down again.

He looked well. He was still moving with caution, but the pain was obviously much improved and the faint lines of strain had gone from around his eyes. The autumn-leaves hair had been neatly trimmed, but the slight breeze from the sea was catching it, ruffling it out of perfect order.

'Do I pass muster, or do you think I require a tonic?'

Alessa blushed, conscious that she had been staring. 'Eat more oranges and drink less coffee and brandy,' she said tartly to cover her confusion.

'Is that all?' Chance glanced up to nod acknowledgement to the waiter bringing Alessa's orange juice, then brought his gaze back to her face. For a man with such warm brown eyes, he had the most penetrating stare. Alessa made a conscious effort not to wriggle under it. 'I had hoped I might be in need of my ankle massaging.'

Alessa narrowed her eyes at him, but did not rise to the bait. 'I should not be here—was there something in particular you wanted to talk to me about, my lord?'

He ignored the question, frowning instead at the statement. 'Why not? This is a respectable place for a lady to be seen, is it not? And we are out in the open. Surely you do not require a chaperon here? I did not mean to put you to the blush.'

He sounded so concerned that Alessa laughed. 'It is a perfectly respectable place. That is entirely the problem—I am not a lady, so I should not be sitting here.'

'Nonsense!' It was said so sharply that she jumped. 'I beg your pardon, but you are quite obviously a lady. You are an officer's daughter.'

In answer Alessa swept a hand down her embroidered bodice and kicked the marketing basket under the table. 'I do not dress like a lady, I have no pretensions to being a lady, and I work for my living. The men watching us will have come to their own conclusions about what we are discussing, and wondering about the price,' she added, slyly reminding him of his earlier error.

'*Hell.*' He swore softly and swept an inimical eye around the arcade. They were sitting at one end and she had her back to the rest of the tables, so Alessa could not see without turning round. Chance raised his voice, fractionally above conversational level. It had a carrying quality. 'If anyone here is foolish enough to be taking an interest in my business, then I am sure it will be a pleasure to discuss the matter further with them, in private.'

There was the sound of chair legs scraping and paper rustling. Alessa had a mental picture of a number of gentlemen hastily turning their chairs away or raising their newspapers protectively.

'I do not think the English have had a duel on Corfu yet,' she remarked objectively. 'They have not been here long enough. I do feel you were little harsh—after all, it is a very easy conclusion to jump to, is it not?'

'I have not apologised for that yet, have I?' His smile was rueful.

I wish it were true, I wish we could… The shocking thought jolted through her, almost wrecking her hard-won poise. 'You did not believe it, in the face of all the evidence—that was apology enough. And I should have thought how it would appear, taking those men into my bedroom. The trouble is, I am too much used to being independent, to relying on myself alone. I do not have to explain myself to anyone.'

'Nor do you have to apologise for supporting yourself. But you should not have to do so.'

'Just because I am English, just because my father was an officer, should I then give myself airs and sit around, reading novels? We would pretty soon starve, my lord!'

'Chance. No, of course I do not mean you should starve out of pride. But neither should you have to work to support yourself if we can locate your family.' He was sounding exasperated, like a teacher confronted with a pupil who was wilfully failing to understand a simple addition.

Alessa found herself frowning back. *We must look a pretty couple, glowering at each other,* she thought, with a flicker of humour. 'Why should they have the slightest interest in me, let alone wish to support me? By all accounts Papa was wild to a fault, Mama was a foreign widow two years older than him and from a country with which we were at war, and they have never set eyes on me in their lives. And I have two children from whom I will not be parted,' she added defiantly.

'Why should you be? Alessa, however unknown, they are your *family.* It is their duty, and I am sure will be their pleasure, to welcome you and look after you. It is not as though you would be imposing on some humble folks who must put money before family. Of course, you would not understand it so clearly, but the English aristocracy would not see a relative fall on hard times.' Chance was obviously in deepest earnest. For some reason he felt strongly about this. Then something he had said penetrated.

'Aristocracy? What makes you think my family is noble? What do you know about them?' *How could he know anything? I never told him my last name.* 'And why should you care, anyway?'

'I assumed,' Chance said awkwardly. He looked uncomfortable, perhaps feeling he had been tactless. 'And I care because I am an English gentleman and it is my duty to care about Englishwomen in distress.'

'Do I appear to be in distress?' Alessa bristled.

'No.' Chance quirked an eyebrow and the simmering tension between them suddenly vanished like a soap bubble in the sun. 'But you look capable of inflicting considerable distress on presumptuous men.'

Alessa bit the inside of her cheek to stop from laughing— Chance did *not* need encouragement—and took a sip of orange juice. It felt very strange to be sitting here, waited upon, in company with a gentleman. 'I do not wish to discuss my English relatives, assuming I have any,' she said mildly.

'Very well.' Chance gestured to the waiter for more drinks. 'May I ask you a personal question?'

'Yes.' Warily. 'I may not answer it.'

'I would hate to do business with you,' Chance said appreciatively. 'All I was going to ask was, do you always wear the traditional costume?'

Alessa nodded. 'Ever since we started travelling in the islands. The French, and now the English, immediately discount you if they think you are just a peasant, and it is much easier to work in.'

'Really?' Chance put one elbow on the table and cupped his chin on his palm. 'Why?'

'There's plenty of movement in the skirt and the bodice,' Alessa rolled her shoulders to demonstrate. 'And no corsets…oh!' *Think before you speak!*

Chance was gazing appreciatively at the minor disturbance caused by her shoulder-rolling. 'Mmm. I see.' He lifted his eyes back to her face. 'You blush so charmingly.'

'Thank you.' Her attempt at dignity only made his eyes

sparkle and a dimple appear at the corner of his mouth. It should have made him look less uncompromisingly male, but if anything, it made his lips seem even more kissable. Alessa shut her eyes for a moment while she got her unruly imagination under control and thought of something repressive to say. 'Of course, I do not wear the full, traditional, costume, which includes the cows' horns.'

'Cows' horns? Now you are teasing me.'

'No, truthfully. The country women braid up their hair and fix a pair of horns into it, then they drape a headscarf over the top.'

Chance reached forward and took her hand. 'Promise me something?'

'What? Not to wear horns?' She should free her hand, of course, that was only prudent and proper. Only his fingers were warm and gentle, their hold compelling, and the faint movement of the tips over her pulse was mesmerising.

'Yes—hell!' Chance dropped her hand as though it had stung him and sat back. 'Lady Trevick and her daughters!'

Sure enough, the Residency ladies were making their way along the Liston followed by a footman carrying parcels. Alessa had never met any of them, although she knew them all by sight, and, if so minded, could have described what they were wearing down to their skins. After all, she laundered all their fine linen.

'So it is.' She frowned at Chance, who was looking decidedly uncomfortable. 'Whatever is the matter?'

'Tip your hat so they can't see your face,' he hissed, leaning forward and batting the edge of the wide brim so it dipped down on the roadward side.

'What? Why?' Then it dawned on her—Chance did not want to be seen by the ladies from the Residency hob-nobbing with some laundry maid. And why would that be? Sheer snobbery? Or perhaps he was courting one of the Misses Trevick. Whatever his motives, it made his protestations about wanting to aid her complete hypocrisy.

She sat stiffly, her hands clasped together on the tabletop, willing the ladies to walk past. Chance was gazing fixedly into his coffee cup, obviously trying not to catch their eyes. A minute passed and Chance relaxed. 'Gone, thank goodness.'

'Really? And why are you so thankful for that?' Alessa jammed her hat back square on her head and got to her feet, making the metal chair legs judder noisily back on the stone terrace. 'Ashamed of being seen with a local woman? Afraid someone might jump to the wrong conclusion?' A sudden, horrible thought struck her. *If it is the wrong conclusion—can he possibly be that devious?* 'Afraid Lady Trevick would be shocked? You, my lord, are a hypocritical *bastard*.'

Alessa snatched up her basket and was down the steps into the roadway before Chance could stand. The other patrons stared without pretence at the interesting scene; Alessa swept them a haughty glare and whisked round the corner. Then she took to her heels, dodging through the crowd, down a side street, away.

Chance stood in the street, craning to see a glimpse of one wide-brimmed hat amongst so many. She had gone. *Hell and damnation.*

'*Signore?*' It was the waiter, black eyes sparkling with interest, obviously torn between his enjoyment of the little drama and worry that the customer might disappear without paying.

'Here.' Chance dug into his breeches pocket and dropped coins on the table, picked up his cane and hat and hobbled, with as much dignity as he could muster, back down the steps and into the street Alessa had vanished down.

He had acted to shield her face without thinking beyond

the fact that Lady Trevick would surely notice the resemblance between his companion and her new house guests. Alessa's reaction was completely understandable: one minute he had been assuring her that she could take her place amidst any company, that her working status was nothing to be ashamed of, and the next he had virtually bundled her under the table to hide her from his hostess.

He would have to find her and explain why—which would mean revealing his suspicions about her relationship to Lady Blackstone before he had properly thought through how he was going to manage the reconciliation. Or before he had done some very basic checking. What if Lady Blackstone's younger brother proved to be alive and well and living in England and Alessa was a far more distant connection?

Chance flattened himself against a wall to make room for a minute donkey laden with what appeared to be a pair of doors, so large that only its head and hooves were visible. He was lost already, although he supposed he had not gone so far that he could not retrace his steps. The alleyway opened into a tiny square with a church on one side and a handsome Venetian wellhead in the centre. He leaned against it to take the weight off his leg and contemplated his options.

Getting back to the Residency seemed an obvious first step—and, if it was possible, to do so without having to walk back along the Liston under the interested gaze of the coffee-shop patrons. *Coward*, he told himself, and grinned in self-mockery.

Then he could write and apologise. No, *that* would be cowardice. He would have to get Roberts to guide him and go and make his peace in person, although he suspected that this time she really would lob the geraniums at him.

Chance raised his head and scanned the rooftops, finding the domed campanile of the church of Ayios Spyridhon. He could orientate himself on that and find his way back. He walked slowly through the maze of streets, pausing now and then to examine a fragment of glorious carving set into a shop front, or another Venetian wellhead with its inevitable lions of St Mark on guard. His instinct told him to hurry, but he controlled it. Straining his partly healed ankle would be foolish and Alessa would be in no mood to speak to him now.

He reached the south door into the church and glanced up to his right. As he thought, there was the end of the Spianadha, and beyond it the road that would take him close to the bay and the Residency. People were coming and going through the church. Part of his Anglican upbringing was slightly shocked by this casual use of the space, but, as he watched from the shadows of the porch, he realised that all of them stopped for a moment, bowing or turning towards the altar and the iconostasis, behind which lay the mummified remains of Bishop Spyridhon, as if seeking approval or comfort from their saint.

Spyridhon could summon storms, they said, had done just that to save the island from the Turkish fleet, and was an all-powerful protector of the Corfiots. Chance doffed his hat and went in into the semi-darkness, rich with incense fumes, lit by myriads of candles reflected in the silver and gold frames of the sad-eyed icons.

As a man, he knew he could approach the iconostasis and pass through it into the area behind the altar where the saint lay, into the area forbidden to women, but he hesitated to do so. As he stood there a young priest, black bearded and smiling, gestured him forward and ushered him through to the ornate tomb. It seemed one could look through a glass panel in the ornate coffin and see the saint. Chance saw a glimpse of a brown, wrinkled face and stepped back, surprised at how powerful the sight was. He waited, not wanting to offend the priest by hurrying away.

Another man in western clothes was standing by the casket, his head bowed, apparently in prayer. Two townsmen entered behind him and Chance realised he would have to wait until the praying man moved to avoid jostling him.

Eventually he raised his head, crossed himself with the elaborate gesture of the Eastern Orthodox rite, and turned to the doorway. Chance followed, but, as they walked down the steps into the body of the church, his ankle gave with a sickening pang. He put out a hand to steady himself and found his arm gripped by the stranger.

'Thank you.' Even as he spoke he wondered if he was using the right language—despite his fashionable clothes the other man had a distinctly exotic air about him.

'Not at all, my dear fellow.' The accent was almost perfect, but behind it there was a richness, an undertone that was foreign. 'Have you turned your ankle? Allow me.' He crooked his elbow companionably and Chance took it, grateful to escape through the north door without falling flat on his face.

'I sprained it badly the other day.' Chance hobbled up the flight of steps to street level. 'I appreciate your help, sir, but I believe I can manage now.'

'Might I give you a lift?' The stranger raised one hand and clicked his fingers. A small open carriage driven by a man in local dress pulled up alongside them. 'I was going to the Residency, but I can drop you anywhere you choose.'

'That is my destination also. Sir Thomas has taken pity on me in my present unhandy state.' Chance climbed in and waited for his rescuer to join him before holding out his hand. 'Benedict Chancellor, Lord Blakeney.'

'Voltar Zagrede, Count—I think you would say—of Kurateni.' The accent was obvious now, rich and unfamiliar. He waved his hand vaguely towards the bay, to where the mountains of Albania loomed, so close that the sea seemed merely a lake, and they the opposite shore. 'My lands lie over there. I go to pay my respects to the Lord High Commissioner upon bringing my ship into harbour for a few days. Your navy is very suspicious.' He chuckled. 'They think all my people pirates.'

Chance settled back into the corner of the seat to look at his companion more easily. The Count was tall, lean, dark to the point of being saturnine, and exquisitely dressed in a combination of western fashion and eastern fabrics that Chance thought would cause a stir amongst the London *ton*. He was not sure he would want to adopt the wide silk cummerbund, but he coveted the Count's soft leather boots with their embossed detailing. The hilt of a knife protruded from the top of the right one.

Altogether a style to make that *poseur* Byron green with envy, Chance mused as Zagrede tossed his luxuriant, oiled, curls back from his eyes and clapped his hat on his head. The ladies at the Residency would be swooning in delight. Just so long as he did not try his charms on Alessa.

Chapter Seven

Alessa waited until the men had vanished through the north door before standing up from the shadowy bench she had been resting on and slipping out of the southern one. The child of an Anglican father and a Roman Catholic mother, she had spent her adolescence being firmly escorted to the local Greek Orthodox church by old Agatha, their nearest neighbour. As a result she was not certain which creed held her allegiance, nor whether the labels mattered so very much in any case.

Certainly she had fallen into the habit of dropping into the church and having a mental conversation with St Spyridhon. Not that she expected this to be anything but one sided, but she found it soothing and a good way of sorting out her true feelings.

Her first instinct, when she realised that Chance was prepared to be downright ungentlemanly to avoid being seen with her, was to run away. That still seemed a sensible solution, and she had somewhere to run to, which was very much to the point.

It was almost three months since they had all visited Liapades on the other side of the island. She still owned a cottage there, and a small patch of land that old Agatha cultivated alongside her own. She should check on Agatha, make sure she needed nothing and was still in good health. Besides, the children were doing well at their lessons and deserved a holiday.

All excuses, of course, but good ones, she assured herself. She was prudent in removing herself from a man who, despite all his protestations, seemed to want not her welfare, but something else entirely. What other explanation could there be? If Chance truly intended to help her find her English relatives and considered her a *lady,* why should he need to hide her from Lady Trevick? If, on the other hand, he was set on seducing her ladyship's laundry maid, that was another matter altogether. Or perhaps he was intent on courting one of the Trevick daughters and dared not be seen with another woman.

Alessa stood, blinking in the sunlight. No, if that was the case, then all he had to do was explain his interest in her to Lady Trevick and all would be well. As it was, things were far from well. Like a fool she had let herself—what?—trust was the word. Trust and like a man when every instinct should have told her to treat him with the utmost caution. And it hurt. Hurt far more than the simple realisation that she had been a fool ought to.

She settled the basket in the crook of her arm and turned off into a courtyard. As she expected, Dr Theo Stephanopolis was sitting in the shade of his vine arbour, benevolently scrutinising four small boys who were all painfully struggling with the series of sums he had chalked up on a board. Demetri was scowling ferociously, his tongue stuck out with the effort of calculation.

'*Kyria* Alessa, welcome.' The old schoolmaster stood up, and his little class scrambled to their feet, grinning in welcome and relief at the interruption to their task. 'Is all well?'

'Yes, indeed, Doctor. But I have come to collect Demetri. We must go to the cottage for a few weeks.' Behind his teacher Demetri was shoving his slate and pencil into his leather satchel, pulling faces at his less fortunate classmates. Alessa caught his mood and felt her spirits lift. But even so, not far under the surface, there was a dull ache of disappointment. Almost, she thought, as she wrote a note for him to run to the Residency with, a feeling of mourning, as though she had lost something.

'Explain that I will let them know when I am able to take laundry again,' she called after the boy as he took to his heels. 'And, Demetri—don't say where we are going!'

Chance found to his amusement that the Residency ladies were completely under the Count's spell and that even Lady Blackstone was willing to be charmed. As for Miss Blackstone, she had obviously dismissed Chance as unworthy of her lures, and was batting her eyelashes demurely at the exotic visitor.

The Misses Trevick, who felt they had prior claim on the Count, were regarding Miss Blackstone suspiciously as Chance slipped away to find the steward and request the loan of a small carriage to take him back into the town. One was not available until later in the afternoon, much to Mr Williams's chagrin at being so disobliging, for Sir Thomas had taken out the larger, and Mr Harrison the smaller.

Chance shrugged. An interval for Alessa to recover her temper would probably be a good thing, however much he wanted to rush over there and explain. He strolled back on to the terrace to find Lady Trevick explaining that the Residency was about to decamp to a summer villa at Paleokastritsa on the opposite side of the island.

'Such an enchanting spot,' she enthused. 'They say Odysseus landed there. Sir Thomas is having a proper road built across to it, as it will make an ideal summer resort.'

She spotted Chance sliding into one of the lounging chairs. 'Do say you will be fit to travel, Lord Blakeney! We are all determined on it. The old road is very rough, but you may ride where the carriage would jolt too much.'

'You are most kind, but I would not wish to intrude. I have already presumed on Sir Thomas's hospitality and your care too long.' *Damnation! The Blackstones are obviously intent on going, Alessa will be here…*

'Not at all. Do consider it, my lord, your company would be greatly valued.'

'Thank you, but I am not certain I feel up to the journey. Perhaps I could see how I am tomorrow?' It galled him to pretend weakness in front of the Count, who directed a look of manly sympathy in his direction that made him grind his teeth.

'But of course.' Lady Trevick smiled understandingly and Chance was allowed to sink back into obscurity behind his newspaper while the girls flirted chastely with Count Kurateni.

Chance was aware of something very like butterflies in his stomach as the Residency groom reined in the small gig as close to Alessa's courtyard as he could get. In order to make her understand, he was going to have to explain his theory about Lady Blackstone before he could test it any further, and he risked all the disappointment Alessa must surely feel if he proved to be wrong.

Perhaps, he wondered as he began to climb the stairs, a more resolute man would endure being misunderstood for however long it took to prove the matter. If that were the case, then he was weak. He was also, he realised as he arrived outside her door at last, ankle throbbing, dangerously close to falling in love with her.

The idea was such a shock that he stood there, stock still,

one hand raised to knock, for a good minute. If she had opened the door in his face, he was sure he would have blurted it out, there and then. But, thank God, she did not.

Chance dragged a hand through his háir as though to re-organise his brain, and knocked. Silence. He tried again, then shamelessly applied his ear to the door panels. Nothing. It seemed impossible. He had rehearsed exactly what he was going to say—up to the point when that thunderbolt had struck him just now—and it had never occurred to him for a minute that Alessa would not be at home to hear him.

He walked slowly down to the next landing. What had she said, when he had woken up? Her neighbour had helped her with his unconscious body. Mrs Reed…Roades… No, Street. He banged on the door. Again, total silence.

Reluctantly Chance descended to the entrance hall. He would be reduced to asking the steward at the Residency, and that would take some tact if the man were not to wonder at his motives.

'Kyrios?' He turned. A slatternly looking woman with a child at her side had opened the door and was looking at him.

'Kyria Alessa?'

The woman stared. 'She…go. Away. Many days.' That appeared to exhaust her stock of English.

Gone? Chance stared back, every modern Greek phrase deserting him for a moment, leaving only the classical tongue of the schoolroom. He made himself focus. *'Yati? Poo? Pote?'*

The woman shrugged, obviously unable to answer *Why, Where or When,* and apparently not much caring either. Chance found a coin in his pocket and gave it to her. *'Efharisto.' Thanks for nothing,* he thought savagely as he limped back to the gig.

Lady Trevick was seated in the shade of the veranda, her daughters dutifully at their embroidery at her side, when he returned to the Residency. 'Ma'am, I feel much more myself. If your most kind offer is still open, I would be delighted to accompany you to Paleokastritsa.' *And I will flirt with all the young ladies and get over this ridiculous feeling that one of my limbs is missing.*

Instantly he was the centre of attention. Lady Trevick was graciously pleased, her daughters clapped their hands and declared it to be delightful, and his presence the very thing to make their house party complete.

Three days later Alessa leaned on the rickety gate that separated her plot of land from her neighbour's. '*Hérete,* Agatha.'

'*Hérete.*' The old woman grinned back, revealing a few teeth and rather more gum. She was the nearest thing Alessa had to a grandmother. Opinionated, independent and fiercely dismissive of all the invaders who occupied her island, she refused to speak any of their languages and attempts to address her in Italian, French or English were met with a blank stare. Alessa suspected she understood more than she let on, but never risked the experiment.

'So.' She grounded her hoe and waddled over. 'You look better than when you arrived, child.'

'I feel better.' Alessa had thrown herself into ferocious cleaning, imagining that she was sweeping Chance out along with the dirt and the spiders. It had almost worked—she only thought of him now at night when the children were tucked up and sleeping and when the moon streamed through her unshuttered window.

It would be early for the ladies and gentlemen gathered at the Residency, she had thought, turning restlessly in her efforts to sleep. They would be dancing and flirting, or perhaps playing cards, or one of the young ladies would be displaying her skill at the piano or harp. For a while Chance had held out the lure of joining that sort of society. Almost, she had begun to weaken, think perhaps it would be better to swallow her pride, find herself an easier life. Thank heavens she had discovered his insincerity before she had let herself be drawn in.

But how could she have overestimated him so? She thought herself a good judge of character. It was finding how wrong she was about that which had plunged her into such a black mood, of course; no one liked realising that they had been a fool. Even Kate, travelling with them because Fred's unit was taking its turn to guard the Residency, had taken the hint and had not ventured to tease.

Agatha was still regarding her quizzically, her little black eyes screwed up against the morning sunlight. 'Tell me about him, then.'

'Who?'

'This man your friend talks about. The one she says strips off so well.'

'*Agatha!*'

The old woman shrugged unrepentantly. 'What good is a man to a young woman if he doesn't have the—'

'*Agatha!*' It was almost a shriek this time. 'His lordship is a very good-looking man with a healthy body. I was looking after his sprained ankle, that is all. Anything else is none of my business.'

'Pah! You need a husband, one who has lots of—' She broke off to illustrate her point with a graphic gesture that had Alessa blushing. 'You can pretend to be one of those silly cow-eyed little prudes, but how is that going to help you get him?'

'I do not *want* to get him,' Alessa protested.

'You blush over him and you say you do not want him?'

The old woman shook her head. 'Silly child. Go and sit on the beach and perhaps the spirit of Nausicaa will come and talk some sense into you.' She waved a hand in dismissal and trudged back to her weeding.

Reluctantly Alessa smiled at her black-clad back. Like many of the Corfiots, Agatha treated the characters from the island's myths in much the same way as they treated their saints. They held conversations with them, discussed their stories as though they lived just around the corner, drew cautions and morals from the tales. Who was she to criticise? She had been asking *Ayios* Spyridhon for advice herself, only the other day.

'She didn't get to keep him,' she called back across the vegetable patch.

'Who?'

'Nausicaa. Odysseus sailed away in the end.'

The only reply she got was a cackle of amused laughter. *Old terror*, she thought affectionately. Perhaps she was right though, maybe an hour on the beach would settle her mind. Alessa picked up her hat and a water bottle and began to stroll down the dusty track towards the bay. The spirits of Nausicaa and her lover were unlikely to visit her on the cobble beach; if they haunted anywhere it was the wide sandy half-moons of Paleokastritsa where the hero had drawn up his ships below her father's palace.

It was a much nicer beach, and perhaps she would take the skiff and sail round the headland with the children and Kate one day. It was too fashionable now that the Lord High Commissioner had taken it up, that was the trouble. Too many officers and their wives filling up the houses for rent, and lodgings appearing wherever an enterprising local family with one of the old Venetian houses could make the necessary improvements.

Alessa found the beach empty. The village children, including Dora and Demetri, were playing in the olive groves and the local fishermen had long gone out. Agatha's little skiff bobbed at the end of its mooring rope in the shallows and the gulls swooped and screamed overhead.

She skimmed a stone into the waves and it managed one bounce and promptly sank, which seemed to sum up her mood. Alone, with nothing to distract her, she had to admit it—she had been attracted to Chance. *No, be honest, it is more than that. You desired him, you were seduced by the idea that if you became a* lady—at this point Alessa gave a piece of driftwood a kick which hurt her toe—*he might want you too.* 'Oh, very likely,' she muttered aloud. 'Lady Blakeney. Ha!'

The tumbled dark rock of the cliffs edging the bay loomed up in front of her. Alessa turned round and began to crunch back through the pebbles at the water's edge. *I suppose I am in love with him*, she thought glumly, just as a wave curled up and sloshed over her feet.

For a long moment it was touch and go whether she sat down on a rock and had a good weep, or saw the funny side of it. Then the sun came out from behind a cloud, catching the crests of the little waves, and a wading bird flew over, piping shrilly. Alessa kicked off her wet shoes and stripped off her stockings, balancing painfully on the pebbles. It was a lovely morning, and she was free from all her responsibilities. If she sat and sulked, what would it make better? Nothing, she decided, gathering up her skirts and wading in to pull on the skiff's mooring line.

The little boat came towards her, bobbing and curtsying. Alessa tossed her shoes into the bottom, tucked the water bottle carefully upright and cast off the rope. She got badly splashed getting in.

'Out of practise,' she grumbled to herself as she settled

down and unshipped the oars. A stiff row around the headland and along the coast to the first really sandy beach would give her so much to think about that men would have no opportunity to intrude. Alessa grasped the oars, squared her shoulders and dug in.

'My lord wishes to hire a boat?' The butler at the Residency villa regarded Chance with barely concealed surprise. 'But there are only fishing boats, my lord.'

Chance turned from looking out over the twin crescents of sand that bit into each side of the causeway from the mainland to the promontory. High above, the monastery stood watch over the little village. He hitched one hip on to the balustrade.

'They are not out every day, not all of them. Could one be hired?'

'Why, yes, whatever your lordship requires. But I am not certain if I can find a crew, not today at such short notice.'

'I do not need a crew.' Chance stood up and squinted against the sun at the half-dozen boats drawn up on the sand. 'I can sail one of those myself.'

'You sail?' It was Count Kurateni, indolently opening one eye as he lay sprawled in a reclining chair in the shade.

'Nothing that small before, but, yes, I can sail.'

'I should have brought my ship around.' The Count pulled himself into a sitting position. 'It is what you would call a sloop, I believe; we could have some fun sailing her.'

'Would you care to come with me in something smaller?' Chance was beginning to enjoy Zagrede's indolent good humour.

'No, no, my friend. I would be seasick in such a cockleshell. And besides, I lie here in the hope of one of the charming young ladies coming out and allowing me to admire her. You go and get covered in fish scales and leave me the field.'

The butler appeared faintly scandalised at the banter. Chance grinned. It was partly to escape being cajoled into rides, picnics, walks on the seashore or the opportunity to read poetry in the shade of the pine trees that he thought of taking out a boat.

'Can you see what you can arrange? If it will help, I will take the boat for the duration of our stay here.'

'I will do my utmost, my lord.' The butler bowed stiffly and left.

'On his dignity,' Chance observed, making himself comfortable on the balustrade and watching as the butler, one of the Greek footmen at his heels to interpret, stalked off down the dusty road to the nearest huddle of huts.

'Old fool.' Zagrede curled a lip. 'I would stand no nonsense of that sort from my servants—you English are too lenient with your butlers and your valets. You treat them like family.'

'How do you treat yours?'

'As part of my—' the Count waved a hand in the air as he searched for the English word '—my clan. They serve me, they fight at my back, they would die for me.'

'I do not believe English upper servants expect that to be in their conditions of employment. You would make the young ladies squeak with terror if they heard such bloodcurdling things.'

'They enjoy it.' The Albanian grinned. 'They think I am exotic and romantic and they would be disappointed if I did not curdle their blood just a little. Do you think I should grow a moustache? A thin one?'

'I could not possibly advise you.' The butler was returning, a local fisherman at his heels, deep in apparent negotiations with the footman. 'It seems I have got my boat.'

'And can escape from the ladies? I wonder why that is, my friend. You are not attracted to boys, I think…'

'Certainly not!'

'You northerners, so fierce on that subject,' he said mildly. 'No, I watch you when you talk to the ladies; you like women, but you do not want any of these—and they are pretty girls, well bred, amusing. So.' He twirled his imaginary moustache. 'You have the wife to whom you are devoted? No. You have the broken heart? Ah, yes, tell me all about her.'

Chance glared at him, then found his lips twitching with amusement. The man was a rogue, and completely without shame, but he was disarmingly friendly.

'There is someone,' he admitted, as much to himself as to the Albanian. 'Whatever there was between us had hardly begun. I did something stupid. And then she vanished before I could try and put it right.'

'Here? On the island?' Zagrede shrugged before Chance could reply. 'No, I see you are going to be all English and gentlemanly and not say more. Never mind. Off you go in your smelly little boat. I will tell the young ladies that you have gone to write love poetry and then you will have to read it to them tonight.'

'If you do any such thing, I will tell them that you will sing beautiful Albanian love songs,' Chance retorted, getting to his feet as the butler reappeared, flushed and slightly dusty.

'But of course. I will do so, with pleasure.' The Count lay back in his chair and closed his eyes. 'I sing magnificently.'

Chapter Eight

The fishing boat skimmed over the water with surprising speed considering its single sail. Chance wrestled with unfamiliar ropes and knots, then settled back, enjoying the sensation of controlling something this small and agile.

The breeze was fresh, but nothing to challenge the sailor in unfamiliar waters, and he set off across the wide bay to the south. There would be a village somewhere over there where he could buy cheese, bread and olives. A flask of rough local wine perhaps.

The thought of the wine made him think of the shock of the resinated wine Alessa had given him and he lost concentration for a moment; the sail flapped and the little boat lost way. As he cursed his carelessness, and sorted out sheets and tiller, he let himself think about her properly for the first time since he had packed his bags and let himself be swept off on this trip.

You took off in a huff, he told himself severely. *You made a mistake and, just because she wasn't sitting there meekly waiting for you to come along and graciously apologise, you are just as cross with her as you are with yourself.*

That was undoubtedly true, and not very helpful. *Am I in*

love with her, or infatuated with her? How do I tell? Part of
a responsible, well-regulated, life back in England was not
getting involved in incautious flirtations or entanglements
with eligible young ladies, and maintaining one's mistresses
with proper discretion and with no illusions on either side.
Eventually one would find a suitable young lady to marry, and
that would be that, although naturally, one hoped for a loving
and affectionate relationship.

'Prig!' Chance muttered. He was finding this self-examina-
tion uncomfortable. He had an uneasy suspicion that he had
been smug, and patronising in his approach to women in the
past. Worse, that Alessa undoubtedly thought so, and could
now add *hypocrite* or *oaf* to that unflattering description.

He also realised, as the boat skimmed closer to the cliffs,
that love her or not, he most certainly was still violently attracted to her.

There was a headland; he tossed up mentally and steered
towards the open sea, only to see a tantalising little sandy cove
open up before him, the sun directly on it. It was quite
deserted, cupped in the jagged cliffs, and on an impulse he
ran the boat ashore, juddering to a halt on the sloping sand.

He was barefoot already. The sea was coolly refreshing as
he splashed ashore and found a rock to tether the boat to, and
his body was seriously overheated. Chance dragged off his
jacket, shirt and loose trousers and, naked, took a running
header into the wavelets. The shock brought him to his feet
on the gritty sand, the water lapping around his loins. 'Brrr!'
It was colder than he had thought, but the clarity was wonderful. As he looked down he could see tiny fish nibbling
around his toes, and already the sun was hot on his shoulders.

Chance plunged back in again and swam strongly towards
the headland. The waves had undercut it; here and there little
caves appeared, the water inside them a deep turquoise.

Where the rock dipped below the water there was a continuous rim of deep pinkish-purple, like a coarse, thick lace. Chance trod water, picking at it. It was like underwater lichen; perhaps the Lord High Commissioner had books in his library that would identify it.

He let himself hang on the surface, face down for as long as he could hold his breath, gazing at the sea floor, crystal clear below him. He began to kick gently, turning his face up for air before drifting on, entranced.

How deep was it? Twenty feet? More? Shoals of fish darted beneath him, rock outcrops were crowned with weed and studded with spiny urchins. He took another breath and saw that the cliff walls were turning inwards, into a deeper cave. Chance let himself drift in, no longer chilled, the heat of the sun sultry on his bare back.

A boat had sunk just inside the entrance, its ribs jutting up bare and stark. Crabs scuttled in and out of its shelter and the sudden flash of a great, sinister snake-like head betrayed the presence of a big eel.

The water's colours, in the shade and out of it, were a delight of lapis and aqua. For the first time in his life Chance wished he could paint, trap this jewel box for ever.

He stirred his feet lazily, hanging motionless above his shadow, almost forgetting to breathe.

The flash of movement at the corner of his vision made him open his mouth and choke. It was large—as large as a seal. But there were no seals. A shark?

Chance spat water and shook the hair from his eyes, scanning the surface for signs of a fin. Nothing. He dipped his face below the surface again and there it was, swimming beneath him. No shark, but a mermaid.

Long, bare, strong limbs propelled her through the water with the grace of a fish. Her hair streamed around her head like a mass of dark weed. She swooped to pick up something from the sea bed, turned and changed direction.

He knew the moment she saw his shadow. Instantly she turned on her back, eyes searching above her, then she had somersaulted, twisting away, back the way she had come.

Surely she had to come up to breathe soon? Chance dragged air into his lungs and set off in pursuit, cutting through the surface, watching ahead for the sight of the dark hair breaking the surface.

She surfaced almost in front of him, so close he had to stop in a flurry of arm strokes and spray. 'You!'

'Alessa?' Chance trod water, stunned. He could rather have believed in a mermaid. 'How did you…?'

'…know I was here?' They spoke across each other.

'I had no idea.' Her hair capped her head sleekly until it reached the water where it separated into fascinating, seaweed fronds. Her shoulders, where he could glimpse them through it, were white, her breasts, moving gently as she trod water, were whiter. 'Alessa, I am sorry—'

How did it happen? She was in his embrace, their wet, naked bodies bumping and slipping together until their arms locked and she fitted perfectly against him. The feeling of his bare flesh was warm, cold, strange against hers, but his mouth was so hot as he took her lips.

She stopped breathing, almost unaware that they were sinking straight down. She opened her eyes and found his open, watching her, so close she could see the deeper flecks, the rim of gold, the dark pupils.

Her own hair was streaming upwards like black flames, his was washed back from his face, but the kiss was too intense, too possessive for her to pull back and scan his features. Her feet touched on sand, her lungs were burning.

Alessa managed to pull back, gesture upwards and, taking Chance's hand, kicked for the surface. They reached it, both gasping, and clung together in the shadow of the cliff.

Chance captured her other wrist and turned on to his back, dragging her with him so she overlay his body. Somehow they stayed afloat, their bodies touching and floating apart. 'God, I want you.' He pulled her closer, wrapped his arms around her, took her mouth again.

And it seemed he did indeed want her; despite the cool of the water, his desire was quite unmistakable. They were sinking again. Alessa, panting from lack of air, desire and a strange, almost wild happiness, freed herself and they rose, gasping to the surface.

'Wrap your legs around my waist.' His eyes were alight with a joyful wickedness.

'Chance, we cannot, we will drown!'

'Possibly—I am willing to risk it.' He lunged for her like a dolphin, smiling, and Alessa broke away and swam hard for the shore, not knowing whether she wanted to be caught or not.

His fingers closed round her ankle as her hands began to scrabble on the shelving beach and they collapsed, tangled in each other's arms where the small waves broke into foam.

'Chance—'

He was pressing kisses into the angle of her neck, but he looked up and must have seen the doubt in her face. 'Let me explain about what happened on the Liston. I acted without thinking, I did not realise how it must seem to you.'

'You did not want to be seen with me by Lady Trevick, I quite understood.' Despite her effort at control she could hear her voice shaking. There was a trace of sun freckles across his cheekbones and his hair was dark with water. She just wanted to kiss him and not have to think, but the desire was draining out of her as the water ran down her back.

'No, you do not. I did not want her to see *you* at all, not yet, whoever you were with. Not until I had made some more enquiries. Alessa—' he sat up, pulling her with him, the water lapping around their waists '—I think I have found your aunt and she is staying at the Residency. You look so much like her, anyone would see it. I wanted to speak to her first, not startle both of you with the news.'

'My *aunt*?' That was too much to take in. But he had not been ashamed to be seen with her, and he had not been pretending a concern he did not feel out of a cynical desire to seduce her—that she *could* understand. 'I thought you had been…that you were…'

'I guessed that must be what you thought as soon as you had run away. I came back once I found my way to the Residency and could borrow a carriage. But you had gone.'

'But why are you here?' The water evaporating off her skin was bringing it out in goose bumps. Alessa shivered.

'Sir Thomas and his family and house guests have all moved to a villa in Paleokastritsa. I came too, and borrowed a boat. It is in the next bay. But you are shivering.' He pulled her to her feet and Alessa let him, still too shaken to be modest, hardly aware of their nakedness as anything other than natural.

'You are so beautiful.' One hand rested on the curve of her flank, the other skimmed down, over the swell of her breast, down the slim waist to the gentle curve of her belly. 'So…' His gaze sharpened, focused, then rose slowly to meet her eyes. Alessa felt herself begin to blush as the look brought her to awareness.

'Alessa, you have never carried two children.'

'No, of course not.' She stared at him, perplexed, then she realised what he meant. 'Oh! You thought Dora and Demetri are mine? For heaven's sake, Chance! How old do you think I am? They are seven and eight. I am twenty four.'

'Yes, I guessed that.' He sounded shaken.

'So you think I was married at sixteen?' Alessa marched over to the pile of her clothes on a rock and scrambled into a camisole and petticoat. They clung unpleasantly to her salt-wet skin, but at least they covered her. She spun round and found Chance was still standing at the water's edge, hands on hips, staring at her. She tried very hard not to stare back. He was so beautiful. More than beautiful—desirable, tempting. Wickedly tempting. She made herself focus on the still-purple bruise on his hip.

'I am not very good about children's ages,' he confessed. 'I have no nephews or nieces. And *have* you ever been married?'

'No.' Alessa turned her back and walked to the edge of the beach where a tumble of rocks lay in the shade of an arching shrub. She sat down and regarded her feet, curling her toes in the dry sand. 'And before you ask, yes, I am a virgin. And, no, I am not in the habit of swimming naked with men. I did not think there was anyone around.'

She risked an upward glance through her lashes. Chance had turned and was standing with his back to her, hands on his admirably slim hips, gazing out over the bay. 'This is a fine mess,' he observed, apparently dispassionately. 'I can only apologise.'

'Why? I expect it was something we both needed to get out of our systems.' Alessa tried to match his tone.

'I certainly have not got it out of mine,' he retorted grimly. 'Now, what are we going to do?'

'Perhaps you could put some clothes on?' Alessa suggested, trying very hard not to stare at the long, hard, male body, and failing.

'Lord! I had forgotten.' To her delight Chance was blushing—at least, the back of his neck had gone scarlet. 'I will be back in a minute.' He took a running dive into the water and swam strongly for the headland, leaving Alessa prey to wildly mixed emotions, and a quivering new awareness of her own body, which made her knees feel weak.

By the time a fishing boat appeared round the headland with furled sail and a respectably, if casually, dressed, gentleman at the oars, she was fully clothed and sitting in the shade of the bush again while she plaited her wet hair.

Chance ran the boat ashore and waded through the shallows to stand in front of her. There was no sign of his limp now.

'Is your ankle better?' Alessa knotted a piece of ribbon round the end of her plait and tossed it over her shoulder. Perhaps if they pretended nothing had happened…

'Yes. Thank you. Alessa, what just happened—nearly happened—just now. That will not happen again.'

Oh. If only… 'Of course not.' She glanced up, noticed the curving branches and the sprays of leaves of the shrub that arched over their heads, and smiled, despite the churning feeling inside her. 'It could not, just here, in any case.'

'Why not?' Chance hunkered down on his heels in front of her with all the flexibility of Demetri.

'This.' She caught a frond and pulled it down. 'This is the Chaste Tree. Virgins are protected by it. The other name is Monks' Pepper.' She rubbed the shrivelled remains of last season's flowers between her palms and held out the hard grains for him to see. 'It tastes like pepper, and it makes men chaste. Which is why it is so good for monks. Try it.'

'Certainly not.' Chance recoiled, sat down on the sand with an undignified thump and scooted backwards out of the contaminating shade. 'I am entirely with Saint Augustine.' She looked puzzled. '"Lord, give me chastity, but not just yet."'

Chance's expression as he eyed the bush warily released

all the pent-up tension in Alessa. The laughter built and bubbled until she could contain it no more. 'You don't need to worry—it doesn't make you impotent,' she managed to gasp, tears rolling down her cheeks. 'Just chaste.'

'You,' he observed severely, 'are very bad for a man's self-esteem. First you rescue me, then you lecture me, now you laugh at me.'

'I expect you deserve it. Have you anything to eat in your boat? I am starving.'

'No, nothing. I was going to sail over to that bay. There must be a village.'

'Yes. My village. Would you like to come and eat with us?' She got warily to her feet, suddenly very shy of being close to him, yet anxious not to let him go now she had found him again. And her head was buzzing with the impossible news that he had found a relative of hers—an aunt, of all things—here on the island.

'Are the children with you?' She nodded, too preoccupied to speak. Chance pulled her rowing boat into the water and tied it to the stern of the skiff before handing her in. 'Is that all your household?' She noticed how competently he handled the little craft, it seemed an odd skill for an English nobleman. Perhaps he kept a boat on the lake that his country house would doubt-less have. She could imagine summer picnic parties, all the ladies in elegant light gowns, the servants spreading a feast on crisp white cloths over an immaculately scythed lawn, the gen-tlemen amusing themselves with sailing boats. Another world...

'Are the three of you alone?'

Alessa started, realising he had already asked her the question. She must have caught the sun—how else to account for this ridiculously light-headed feeling? 'My friend Kate Street is staying with us. And old Agatha lives next door. She is the nearest thing I have to a grandmother, I suppose.'

'I should have checked further.' Chance frowned. 'I was so pleased having identified your aunt and linked her to your father that I didn't note the rest of the family, although your paternal grandfather is dead, I'm afraid. You have an uncle, as well as the aunt on your father's side. Your father *was* the Honourable Alexander William Langley Meredith?'

'Yes.' Alessa nodded, noticing the look of relief on Chance's face. He had told her more abruptly than he intended in the shock of their meeting. How would she feel if he had made a mistake? Disappointed? She was not at all sure how she felt now, when it seemed he was correct. 'Yes, Captain the Honourable Alex Meredith.' She hesitated, then stretched out a hand to touch his as it lay relaxed on the tiller. 'Thank you.'

'You are not sure you truly are grateful, are you?' His smile was disarmingly rueful. 'You must understand it would be dishonourable of me to abandon an English gentlewoman.'

'Even one who was not in distress?'

'Even so. When you are safely back in England, you will realise it was the right thing to do, believe me.'

Alessa eyed the elegant, assured profile as Chance scanned the shore ahead, adjusting the steering towards the pebbled beach. So arrogantly sure of himself, of his place in the world. So certain he knew what was best for her, and so fixed on following the dictates of his honour, whether she wanted it or not. She should dislike him and resent him, and part of her did. But the other part yearned for him and for the feel of his mouth on hers again, the touch of his hands on her body, the times when they seemed so much in harmony they hardly needed to speak.

'There.' She pointed. 'The children have come down to the beach.' The entire village gang of under-tens was skirmishing along the shoreline, skimming stones, splashing in the surf, playing tag.

'Where did you find your two?' Chance was smiling at the sight and her heart warmed to him. Unbidden the thought struck her: *He would make a good father.*

'Demetri's father was in the boat with my father when the storm caught them. He never came home either, and his wife had died the year before. Dora I did, literally, find that same year. She was sitting by the side of the road, blood all down her face, crying and clutching a filthy rag doll.

'Eventually I found the priest of her village. Her mother was a widow who took up with a fisherman who beat them both. One day he went too far and the woman died. Dora ran away.' She shrugged. 'She had no one to look after her, so she stayed with me. Now they think they are brother and sister and I do not remind them of the past. One day, perhaps, they will want to ask.'

'When you take them to England, Demetri will do well at school. He will grow up an English gentleman.'

'He is Greek, Corfiot,' Alessa said sharply.

'When he is a man he can choose what he wants to be. And Dora will marry—' He was cut off short by Alessa's muttered exclamation. 'What? Do you not believe in marriage?'

'Perhaps. It is not the be-all and end-all. And who will want to marry a Greek peasant girl in England?'

'Someone who wishes to ally himself to the Merediths by marrying their ward. Your life is going to change in ways of which you have no idea, Alessa.' Chance lifted a hand in greeting to the children who had gathered round the landing stage, calling and waving.

Whether I like it or not. Alessa stood up as the skiff grounded and untied the painter of the rowing boat, tossing it to Demetri to make secure. He scrambled to take it, greeting her with his wide, affectionate grin. *An English gentleman, with all the advantages that would bring him. What could he become, given the opportunity? And Dora? A whole world would open up to them. Am I being selfish, or just proud?*

'See who I have found,' she greeted them as she hopped out of the boat into the surf. 'Lord Blakeney is coming to eat with us—will you run on ahead and tell Aunt Kate?'

'*Yia sou.*' Chance smiled at the children.

'*Yia sas,*' they chorused back, wide-eyed at his sudden acquisition of a colloquial phrase, then took to their heels and headed up the steep hill.

'You have been learning modern Greek,' Alessa commented as she led the way over the shingle to the foot of the track way.

'I have about ten phrases now. I try to practise on the servants, but they all think I am mad and insist on addressing me in English, so I am not making much progress. When I get stuck I start to think in classical Greek and then I get in a muddle.' He reached out, took her hand and tucked it into the crook of her arm. 'This hill is devilishly steep.'

'But not long.' Alessa felt curiously breathless, despite having walked up and down that same hill countless times. Chance's body was warm against her wrist, and the linen shirt was still damp from where he must have pulled it on over his wet body. She could feel her cheeks colouring. 'See, there is the cottage.'

The stone building nestled into a bank, shaded by olives behind and a big pine at the side, leaning as though for companionship against Agatha's smaller house. Alessa felt a warm tug of affection for it. 'Home.' *Could I leave here?* And the feeling that ran through her was fear.

Chapter Nine

Chance felt Alessa's body stiffen and glanced down, but he could not see her face under the broad brim of her hat. Instead he studied the reception party—he was not certain he would call it a welcome party—which was clustered around the gate.

The children were certainly pleased to see him, but the two women were another matter. The younger, a buxom wench with a tangled mop of red hair, her muscular arms crossed under a quite magnificent bosom, was regarding him with a look that held both curiosity and assessment. He stared back with a certain degree of *hauteur*, expecting her to drop her gaze, but she just grinned back unrepentantly. This, presumably, was the friend who had helped undress him and put him to bed; from the wicked twinkle he was quite sure she knew that he knew it, and was watching him for signs of discomfiture.

Chance drew on several years' experience of dealing with alarmingly forward young matrons and maintained his composure. The other woman was another matter altogether. Apparently as old as the olive trees behind her, brown, wrinkled and with every sign of being as tough as old boot leather, Agatha regarded him with sharp black eyes from under an elaborately draped headscarf. That, no doubt, concealed a substructure of cows' horns.

Chance conjured up a mental picture of the full set of Almack's patronesses at their most critical and produced a charming smile. The shrewd old eyes narrowed.

'*Kalíméra*,' he said politely.

'*Yia sas.*' *Health to you.* The old woman produced the phrase like a threat.

Mrs Street smiled more broadly. 'Good day, my lord. A pleasure to meet you again.'

Beside him he heard the sharp hiss of Alessa's indrawn breath. 'I regret I have no memory of our first encounter, ma'am,' he replied. 'You have the advantage of me.'

'*Kyria* Agatha, Mrs Street,' Alessa snapped, almost pulling him through the gate so that its two guardians had to give way in front of her. 'I hope our *guest* will not have to wait long for some refreshment.' Her voice had all the steel chill he had last heard reproving him; now he found himself enchanted by it. She was flustered and defensive, for all that she was trying to conceal it, and the only reason for that could be him.

Which means, Chance mused, allowing himself to be pulled by the children to a bench under a vine arbour, *that she is not as unaffected by what happened in the bay as she would like to make out.*

He should be ashamed of himself, he knew. On one level he was—no gentleman should take advantage of a lady like that, however surprised he was by the encounter, and however extreme their state of undress. On the other hand, his body still ached with the memory of hers in his arms, of the silken slide of wet skin against his, the heat of her mouth, passionate—innocent—under his.

He wanted her, and what was even more imperative, he wanted her to want him. What had she meant when she said, *I expect it was something we both needed to get out of our systems?* That she had been curious and now her curiosity was satisfied? Somehow he felt as though his for her never would be.

Demetri and Kate Street were bringing over a table, Dora lugging a chair behind them. Chance tried to get to his feet and found himself pushed down on to the bench again by a small, firm hand on his shoulder. 'Sit, please. You are our guest.'

Food began to appear. A plate of olives, black and green in a golden pool of oil. Cheese lying on a vine leaf. A craggy loaf with a dangerous-looking knife stuck into it and a dish of pale butter, and finally a gnarled, U-shaped sausage that looked as though it had been hanging in the rafters for months. Old Agatha began to slice it, revealing a deep crimson interior, richly flecked and marbled with white like a piece of porphyry. Chance felt his mouth begin to water as the boy hefted a pitcher of water on to the table and Alessa added a jug of wine.

'Sit, everyone.' Alessa gestured to the table and they sat around. She began to pour wine into beakers, a splash for the children, topped up with plenty of water: half and half for Kate Street, herself and him; undiluted for Agatha.

In the dappled shade with the sun glinting off the waves in the bay below, Chance felt himself relax. He had not realised just how tense he had been. Now he felt a kind of happiness he could not entirely define.

'Would you cut the bread, my lord?'

He reached for the knife, suppressing a smile. Alessa's tone would not be out of place in a Mayfair dining room, asking him to pass the caper sauce or carve a capon. It was difficult to create a creditable slice of the rustic bread, but he persevered, passing each slice as it was cut. The children exhibited perfect table manners, he noticed, sitting quietly and handing olives or the cheese without being asked. He smiled at Dora and was rewarded by her flashing, mischievous smile in return.

She would be enchanting, all dressed up in English style. Would she like a pony? he wondered. When Alessa was home in England where she belonged, the children could have whatever they wanted—her long-lost family would dote on them, surely.

He glanced across at Alessa and saw she was gazing round the garden, an expression of quiet contentment on her face as she took in the neatly tended rows of vegetables, the chickens that had strayed from Agatha's plot and were chasing a spider, and the vine, which scrambled over the front wall. His pleasure vanished, replaced by a chill stab of doubt. This was her home now, and she was happy. Was he wrong, after all, to want to take her away from it?

Then he looked at the old woman's work-gnarled hands, Kate Street's reddened knuckles, the careful, loving mends and darns in the children's clothes. Yes, of course he was doing the right thing; she might think she was happy now, but this was not what she had been born to. In society she would flourish, and the children with her.

He looked at Alessa again, and this time caught her eye. Off guard, she smiled at him and his heart seemed to flip in his chest. All the sound in the garden stilled to nothing. The sensation lasted a moment only, then she glanced away and hearing returned.

'Are you staying locally, my lord?' It was Mrs Street, managing to sound perfectly respectable, despite the impudent glint in her eye.

'The Lord High Commissioner has taken a villa at Pale-okastritsa. I am his guest.'

'Then my Fred and his lads are guarding you,' Kate Street said with simple pride. 'Smartest lot in the army, my Fred's lads.'

'Sergeant Street, is it? I must look out for him.'

'I'm not married to Fred Court, Lord love you!' The redhead snorted with amusement, caught the sharp edge of Alessa's meaningful stare and glanced at the children, then added, 'Not that we'll not be getting round to it, some day.'

There didn't seem to be much to be added to that, so Chance turned to the old woman who was steadily demolishing bread and cheese despite an apparently total lack of teeth. 'Do you speak English, ma'am?' A blank stare. He did not feel up to making stumbling conversation in Greek, but surely she would have acquired some Italian from the long-time rulers of the island. *'Parliamo inglese, signora? Italiano?'* The stare this time was positively frosty. He was beginning to see where Alessa might have acquired her more forbidding expressions.

'*Kyria* Agatha speaks only Greek,' Alessa explained. 'Would you like some more wine?'

When they finished the meal she pressed Chance back into his seat again and cleared the table with the help of Kate and the children. They vanished inside, leaving him alone with Agatha. Chance ventured a smile, forcibly reminded of the dowager Lady Lakenheath at her most formidable. He had a sudden weird vision of both old ladies at Almack's and kept a straight face with an effort.

The old woman adjusted her head scarf with a flick of one hand, straightened up and regarded him with intelligent, inimical, black eyes. 'If you hurt my child, I will make you sorry you ever came to *Kérkyra*, lord.'

For a moment Chance thought she had spoken in Greek and that by some miracle he had translated it instantly, then he realised that she had addressed him in perfect, if heavily accented, English.

'I would not dream of it,' he retorted, shaken out of his poise by her attack.

'Pah. You think you love her? It is easy for men to love, to forget and to love again. You are all the same. For women, not so easy. So I warn you, English lord, so you know I watch you.'

'I do not love her,' Chance denied, wondering even as he said it if it was a lie. 'And I will not hurt her. I just want to help her find her own people again. And I thought you did not understand English.'

The only answer he got was a cackle and one wrinkled eyelid dropping in a wink. When Alessa reappeared Agatha was sitting back in her chair, eyes closed, apparently asleep, and Chance was flicking olive pits at the chickens, who chased them hopefully.

Alessa leaned against the olive tree and watched. The tall man in the sailor's clothes leaning back at his ease on the bench next to the sleeping old woman—they made an incongruous pair. However he was dressed, however tousled and salt-sticky his hair, Chance looked like the English gentleman he was. Agatha looked as though she had grown out of the rocky soil.

She was in love with him, there was no denying it, however hard she tried. She had struggled with her feelings, even as she worked with the children and Kate to clear up the meal, telling her friend about some little item of local gossip, daring her with her eyes to say anything about Chance in front of the children.

At first her startled mind told her this certainty was simply a physical reaction, and the extraordinary way she felt was only her response to her first real sexual experience. But as the minutes passed she knew it was not just that. There was excitement, a strange quivering ache deep inside her, a frightening awareness of her whole body. But there was also a feeling of tenderness and yearning that made her want to go and touch him, hold him, feel his breath against her skin, feel his heart against hers, and never, ever, let him go.

Alessa folded her hands tightly together and walked up to the table. Chance tipped back his head and smiled lazily up at her and all her doubts vanished. She could have stood there all day, locked in that warm brown gaze. The breeze caught the branches of the olive tree, flicking the leaves and scattering bright sunlight across Chance's face. He squinted his eyes against it and the trance was broken.

Time to face reality. 'Chance—will you tell me about this lady? About my aunt?' How strange that sounded. *Aunt.*

'Yes, of course.' He sat up straight and moved along the bench to make room for her.

'No, not here. In the olive grove, where we will not be disturbed.' It was too soon to let other people know about this, and certainly too soon for the children. Later would be time enough, if Chance proved to be right and this unknown relative acknowledged her.

Alessa took his hand without thinking and led him away, round the side of the cottage and up the hillside until they were in the strange greenish-brown shade of the olives. 'Here.' It was a favourite spot, a mossy bank that must, in ancient times, have formed a boundary between different owners' plots of olives. They sat and she wriggled back against a gnarled trunk. 'You can see the sea—look.'

She raised her hand to point and realised it was clasped with Chance's. Both sets of fingers were brown with sun and wind, but hers looked tiny against his. Chance let his hand rise with her gesture, then, instead of opening his fingers, he raised her hand to his lips and let them touch the back of it.

'*No.*' Alessa jerked her hand away. It was like the strange pricking sensation you got when you rubbed silk against glass. Papa had used to do that to make paper dolls dance for her and she used to giggle and shriek if her fingers touched the magic tingle. Now, she had no inclination to do either. 'No,' she repeated, this time more moderately, disentangling herself. 'We have been imprudent enough for one day.'

'Is that a promise for another day?' he asked softly.

She shot him a reproving look, but he was leaning back against the tree, not looking at her any more.

'These olives are odd; different from the ones I have seen in Italy and France. Bigger, and the trunks look as though they are made out of ropes and net, all tangled together.'

'I know.' Alessa snatched at the neutral topic gratefully. 'It is Venetian, I believe: nowhere else are there olives pruned like these.'

Chance was silent for a moment, twirling a twig between his fingers. 'We did not come here to flirt, nor to discuss olives. I wish I had handled this better, made sure of my facts before I told you anything.'

'Tell me what you believe.'

'Your eyes and eyebrows are very distinctive; I would guess from what I know now that you inherited them from your father.'

Alessa nodded. 'Papa had always referred to them as the Meredith witch-eyes. Legend has it that one of our ancestors seduced a witch and then left her. She deposited her son on his doorstep nine months later. Personally I think any self-respecting witch would have left a curse, not a baby.'

'Perhaps she loved him,' Chance speculated, suddenly turning his head and fixing her with a direct look. 'It does happen.

'Anyway, I was in the courtyard at the Residency. You had just run away and left me, and Lady Trevick arrived home with her new houseguests: Lady Blackstone and her daughter Frances. For a moment, when I saw the daughter, I thought she was you—you could be sisters. There is no mistaking the resemblance, nor yours to Lady Blackstone.

'I checked the *Peerage*. Lady Blackstone was Honoria Meredith, the sister of the fourth Earl Hambledon—Edward Charles Meredith. And the *Peerage* mentions one other brother, the Honourable Alexander William Langley Meredith. There is nothing else about him—no marriage, no death. Nothing. But I remembered you told me your real name was Alexandra. On the beach you told me your father's name—it cannot be a coincidence.'

'No.' *How strange I should feel like this—numb. Not afraid, not happy, just numb.* 'No, it cannot be coincidence. Chance, she will not want to acknowledge me.'

'I think she may be here to look for you. She is travelling to meet her husband in Venice, but this is by no means the logical route for her to take. In fact, it is positively perverse. When I probed she became evasive, but Lady Trevick let drop that she thinks Lady Blackstone has family connections with the island.'

'Why should she search for me?' Alessa heard the bitterness in her voice and suppressed it. 'After Mama died Papa wrote to his family, to ask for their help for me; but the letter was returned by my grandfather's lawyers.'

'Did they know where you were at that time?'

'No, only that we were in the Mediterranean. But now the war is over, I suppose it would be possible to find out where my father was based.'

'Could it be that your grandfather never forgave your father for whatever had caused the breach between them, and for your father's marriage, but now he is dead his children wish to make amends?' He swivelled on the bank to face her. 'Lady

Blackstone is going to make the journey to Venice, so she plans this detour in the hope of finding you.'

It was logical, and it held out the hope that her aunt—if she thought the word often enough it would begin to sound less improbable—her *aunt* would want to acknowledge her.

'Has she made any enquiries about me, I wonder?' She bit her lip, frowning down into the bay below them. 'But no one here knows my true name.'

'I will find out what she is about, as tactfully as I can. Do not frown so, Alessa, you will develop wrinkles.'

She ignored his teasing tone, a new worry building. 'I cannot just impose myself upon them. Why should they support me?'

'Because you are their niece and it is their duty. But your father, even if only a younger son, must have had some assets—some land, some investments sitting there earning interest. There will be back pay owed by the army.'

'But if his family thought he was dead…'

'They have to wait seven years to presume that. The War Office would have given them the date of his death if they had enquired and they would have no reason to suppose you too had died. That money and land will be in trust somewhere and it is yours by right.'

She had never thought of that. Money for Demetri's education, for a dowry for Dora, modest independence that depended on no one, least of all the family who had turned their back on Papa. 'If I do not have to be dependent on them,' she began hesitantly, 'then perhaps…'

'I will sound out Lady Blackstone as tactfully as I can, and let you know. There is no need for you to confront her before you are both fully prepared.'

'I do not remember England, not really. It was cold and grey and damp and Papa was not in a good mood, that much I do recall. Does the sun shine in England?'

'Occasionally.' He was amused by her doubt, she could tell. 'But the rain has its advantages. The grass is green and lush all year, the rivers run full and the English umbrella industry flourishes.'

'That is very gratifying,' she retorted tartly. 'Will you return to England?'

She wished the question back as soon as the words were out of her mouth, but Chance did not appear to take them as some sort of flirtation. He was getting to his feet, careless of the moss and twigs clinging to the loose cotton trousers and belted shirt. 'Home? Yes, I expect to travel on from here to Venice, then back overland. I haven't decided on the exact itinerary yet, but home for Christmas, then I shall be at my mother's mercy for the Season.'

'Will she expect you to squire her around to all the balls?'

'That, and to escort my sisters. But her main intention is to find me a wife.' He said it so carelessly, jumping down into the hollow track that ran down to the village, that for a moment she missed his meaning.

So, why are you surprised? Of course he is going to be looking for a wife. And, of course, he expects to find her among the eligible young ladies of London. What do you expect, that he would turn and take you in his arms and say, 'But I have no need to search, she is here'?

Without waiting for Chance to turn and offer her his hand, Alessa jumped down beside him and took the lead as the track turned downhill, curving under the spreading shade. By the time they regained the cottage she would have her emotions under control and a serene smile back on her lips to ward off the speculation in all those watching eyes.

Chapter Ten

Chance steered the fishing boat into the bay under the looming monastery where Odysseus had once been washed ashore, to be received by the Princess Nausicaa. He hoped it was an omen. Alessa had shown no reaction to his remark about seeking a wife. Had she not understood his hint? Probably not. More and more the feeling was growing within him that she was the only woman he wanted in his life. But to court her now, marry her out of hand before her status was confirmed and her place in English society established, would always brand her as 'that Greek girl Blakeney picked up on his travels.'

No, Alessa was going back as Miss Meredith, the eminently respectable daughter of a war hero and the niece of an earl. Could he explain that to her? He had started to frame the words in his head half a dozen times, only to realise that, however he put it, she was going to be deeply offended. Her independence, her work, her adopted country were all sources of pride to Alessa. Back in England it would come into perspective and his courtship of her would appear the honourable thing he intended it would be.

As it was, if he made any declaration now…

'Are you going to sit in that boat all night, Benedict my friend?' Zagrede was standing on the sand regarding him. He cut an exotic figure in the evening light with loose trousers, a flowing silk shirt and a scarlet sash into which was thrust the long dagger he never seemed to leave the house without.

'No. Here, take the rope.' Chance threw it, admiring the nonchalant, one-handed catch. The Count stooped to flip the rope around the metal stanchion protruding out of the sand and Chance vaulted over the side into the few inches of water. 'You look fit to repel pirates with that sword.'

'This? This is merely a *thika*, a knife. This is not a sword.' He turned and began to walk companionably back up the beach at Chance's shoulder. 'I have come out to escape the young ladies; I do not feel capable of managing them all by myself.'

'You amaze me, Voltar.' It seemed odd to be using first names, but the Count appeared to expect it. 'Surely a man of your address should have no trouble with three young ladies.'

'But I do not want three,' the Albanian said plaintively. 'I only want one.'

Ah. That explained it, although Chance was not anxious to find himself in the position of distracting two susceptible damsels while the Count carried out his courtship of the chosen one. 'Which is the lady with whom you wish to…dally?'

'Oh, any of them would do.' He seemed impervious to Chance's stare. 'They are all handsome, all well bred and all, no doubt, well monied. Is that the word?'

'Well dowered?' Chance suggested, fascinated by this cold-bloodied approach.

'Yes, that is it. A wife would be desirable at this stage of my affairs. Mistresses I have, many of them, and children, but legitimate sons I do not have. A man has to think of these things.'

'Indeed, yes.' Chance was beginning to think of little else but marriage and heirs. Or, if he was to be honest, the getting of heirs with Alessa. 'But an English wife for an Albanian Count?'

'The English have much power now in these seas. It would be a good—what is the word?—tactic.'

They reached the roughly cobbled street. Chance kicked the worst of the sand off his feet and pushed them into the shoes he had carried off the boat. Just how powerful in his own country was Zagrede? He seemed to be thinking like a princeling, not a minor aristocrat. And yet, he mastered his own ships, which argued more the merchant than the prince.

'Well, you tell me which one your fancy alights upon,' he said with good humour. 'I'll do my best to flirt with the other two.' *Just so long as that does not involve getting on the wrong side of Lady Blackstone.*

There was no sigh of any of the other guests as they regained the villa. Chance climbed the gleaming chestnut wood stairs to his rooms and threw himself with gratitude into the waiting bath of cool water that Alfred had standing ready. He waved aside the valet's suggestion that 'my lord might wish to have his back scrubbed' and slid down until his head was submerged, surfacing only when his breath ran out. He lay back against the high curve of the tub while the salt sluiced from his skin.

How did Alessa wash in that little cottage? No deep marble bathtub for her. No respectful servants tapping on the door to offer steaming jugs of fresh water, no heap of soft linen towels. The image of her standing naked at a wash stand had its inevitable effect and he grabbed the long-handled brush and scrubbed his back mercilessly as a distraction while he rehearsed his tactics for approaching Lady Blackstone. 'Indirectly,' he murmured, 'that's the way.'

Later, as the house party gathered on the terrace overlooking the bay before dinner, he found himself beside his hostess.

Lady Trevick was fanning herself while keeping a wary eye on the Count's flirtation with the young ladies.

'A charming gentleman,' Chance observed.

'Yes. Yes, certainly. Perhaps a little *too* charming.' Lady Trevick frowned as both her daughters succumbed to blushing giggles at some sally.

'But then, who can blame him, surrounded by such delightful young ladies? Has Lady Blackstone made any progress with her search for her family connection on Corfu?' Lady Trevick glanced at him and he added smoothly, 'You mentioned it the other night.' She had hardly alluded to it, in fact, but now, with any luck, she would imagine he knew far more than he did.

'I believe not.' She glanced round, lowering her voice. 'A tragic case, I understand—her younger brother, estranged from the family, an unsuitable match and, I very much fear, a child of the union adrift somewhere in the Mediterranean.'

'Frightful! I presume Lady Blackstone has only just become aware of the child's existence?'

'Ye…es.' Lady Trevick looked a little doubtful. 'That must be the case, I am sure.' She brightened. 'Lady Blackstone has been discussing it with my brother's secretary, Mr Harrison.'

'Indeed.'

Lady Blackstone came out on to the terrace, sized up the little group around the Count at a glance and skilfully cut her daughter out of it, steering her towards Chance and their hostess.

'If you will excuse me…' Lady Trevick cast a slightly hunted look at her own daughters '…I must go and have a word with the butler. Perhaps you will keep an eye on the girls, Lady Blackstone?'

Miss Blackstone drifted a little apart to turn her back on the terrace and affect an interest in the view. *Perfect.* He was alone with his quarry.

'I do hope you will pardon a personal observation, ma'am, but what very striking and lovely eyes Miss Blackstone has. It is quite obvious that she has them from her mama.'

The older woman inclined her head graciously, a smug smile tugging at her lips. 'You are most kind, my lord. Of course, Frances is much admired, but I have to admit that I, in my youth, was complimented upon those features.'

'A family characteristic, I collect?' Chance managed a puzzled frown. 'Which makes it very odd, for I know of another young lady on the island with just such striking eyes and brows.'

'You do? How extraordinary. Under what circumstances?' *Touché.*

His timing was perfect; the butler was just emerging to announce dinner. 'She saved my life,' he said simply. 'Please excuse me, I believe in Sir Thomas's absence I am taking in Lady Trevick, and here comes the Count to claim your hand.'

A prolonged dinner would give her ladyship plenty of time to recover from the shock and any defensiveness and to get her own story arranged. The less embarrassment she felt discussing such a sensitive family matter with a stranger, the better it would be for Alessa.

Chance assisted his hostess into her seat, declined her flattering invitation to take the head of the table and sat at her right hand, paying Lady Blackstone at the other end no attention whatsoever. Whatever happened, he wanted no suspicion to arise that he and Alessa were anything but chance-met strangers, thrown together by the drama of the attack upon him. It was going to be difficult enough hiding the fact that Alessa took in washing.

His ploy worked. As they strolled out again into the moonlit evening Chance found himself neatly steered into Sir Thomas's study, its doors opening out a little way along the terrace.

'Ma'am?'

'This young lady you referred to.' Her ladyship was too agitated to apply any poise to her questioning. 'What is her name?'

'Alexandra.' He saw the name strike home—the green eyes watching him widened. 'I do not know her family name. How delightful if she should prove to be a distant relative of yours.'

'How old is she?'

'Perhaps twenty-four or five. I was waylaid by thieves one evening, just outside her door, and took refuge in her house; hence the injuries that left me limping until a few days ago.'

'And what are her circumstances?' Lady Blackstone's fingers were tight on her fan. She seemed to be holding herself still by sheer force of will. Chance felt a flash of sympathy. What must it be like to be so close to finding an unknown niece, the only child of a long-lost brother? Whatever the rift that had driven Meredith from his family, there must have been happy childhood memories this elegant, apparently assured lady cherished and mourned for.

'She supports herself modestly, but respectably, by making herbal remedies. *Kyria* Alessa, as she is known, supplies the Residency among many other establishments. She lives with a female companion and with two orphan children she has rescued—she's funding their education.' To describe Kate Street, whom he had every suspicion had at some time earned her keep as a game pullet, as a *female companion,* was stretching truth to its limits, but he sincerely hoped Kate would never have to meet Lady Blackstone.

Honoria Blackstone looked at him sharply. 'The children are not hers?'

'Not in the family sense, no. But she regards them as her charge, having taken them in.'

'I see.' She walked away from him, the short train of her

evening gown swishing softly over the wide boards. 'I suppose it is just possible that she might be a connection. I will call upon her when we return to the town.'

'She is staying only a short distance away. I met her by accident today, which is what called her to mind; it seems she has brought the children away for a short holiday in the next village. They have come to visit an old woman for whom she feels a responsibility.'

'Quite a philanthropist, this young person.'

Chance winced inside at the sharp edge to Lady Blackstone's voice. She was wary, unwilling to accept anything until she saw the proof.

'Indeed,' he responded, concealing his feelings. 'From what I have seen of her, she has all the instincts of a lady. Should I bring her to speak to you, ma'am? Tomorrow, perhaps?' Chance had no intention of leading Lady Blackstone up a mule track through the olive groves to call on a humble cottage, still less to be glowered at by old Agatha.

'Yes. Very well. It is probably a coincidence and she is no connection, but, naturally, I would like to know. Three o'clock tomorrow, if that can be arranged.'

'I will send a note.' Chance affected a tone of disinterest. 'Doubtless the villa staff will be able to find the right direction.'

Alessa turned the note over in her hands, folded it, unfolded it, then finally smoothed it out on the table and read it through. It was the first, and probably the last, letter she would ever have from Chance and ridiculously her fingertips traced the bold black slash of his signature. He had written nothing that hinted at any sort of relationship between them. Was that tact—or simply that he did not regard what had happened as of any significance?

Lady Blackstone thinks it possible you may be a family

connection, and naturally would like the opportunity to meet
you. Three this afternoon would be convenient to her ladyship.
I believe it will not be necessary for you to be accompanied
by anyone else from your household, including your female
companion, as Lady Blackstone will, of course, be able to
chaperon you.

Amused by the idea of Kate as a lady's companion, Alessa
took the hint. Chance had prepared the ground, now it was
up to her, if this Lady Blackstone truly was her aunt, to establish herself with credit.

Alessa borrowed Agatha's white mule and set out at two
wearing her Sunday best. She had no fashionable clothes, only
the traditional island costume she had worn for years, but this
dress was her finest, the edge trimmed with old embroidery.
Her stockings were pure white, her blouse full-sleeved and
inset with lace. On her head she had perched a pert saucer of
a straw hat with broad black ribbons tying it behind her
chignon, and her mother's filigree earrings dangled in her ears.
Lady Blackstone might be startled, but she would have no
reason to reproach her niece for shabby or immodest clothing.

'Alessa!' Chance appeared as she rode into the yard at the
back of the villa. 'You look very fine.' He lifted her down from
the mule, stepping back to admire her while keeping his firm
hold on her waist. His hands were warm and strong and the
memory of how they had felt on her naked skin brought the
heat to her cheeks. 'Come along inside and I will tell you what
I have said to your aunt.'

'You are sure she is?' Alessa let herself be pulled inside,
through the back door and along the shadowy corridor that led
towards the front.

'Beyond doubt. Here, this should be safe enough.' He
stopped outside an empty storeroom and ducked inside. Alessa

followed and listened, nodding at intervals as he described his interview of the day before. 'Lady Blackstone is cautious, which is understandable, but you will win her over,' he concluded. Alessa did not speak, her mind whirling with the realisation that this, after all these years, was the moment when she would meet a member of her family. How did she feel?

'You look pale.' Chance was regarding her closely in the gloom.

'I am nervous,' Alessa confessed. He still had hold of her hand and she gripped it hard. 'Will you come in with me?'

'No, better if this is in private. And I do not want to let her guess how well we know each other: she might imagine some impropriety.'

And she would be correct! Alessa did not say it out loud, but the sudden spark in Chance's eyes told her that his thoughts had meshed with hers.

'A kiss for luck,' he said huskily, and drew her into his arms. It was the first time he had kissed her properly, not under water. The sensations were the same, yet startlingly different, for now, without her senses filled with the scent and the noise and the taste of the sea, she could smell his skin, hear her own pulse thudding, savour the taste of his mouth as he explored hers.

It was extraordinary how her body knew how to fit against his, how her soft curves met the long, hard masculine lines. How did her fingers know what the crisp hair at the nape of his neck would feel like as they tangled in it? Why did her lips part under the demand of his to allow the intrusion of his tongue?

Chance thrust into the moistness, and she yielded to him, quivering as the dart of his tongue sent a stabbing demand into her loins. Crushed against him, her breasts felt swollen, the nipples, peaking against the tight constraint of her laced bodice, ached.

His hands slid down, cupped her buttocks, lifted her against him, while his mouth continued to plunder hers. It would have been arrogant, this mastery of her body, if she had been anything but an equally willing participant. Now, moulded against the exciting evidence of just how aroused Chance was, Alessa quivered in response, her mind cloudy with the force of her body's responses.

The heavy strike of the big hall clock cut through the room, drowning the sound of panting breaths and rustling clothing with as much force as though it had been in there with them.

'Hell!' Chance freed his mouth, let her slide down the length of him until she was standing again, and closed his eyes for a moment. When he opened them again his gaze was wide and black and his breath was coming fast and short. 'Hell,' he said again, stepping back and tugging his coat and neck-cloth into some sort of order.

There was no time. No time to talk, to question what had just happened, and why. Alessa looked round wildly for a mirror.

'Out here.' There was one hanging, dust-smeared, in the passage. Her frivolous hat had tilted crazily over one eye, an earring had knotted itself up in her hair and her neckline was all awry. She had no recollection of Chance even touching it.

Frantically Alessa straightened and tidied, half-aware that behind this whirl of activity she was avoiding talking to Chance or thinking about her own wanton behaviour.

'You'll do.' He opened the door and pushed her into the hallway only to come face to face with the startled butler. 'Really, *Kyria,* I wish you would find something to ride other than that half-broken mule!' he scolded. 'I feel I have been dragged through a hedge backwards, trying to stop it just now as you hurtled into the yard.

'Ah, Wilkins. This lady is here to see Lady Blackstone.'

Alessa felt Chance give her a little push and managed a

smile for the butler. 'Miss Meredith.' How strange those words sounded. How long was it since she had spoken them? 'Her ladyship is expecting me at three.'

'I will take you straight in, Miss Meredith.' She was aware of a skilfully concealed, all-encompassing survey of her attire, but Wilkins was too well trained to betray surprise at the combination of her costume and her name.

She glanced behind her, but Chance had gone. Well, she was used to being all alone. What was the worst that could happen? That this Lady Blackstone would refuse to acknowledge her? She would be no worse off if that were to happen, when all was said and done.

'Miss Meredith, my lady.' She was into the room before she could collect her thoughts. The woman who turned from her contemplation of the bay was tall, slender, with black hair streaked dramatically with silver at the temples. But it was her eyes that riveted Alessa's attention. No wonder Chance had seen the resemblance: identical green irises and the slanting brows to those that looked back at her from her own reflection were fixed on her face.

'Ma'am.' She dropped a curtsy, keeping her head up and her expression calm. But inside her stomach was churning and her mouth was as dry as ashes. This was her father's sister, she had no doubt, and it was as though his ghost had entered the room too.

'You are Alexandra Meredith?' Her aunt's voice was cool, but not hostile. Alessa nodded. 'And your parents?'

'My father was Captain the Honourable Alexander William Langley Meredith,' she said, hearing the pride in her own voice as she said his name. 'He was the son of the third Earl of Hambledon. My mother was Thérèse Bonniard, the widow of a French royalist.'

Lady Blackstone turned abruptly, but not before Alessa

caught a glint of moisture in her eyes. 'Forgive me, but they were married?'

'Yes, ma'am. I have all my papers here.' Alessa opened the leather pouch that swung at her waist. 'My father's passport and army papers, the wedding certificate and my birth certificate.'

She held them out, but Lady Blackstone remained standing, apparently transfixed by the view through the open doors on to the terrace. Alessa laid the grubby, water-stained documents on a side table and stepped back. 'When did he die?'

'Almost six years ago. He drowned in a storm. Papa was an intelligence officer.' Alessa waited a moment—there was no response. 'I am very proud of him. I do not understand why his family turned their back on him.'

'Oh, it was so long ago.' Her aunt sounded weary. She turned, picked up the papers, one after another, and glanced through them. 'I really do not need to see these, do I? You are Alex's daughter—how could I mistake you? We knew about the marriage, all that time past, but my father was adamant: once the black sheep, for always the black sheep.'

'Papa used to say he had been very wild.' If truth be told, he was never anything else.

'He was certainly that. If he had set out to alienate his father's good opinion and scandalise his every value, Alexander could have not done better. ' Lady Blackstone put down the papers and raised her eyes to Alessa's face. 'What do you want of your family?'

'Acknowledgment, perhaps. Nothing that is not mine.' She had not known what to expect; certainly not this cool, contained emotion, icing over the tears that she had surely seen welling just a moment ago. 'I assume that Papa had some small inheritance that would come to me? If that is the case, then I would want to return to England and claim it, decide whether I could make a life there. If there is nothing…why, then I will stay here, where I can support myself.'

'Or you could stay here and our attorneys could make financial arrangements.' So, there was to be no rush to welcome her to the bosom of the family. 'There is a small manor in the depths of the Suffolk countryside. Perhaps a thousand pounds a year. You could live like a queen here on that, I imagine.'

Alessa did a rapid conversion into Venetian *ducats* and French *louis*. Her aunt was not exaggerating. Nor did she want her back in England. She, the daughter of the brother loved and lost, stirred up too many memories. Perhaps her aunt felt guilty that she had not stood up for her younger brother. Perhaps the French wife was still too much to swallow. Or perhaps it was simply that this stranger with the same eyes, standing in front of her with a well-bred English accent and dressed from head to foot like a Corfiot peasant at a festival, was simply too difficult to imagine in London society.

I am not going to beg her to take me back. Anger and pity and disappointment and a welling relief all mingled inside her. With a thousand pounds a year she and the children would never want and she could give them everything they deserved. Only now did she realise why England had seemed so attractive. In Corfu she would never be able to meet Chance on equal terms. *Nor will I be able to watch him courting and taking a wife.*

'I think that would be—'

'Mama! May I go out in a boat to sail around the monastery rock? Oh! I am sorry, I did not realise you had anyone with you.'

Into the room came a girl who could be her sister, her arms linked through those of a staid-looking gentleman on one side and a glamorously exotic character who Alessa immediately recognised on the other. Everyone in Corfu Town knew the

Count of Kurateni by sight. And of course the staid gentleman was Mr Harrison, the Lord High Commissioner's secretary.

All three stared at Alessa. Mr Harrison found his voice first. '*Kyria* Alessa, I did not look to see you on this side of the island.'

The Count, without the added confusion of prior acquaintance, shot one penetrating glance around the three women in front of him. 'You have found a relative, Lady Blackstone! What a charming event—my congratulations.' He stood there positively radiating good will, curiosity and a complete lack of understanding that he was intruding.

Then Alessa saw the mischief and intelligence in the black eyes and realised he knew just what he was doing. The Count scented scandal and entertainment and he was going to indulge himself.

'But, Mama, who is this?' The girl freed herself from the men and came up to Alessa, her hand held out, a frank smile on her face. 'How do you do? I am Frances—I am sure we must be cousins.' She half-turned as she spoke, bringing Alessa with her so they stood side by side in front of the mirror. 'Just look!'

'Frances, you are interrupting a private meeting—' But Lady Blackstone's reproof was lost in the sound of the two Trevick sisters calling for Frances.

'Did your mama say you could go?' Then they were into the room, closely followed by their mother and, sauntering in with an expression of mild boredom, Chance.

Now the cat is out of the bag with a vengeance!

Lady Trevick was regarding this crush in the small sitting room with well-bred surprise. It left Lady Blackstone no options. 'Lady Trevick, the most fortunate circumstance—this is Alexandra Meredith, my long-lost niece. My youngest brother's child.'

Chapter Eleven

'My dear, what a tale you must have to tell.' Lady Trevick swept forward graciously. 'Welcome. Is your mama with you on Corfu?'

'Both my brother and his wife have tragically passed away.' *That establishes my legitimacy in front of everyone,* Alessa thought, chiding herself at once for being uncharitable. Her appearance must be the most incredible shock to her aunt, and, after all, although *she* knew she was a respectable young woman, her new aunt most certainly did not.

Then the unpleasant thought struck her that she was no longer quite so respectable. If anyone had seen her only half an hour ago, let alone in the bay yesterday, she would be ruined. Instinctively she looked at Chance and found he was frowning. Perhaps he had imagined her receiving a more rapturous welcome.

'I am Sir Thomas's sister,' Lady Trevick was explaining. She had no way of knowing that the young woman in front of her had probably washed all the linen she was wearing now, and, mercifully, Mr Harrison did not feel it necessary to point this out. 'These are my daughters Maria and Helena.' The two smiled warmly, obviously agog with curiosity.

'The Earl of Blakeney; the Count of Kurateni.' Both gentlemen bowed and Alessa dropped a small curtsy. Chance's expression was one of polite interest, although she could read the approval and encouragement in his face. The Count was openly admiring.

'And so, an English lady here among the Corfiots,' he marvelled, obviously quite uninhibited about saying out loud what everyone else was wondering about. 'And how have you lived? Are you married?'

'After my father died, I lived with *Kyria* Agatha, an elderly widow who taught me about herbal medicines and remedies. When I was old enough I moved to Corfu Town and set up in business, selling my herbs and salves.'

'All alone?' Helena Trevick was wide-eyed.

'With the two children I have adopted. The English wife of a sergeant in the garrison here lives with me also.' Well, it was almost true: Kate was virtually Fred's wife, and living on the floor above in the same house was, more or less, living together.

'Let us all go out on to the terrace and leave Miss Meredith in peace with her aunt,' Lady Trevick said firmly. 'You must have much to talk about. And, of course, if you would like to stay here with Lady Blackstone, Miss Meredith, I would be only too delighted.' Sweeping the girls and gentlemen in front of her, she cleared the room, shutting the doors behind her with a click.

Alessa was left confronting her aunt. Lady Blackstone smiled. It was strained, perhaps, but it was certainly the most friendly gesture she had made yet. It seemed the intrusion of so many people had helped her overcome her shock.

'Of course, you will stay here.'

'But, ma'am—the children.'

'They can stay for a few days with your companion and

the old lady, can they not?' Her aunt came over and took her hands. 'How else can Frances and I get to know you better? Alexander's child—it hardly seems possible,' she added, almost to herself. 'Do you take after your father, my dear?'

'Am I wild, do you mean? No, I think not,' Alessa replied with a smile. 'When Papa was alive, I had to be the sensible one, and living in disguise on an enemy-occupied island teaches one caution and discretion. Since he died I have had to earn my own living.'

'You certainly still speak like a lady, and carry yourself like one. ' Lady Blackstone studied her. 'Do you have other clothes?'

'Only Corfiot dress, ma'am.'

'I wish you to call me Aunt Honoria. The elder Miss Trevick is much of your size; perhaps she will lend you something until we can find a dressmaker. I will ask Lady Trevick while I am speaking to her about your room.'

'Thank you, Aunt Honoria. Should I come back tomorrow morning?' Her aunt was right to expect her to stay, and surely the children would understand if she was only away a few days.

'Certainly not! Why are you running off? Now you are here, you must stay.'

'No, ma'am. I am sorry, but I borrowed the mule, and I cannot just walk off without letting everyone know where I am. I will return tomorrow.' The older woman stared at her, obviously taken aback by this show of independence and Alessa felt a qualm about just what she was letting herself in for. 'Good afternoon, Aunt, and thank you.' She bent forward and kissed the smooth cheek, startling herself almost as much as Lady Blackstone by the gesture, then turned and was out of the door before any further objections could be made.

In the hall she hesitated. What to do now? She had no idea how one went on in a big house with servants. Should she wait for someone to appear and ask for her mule to be brought round? Or leave by the front door and walk round to the back? Or perhaps she could slip out through the servants' entrance, the way they had come in.

'*Alessa!*' It was Chance, beckoning her out on to the terrace. 'It is all right: they have gone to look at the sailboat the Count has sent for. Lady Trevick cannot decide whether to approve it for a pleasure trip.'

'Thank goodness, I was afraid they would all be out here talking about me.' Her knees felt weak now and she sank gratefully on to a cushioned bench under the shade of an arbour.

'I imagine they are talking of little else.' Chance hitched one hip on to the balustrade and grinned at her. 'How do you feel?'

'Confused, overwhelmed, undecided.' Alessa glanced along the broad sweep of the terrace, but all the doors were closed. 'My aunt is not very pleased to see me. Relieved, perhaps, that she has found me, and that I am accounted for. But you know, if she had discovered that I had died as a child, or drowned in the boat with Papa, I believe she would have been—not pleased, but guiltily relieved about that too.'

'I am sure that cannot be the case, and she is simply naturally reserved.' Chance frowned. Suddenly he seemed distant and starchy, disapproving of her coolness about her aunt. But why should she be a hypocrite and pretend she did not notice Lady Blackstone's lack of enthusiasm? Or did he expect her to be such a conventional little miss, so lacking in self-sufficiency that she would simply throw herself uncritically on her relatives' protection? She had expected him to understand and offer some support after that difficult interview. 'It is just that you are strangers and you do not know her yet,' he added. Alessa was aware of a glow of anger overcoming her momentary weakness.

'There is money, as you thought.' She pushed her papers more securely into her leather pouch and secured the toggle.

'My aunt suggested she would make arrangements for it to be paid to me here, so I could stay on the island—presumably so I would not be an embarrassment to the family in England. Then when everyone appeared she seemed to change her mind. She wants me to stay here at the villa for a few days at least.' She hesitated, her gaze fixed on her clasped hands as she thought. 'It is very awkward.'

'I am sorry!' Chance made a move to hold out his hand, then jerked it back. 'I should never have kissed you like that. I had no wish to make things more complicated for you.'

'Oh, that,' she said flatly. Did men think that the entire world revolved around them? Probably, she thought irritably. 'No, that was not what I meant. I mean it is awkward about the children.' And it had been what she was thinking about, if only to prevent her mind dwelling on that hectic, crowded, insane minute in the dusty storeroom. Which made her a hypocrite for being angry with him for leaping to the conclusion that she *had* been thinking about it... *Oh, damn and blast!*

'I see.' Now she had wounded his pride. In some ways it was much easier to deal with Chance when she was cross with him and the desire to be in his arms was buried. *Over-amorous, arrogant male aristocrat. Oh, but I love you.* 'I suppose you do not have any concerns about sleeping and living in the same house as me, after what happened?'

'None at all.' She got to her feet, smoothing down her skirt with a decisive sweep of her hand and managing to look at him without focusing on the tiny details that were beginning to obsess her: the arch of his brow when he was thinking, the tiny scar on his left temple, the whorl of his ear. 'I will, after all, be very adequately chaperoned here.'

She realised that she had done nothing to deal with the events in the bay yesterday—and look where that had led her.

She should have said something at the time, made it quite clear that she was chaste and fully intended staying so.

Yesterday. Yesterday they had probably done what any two people with a moderate degree of attraction to each other would have done if they found themselves without clothes, shaken by the shock and uninhibited by fear of discovery. And he had not, after all, pressed her once he had realised she was a virgin.

'So you will be safe from me, you mean?' His voice was suddenly harsh and Alessa glanced up to meet angry brown eyes. Her own smouldering temper and embarrassment flared up.

'Yes. I believe it should be quite clear now that I am not going to accept being any man's mistress. I would not have considered it before, and now, after all, I have the protection of my family, the Commission, my own money.'

'Who said anything about mistresses?' Chance demanded. They were both on their feet now, facing each other, only some residual awareness that they could be overheard keeping their voices down to an angry hiss.

'That was what you thought, was it not? Why you wanted to make love to me in the bay yesterday? You thought that I was a widow and that I might be willing.'

'Damn it, you *were* willing, virgin or not. And the thought of making you my mistress never entered my head!'

'Really? So if you came across Maria Trevick or Frances Blackstone swimming in the bay, you would make love to them?'

'No, I would not!' He was furious now, and so was she, even if she was dimly aware that it was herself she was most angry with. 'But then I do not—' Chance broke off, glaring at her, the colour high on his cheekbones, his eyes hard.

'Do not what?'

'Desire them, damn it.' *Was that really what he had been about to say?* 'Alessa, why are you so angry now? It was all right between us afterwards yesterday. It was all right an hour ago when you were kissing me. What has changed? The acquisition of some rich relatives and an inheritance? Do you expect a proposal of marriage now when you did not before? Well, you can join the house party here and learn the art of flirtation, and who knows what might happen. The Count is looking for an English wife, I believe.'

'Why, you arrogant—'

'Your mule, Miss Meredith.' It was Wilkins the butler, face impassive. *What had he heard?* Alessa got to her feet, looking at Chance, but he appeared merely a trifle bored, lounging against the balustrade.

'Thank you, Wilkins. Lady Trevick has invited me to stay here.'

'So I understand, Miss Meredith.'

'I shall be arriving tomorrow morning.'

'Very well. To which address shall I direct the footman and the trap to collect you and your luggage?'

'I am afraid the track is not suitable for wheeled vehicles. I will ask a neighbour to lend me mules and one of the boys will take them back, I am sure.'

'It would be easier by sea.' Chance stood up. 'I shall bring a boat into the bay below the village at ten, if your friends will be able to transport your luggage down.'

Oh, really? And just what did he expect would happen once they were alone again in a boat?

'Thank you, my lord,' she said sweetly, with a smile for the benefit of the waiting butler. 'But I am sure that would make me feel unwell—the action of the boat, you understand.'

'I understand perfectly.' Chance smiled too; Alessa only

hoped the butler was deceived by it, for she was not. He was furious with her. Why had she been worried at the thought of the boat? He probably only wanted to spend the journey by sea quarrelling with her.

With a tight smile she walked away from him, followed by Wilkins, and did not look back.

'Hell and damnation! Double damnation.' Chance flung himself on to the bench where Alessa had been sitting and dropped his head into his hands. He felt like tearing his hair out, but that was not going to get him anywhere. He leant back against the uprights of the arbour and tried to think. What had gone wrong just now?

Alessa had been upset over her encounter with her aunt, which was to be expected. It must have been emotional for both of them, and, unused to society and the manners that prevailed in it, Alessa had not understood the reserve that must be habitual with her aunt. Lady Blackstone would have been trying to soothe Alessa's fear of change with the offer to have her inheritance sent here to Corfu, but it was unthinkable that she could have meant it. Her plan would have been to wait until her niece was calmer and more used to her new family before explaining that, in reality, she had no choice but to take her back to England.

To leave her, the granddaughter and niece of earls, to live unmarried and independent on a Greek island? Unthinkable. People would consider her no better than that outrageous Stanhope woman, gallivanting around the Mediterranean with her lover. And Lady Hester Stanhope was a good ten years older. Alessa would be ruined—and worse, the Lord High Commissioner, one of the most influential people in the entire area, would know of it, to the shame of her new-found family.

But trying to explain that to Alessa, just at the moment,

would be futile. She was too proud and too independent and it would take several weeks living in the company of English ladies before she realised that and changed her attitude.

Chance got up and walked across the terrace, just in time to catch a glimpse of the white mule, Alessa sitting sideways on the big wooden saddle, vanishing up the track. That ridiculous hat! He could imagine it, decked with wild flowers on some village saint's day.

Her reaction to her aunt was one thing, and a problem that time would solve. But what had just gone so wrong between them? Had she truly believed he was intending to make her his mistress? But if so, why had she not said anything as they sat on the beach yesterday? Or today, when that tide of passion had washed over both of them in that musty little storeroom? Could it be that she had been expecting a *carte blanche* and would have accepted it—until she discovered that she had an inheritance that would make her independent? Did she believe now that she could catch other men, receive proposals of marriage?

Certainly she could have that expectation. If her aunt was careful how she introduced her back into the polite world, and Alessa was discreet, then the well-connected Miss Mcredith, daughter of a military hero and in possession of a respectable competence, could expect to have no difficulties on the Marriage Mart.

And if he told her he loved her now, she would imagine that he was trying to excuse his behaviour in making love to her and perhaps that he had decided that she would be an proper connection as a wife. That there were many far more eligible than she Alessa would have no way of knowing with her complete ignorance of the society. Nor could she have any inkling of his wealth and his connections. The Earl of Blakeney might marry where he wished.

'*You arrogant…*' The echo of Alessa's furious, unfinished insult cut across this complacent reflection. She was probably right, damn it. His family and friends would say he had every justification—not for arrogance, of course, but for proper pride and a sense of his own worth. But Alessa was the woman he wanted to marry, the woman he was in love with, and if she thought him arrogant, then he was just going to have to prove to her that she was wrong about him.

'Benedict, my dear friend.' It was Zagrede, strolling—or perhaps prowling was the better word—out on to the terrace. 'Come for a sail with me in my skiff. The ladies can watch from the shore, admiring our manly ability to tame the treacherous ocean, and then perhaps Lady Trevick will soften and let us take the young ladies out tomorrow.' He lounged gracefully against the balustrade.

Chance admired the showmanship, could appreciate the effect it must have on the ladies, but at the same time, he recognised something dangerous in the Count. This was not some charming mountebank, pretending to an exotic glamour. This man could use the knife in his belt and would kill to defend what was his with very little compunction. In fact, he thought, agreeing with a smile to Zagrede's proposal, he would probably kill to acquire what he wanted. A powerful friend in this part of the world, and a very dangerous enemy.

'And where is our new houseguest?' the Count enquired, padding along at Chance's elbow as he went inside to change. 'She is a very unexpected and very lovely young lady; I look forward to getting to know her better.'

'I'd wager you do,' Chance said, realising the moment the words left his lips that they were not delivered in the light tone that should have convinced Zagrede that he was simply jesting. The Count sent him a penetrating look as he shouldered open his bedchamber door. Chance had too much sense than to make things worse by attempting to explain his abruptness. Furious with both the other man and himself, he caught himself before he could give in to his instinct to turn and snarl 'You cannot have her—she is mine' into the Count's face.

Lord, he is making me as much of a savage as he is! His sense of the ridiculous surfaced and, instead of snarling, Chance turned and promised to be down at the beach in ten minutes.

Tomorrow Alessa would be in this house. He must treat her no differently to any of the other three young ladies and she would learn to trust him again, just as she would learn to accept the inevitability of her return to England.

'You are leaving us!' Dora's eyes were huge with welling tears. 'You are going to go away and leave us.'

Alessa pulled the child tight against her, her heart aching at the alarm in the little girl's eyes. She had been abandoned once before and the insecurity ran deep. 'No, I promise you, I will never leave you. I am going on a visit, that is all. I have found my aunt and she wants to get to know me better. Then, after a few days, she will get to know you and Demetri. But it is a big shock, finding me. I think she would like to take things a little bit slowly, and it is not her house, so inviting three people to stay is difficult.'

She reached out her free hand and caught hold of Demetri. Too much the man to cry, she could read his emotion in the set of his jaw. Hugging both children to her, she went and sat on the bench under the olive tree. 'It would be very difficult for me to go if you were not both so grown up and sensible.'

'Why?' Demetri sounded gruff.

'Because who will be host to Aunt Kate? And who will keep Aunt Agatha company?'

'I will be in charge?' His eyes were bright with pride now, and she could have sworn he had puffed out his chest.

'You will be in charge of security and the garden and the chickens and Dora will be in charge of the house and making Aunt Kate feel at home and visiting Aunt Agatha. What do you think? Can you do it?'

They both nodded, faces solemn, all tears forgotten. 'Good. I knew I could rely on you. And guess what—there is even more important news for us than just my new aunt. We can go to England.'

'England? All of us?' Demetri demanded.

'Yes, all of us. And you will go to school there and grow up to be a gentleman and Dora will have a governess and learn to play the piano and have lovely dresses.'

'Will I have to be an *English* gentleman?'

'You will be both a Greek gentleman *and* an English gentleman and then when you grow up you can chose to do what you want, where you want.'

'It rains all the time in England, Aunt Kate says so.'

'Not all the time, but it is not so hot as here and olives and vines do not grow.'

'Aiee! What do people eat then?'

'Lots of meat and cow's milk and cheese and many vegetables and fruits. And we will visit London, which is the biggest city in the world.'

'Bigger than Corfu Town?' Dora's eyes were popping.

'Bigger than the whole island.' The children were speechless. Alessa cuddled them close, her eyes meeting Kate's over the top of their heads. Was she doing the right thing? Yes, surely to give them all the opportunities and the choices in her power was right.

'We will all be fine,' Kate reassured her, her smile rueful as she took in the fierceness of Alessa's hold on the children.

'In three days from tomorrow, I want you all to come down to the villa to meet Lady Blackstone, my aunt,' Alessa declared. It was as long as she was prepared to be parted from the children and Aunt Honoria had to meet them sooner rather than later. She could hardly drag them off on a long voyage with a woman they did not know.

'All of us?' Kate's eyebrows had shot up.

'Yes, all three of you. I told my aunt that I lived with the wife of a sergeant of the garrison, she will expect to meet you.'

'Lumme.' Kate, for once, looked nervous. 'It'll be Sunday best, a fichu for decency and my hair braided up, I suppose. One look at me and her ladyship'll jump to all sorts of conclusions about my past, and that won't do you any good, even if she will be accurate, most like.'

'I am not ashamed to be your friend.' Alessa stretched to press Kate's hand. 'But I think she may be rather…conventional, and I shock her already, so we had all better be on our best behaviour.'

'Right you are. And what about his lordship, then? He's living there, isn't he? That'll be cosy.'

'Dora, would you run along to ask Dinos if I may borrow his mule and the pack saddle tomorrow morning? And, Demetri, can you find my two portmanteaux? I pushed them up into the hay loft.'

She watched until the children were out of earshot. 'We quarrelled. He seemed to think that…that we could be…and I did encourage him, only…' Her voice trailed off. 'Anyway, we quarrelled.'

'They're mostly all the same, men,' Kate said gloomily. 'My Fred's all right now, but talk about marriage and he wriggles like an eel on a hook. But lords and the like, they're worse. They're tricksy and they expect to get what they want, pay for it or no. Are you in love with him?'

'Yes,' Alessa said baldly.

'Does he know?'

'No! Good Heavens, no. I mean, when he kissed me, I kissed him back, but that doesn't necessarily mean I love him, does it? He wouldn't jump to that conclusion because I let him? I rather more than just let him kiss me, if truth be told,' she added with a burst of candour.

'Lord love you, no.' Kate grinned broadly. 'With a well set-up young man like that, to say nothing of the title and the money and everything, he won't think twice because a girl's willing. Why, I expect he's beating them off with a stick daily. You kissing him with unmaidenly enthusiasm is not going to make him suspicious, I'm sure. They all think they are God's gift to womankind anyway.'

'Thank goodness,' Alessa said devoutly. 'This is going to be hard enough, without him guessing.'

Chapter Twelve

Alessa approached the villa with butterflies in her stomach. She could not remember feeling this nervous for years. Since she had taken charge of the household she had learned to stand up for herself, think through what she wanted, and work out how to set about achieving it. No one else was going to do it for her. For a woman alone that had meant nervous sensibilities were an impractical luxury, and maidenly dithering and indecision got her precisely nowhere.

The problem now was that she was not at all sure she knew what she wanted, nor how to behave while she was finding out. Uncertainty was a more trying state than she had expected. With a silent request to Saint Spyridhon to suppress any tempests in her vicinity, she led her borrowed mule into the courtyard.

Two grooms immediately hurried to her side, one to take the leading rein, the other to lift down her luggage. They were less skilled than the butler in concealing their surprise that a guest at the High Commission villa would arrive at the back door in peasant clothing and leading her own mule.

'Thank you.' Alessa nodded to them and turned to young

Yanni, whose father had lent her the mule. '*Efharisto*, Yanni.' She pressed a coin into his grubby fist and he grinned, took back the leading rein with a proprietorial air and marched away, his bare feet kicking up the dust. He would go straight off to Demetri and report, she knew. It was as if her last link with her little family was broken.

'This way, if you please, Miss Alexandra.' The groom gestured to the back door and Alessa preceded him into the gloomy corridor she remembered from the day before.

Miss Alexandra. That seemed belittling after the dignity of *Kyria*—Mistress. The title was given with respect, according her the status of a married woman, and an independent economic entity. And Alexandra. No one had called her that for years, not since they had settled on the island and her father had changed her name for something 'more Greek'. At the time she had protested—no one she had met was called Alessa, and anyway, what about Alexander the Great?

He was a Macedonian, her father had said, brooking no argument. Only later she realised he was pained by recalling her mother saying her name, the French accent drawing out the four syllables luxuriously.

Now she was reduced to the status of an unmarried girl. Well, she must learn to bite her tongue and put up with it. To fall out with her newly discovered aunt was both ill mannered and unproductive.

Ushered briskly along the passage, she was past the storeroom where yesterday she had so shamelessly returned Chance's passion, and through the door into the hall, before she realised it.

Wilkins the butler was waiting for her. 'Your luggage has been taken up, Miss Alexandra, if you would please follow me. Miss Blackstone's woman will be waiting upon you and has selected some gowns for your approval. Miss Trevick has lent some items as well, I understand. The sempstress from Corfu Town will be calling this afternoon with some samples.'

From Corfu Town? Already? Aunt must have sent for her as soon as I left. Something else struck her as an anomaly. 'Wilkins.'

'Yes, Miss Alexandra?' He paused on the landing.

'I would prefer it if you would address me as Miss Meredith. I have no elder sister.'

The butler paused, just long enough for her to be seized with doubt. That was correct, was it not? The elder daughter was addressed by the family surname, the younger ones by their first names?

'Of course, Miss Meredith. My apologies. I will instruct the other staff.'

That was a relief. She had succeeded, perfectly politely, in putting the top-lofty butler in his place and asserting that she was not the poor relation. Now all she had to do was to deal as confidently with the residents of the villa.

Her bedchamber was a revelation. Wilkins opened the door, ushered her in and removed himself with a bow. Alessa found herself in a chamber as large as her entire apartment in the town, confronting a neatly turned out maid who was laying a bewildering array of clothing on the wide bed.

'Miss Alexandra.' The girl bobbed a curtsy. 'I'm Peters, miss, and Lady Blackstone says I'm to look after you as well as Miss Blackstone.'

'Thank you, Peters. I hope it will not make a great deal more work for you,' Alessa said pleasantly, closing the door behind her. 'And it is Miss Meredith, by the way.'

'Yes, Miss Meredith. I'm sorry, Miss Meredith.'

'You were not to know.' The girl shot her a grateful glance that gave Alessa a momentary qualm about the usual temper of Lady Blackstone if the maid was so nervous. 'Now, what are all these clothes?'

'What Miss Blackstone and Miss Trevick have lent, Miss Meredith.' The girl hastened to display the best items. 'Her ladyship said you were taller than Miss Blackstone, but she's lent stockings and a shawl and such like.' She eyed Alessa's clothes warily. 'That's a very pretty outfit, miss.'

'Yes. My Sunday best, but I will not wear it here. What would be suitable now, Peters?' The maid's eyes widened. 'I have not worn anything but Greek costume since I was much younger, so I am relying on you to tell me how to go on.'

'Yes'm.' The concept seemed to have struck the maid dumb.

'I think I would like a wash before I touch any of those lovely things,' Alessa added with a smile. 'I have walked two miles and I have been leading the mule, so I am a little dusty.'

'Would you like a bath, Miss Meredith?'

Alessa was about to protest that it was far too much trouble to carry water up all those stairs, then caught herself just in time. At the top of her house it was hard labour to carry up water; now she was in a villa full of servants, and she would be expected to behave as though she was used to that.

'Yes, thank you, that would be very welcome.'

'If you go through to the dressing room and get undressed behind the screen, I'll ring for the bath directly, miss.'

There is a dressing room as well? Amid a swathe of linen towels on the polished boards, an embossed leather screen gave privacy in a corner and presses and drawers stood empty, waiting for her new clothes to fill them.

'They are on their way up, Miss Meredith.' Peters came bustling in, a robe draped over her arm, and shooed Alessa behind the screen. 'I'll just undress you, miss.'

'Oh! No, I can manage.'

'But your stays, miss?'

'I do not wear them.' Alessa began to unlace her bodice, slipped it off and unhooked her waistband, stepping out of the wide black skirt to stand in front of the bemused maid in petticoats and blouse. She untied her garters and unbuckled her sturdy black shoes, rolling down the white stockings before a thought struck her. 'What about shoes?'

Peters seemed too stunned by the revelation about stays to take in what was being asked. 'Shoes, miss? Oh, kid sandals, I should think, with this gown.'

'I do not have any shoes, other than ones like this, Peters.'

''Strewth, miss.' They both regarded Alessa's bare feet. 'They are a bit big...I mean, a bit bigger than the other young ladies.'

'I am on them a great deal,' Alessa said ruefully.

'I don't mean they're enormous, miss. I could lend you some of my indoor shoes and then the sempstress could tell the shoemaker to come out, when she gets back.' Peters hitched up her skirts and placed one foot next to Alessa's.

'A perfect match. Thank you, Peters.' She began to unbutton the blouse, feeling curiously shy. The maid was used to undressing and dressing ladies, it was her job. But it felt so strange to be waited on.

'Miss Meredith?' Peters ran appreciative fingers over the fine white-work on the sleeves before folding the blouse over her arm. 'Can I ask, miss, why you haven't...I mean, I don't want to pry or anything.'

The thud of feet over the boards heralded the entrance of footmen with hot-water jugs. Alessa waited until they had finished, then stepped out of her petticoats and handed them to the maid. 'No, I do not mind questions, Peters. I will tell you about why I am here on Corfu, and you may tell the other servants too, if they should ask.'

* * *

The tale lasted until Alessa had taken her bath and was swathed in a large towel. Everything she had related was true, except for her role with the laundry of the Commission's ladies and the fact that she knew Lord Blakeney.

'Coo!' Peters's eyes were wide. 'That's just like one of those novels, miss, ever so exciting. No wonder you haven't got the clothes.'

'And I do not know much about how to go on in society either, Peters. I am going to have to rely on you to make sure I am wearing the right things all the time.'

'Right, miss. Well, it's a chemise first and then the stays.' Alessa's expression must have registered, for the maid chuckled. 'You won't get into these gowns unless you lace, miss, but I won't do it too tight, don't you worry.'

Alessa walked downstairs an hour later, convinced that if this was loose lacing, then she would faint if Peters tried anything tighter. But the effect on her bosom was startling, even under a carefully draped fichu, and it certainly made one slow down and walk with elegance. Used to rushing everywhere, Alessa felt a little like a hobbled mule.

Peters had brushed out her hair and braided, pinned and pleated until it bore as close a resemblance to a fashionable style as possible without the attentions of a hairdresser and hot irons, and Alessa had stared back in wonder at the stranger with her face in the glass.

Even Wilkins unbent a touch as she reached the foot of the stairs. The butler emerged as though by magic and smiled primly. 'Very nice, Miss Meredith, if I may be so bold as to comment. Quite the transformation scene. The ladies are in the front reception room.'

Thank goodness, only the ladies. The thought of meeting

Chance again under Aunt Honoria's critical eye was daunting, although it had to be faced sooner or later.

Music flowed from the half-open door. Alessa slipped in and regarded the scene unobserved. Lady Trevick was reading a journal and Lady Blackstone was writing at a desk in the window embrasure. On the other side of the room Maria Trevick picked her way through an air on the piano and her sister Helena and Frances Blackstone appeared to be trying to make something out of cardboard and sewing silks.

Then the girls glanced up and saw her. 'Oh, Cousin Alexandra—you are here!' Frances jumped to her feet, her slightly plump face beaming, and Maria lifted her hands from the piano keys.

'Ah, welcome, my dear.' Lady Trevick's assessing gaze transformed into a smile of approval. 'How nice you look. Is your room to your taste?'

'It is delightful, ma'am. And I must thank Miss Trevick and Miss Blackstone for lending me clothes, and for the help of the maid.' She glanced across to where Lady Blackstone had laid down her quill and was studying her. 'Good morning, Aunt Honoria.'

'Good morning, Alexandra. I must say you look very well, very well indeed. Did Peters tell you that the dressmaker is coming this afternoon?'

'Yes, Aunt Honoria, thank you.' What was she expected to do now?

'Do you play the piano?' Maria was at her side.

'No, I am afraid I play no instrument. You seem to be very accomplished.'

'Thank you. Never mind about not being able to play— the practise is an awful bore, so just be glad you have escaped that. Although...' she lowered her tone, leading Alessa towards the table and the other two '…it is very good for flirting with gentlemen when they turn the music for you.'

'Come and help us.' Her cousin patted the chair next to her. 'We are trying to make this reticule from a pattern in *Ackermann's Repository*. It says it may be easily made up with a little care. We've had three attempts to cut it out, and it still looks lop-sided.'

'Perhaps if we trace off the pattern on this thinner paper and then fold it in half…' Alessa was working as she spoke. This was like making paper castles with the children. 'And then cut round and open it out. There—is that better?'

'Wonderful.' Frances applied the pattern to a fresh piece of cardboard and began to trace round it. 'What shall we cover it in?'

An hour later the reticule was nearing completion, but Alessa could not believe that the four of them had spent so much time on a frivolous piece of handwork. Nor could she recall having sat still for so long without doing something useful for an age. She glanced anxiously towards her aunt, who was making inroads into what seemed to be an inexhaustible pile of correspondence.

'I feel I ought to be doing something useful for Lady Blackstone,' she whispered.

'Goodness, Mama will soon tell us if she needs anything,' Frances responded. 'You are here as my cousin, not a paid companion. I am sure you need a rest as well, having to earn your living making all those medicines and things. And don't you have two children living with you? Still, I expect your chaperon helps look after them.'

'Yes, but… Yes, of course.'

'What sort of medicines do you make?' Helena put down the needle she was trying to thread. 'Love potions?'

As it happened Alessa had both a medicine for inflaming male passions and one for damping them down in her repertoire. Both had been taught her by Agatha, although she had never had cause to prescribe either. However, she suspected that a potion to make a man 'as virile as a rutting boar' was not quite what Helena had in mind.

How young these girls seemed, playing with their fashion journals and dreaming of flirtation. Still, she had to live with them, if only for a while. She must try and enter into the spirit of life here. 'For whom do you want it?' she enquired conspiratorially.

Helena giggled and blushed. 'She thinks she's in love with the Count of Kurateni,' Maria whispered.

'Oh, Voltar…' Frances sighed gustily, ducking as a balled-up skein of sewing silk flew at her.

'He seems to be very handsome and charming,' Alessa said diplomatically. 'Have you known him long?'

'Only from a distance.' From Helena's gusty sigh, Alessa rather gathered that this had lent enchantment to her infatuation. 'He visits Uncle Thomas on business sometimes.'

'I think he is a pirate—what do you think, Alexandra? Have you met him before?'

'No, never, but anyone living in Corfu Town would know him by sight—he is a great trader and his ships are often in the port. What about you, Maria? Do you have a beau?' For some reason this reduced Miss Trevick to silent confusion.

'She is in love with someone, but we don't know who, she won't tell, the sly thing,' Frances announced.

'Well, at least I am not throwing out lures to the Earl,' Maria retorted.

'More fool you,' Frances said pertly. 'I think he is *gorgeous*. What do you think, Alexandra?'

'Very handsome,' Alessa pronounced judiciously, 'but very

arrogant too, don't you think? He looks it anyway. And he expects to get his own way in everything, I have no doubt.'

'So hard to please!' A masculine voice behind her made her jump and reduced the other three, all sitting with their heads close together, to blushing confusion. 'Who is this handsome man you are so critical of, Miss Meredith? Does he know your harsh opinion? The poor creature must be desolated, all hope lost, if he does.'

'You are *dreadful*, Count.' Helena gazed at him wide-eyed. 'Don't you think he is dreadful, Lord Blakeney?'

'I am sure of it.' Chance strolled in and, catching one of the remaining chairs set at the table, spun it round and straddled it, his chin on his clasped hands resting on the back. His eyes roamed round the four flushed faces before him. 'What has my friend Zagrede done to offend you ladies this morning?'

'Miss Meredith was expressing the harshest opinion of some poor, weak man and I came to his defence, that is all. So fair, and yet so cruel.' The Count dropped one lid in a slow wink that sent Helena into stifled laughter.

'Who is this unsatisfactory creature?' Chance's brown eyes studied Alessa, leaving her in no doubt he knew perfectly well who she had been criticising. She returned his stare, as coolly as he sent it.

'I dare not say, and if I did, the poor thing would not recognise himself, such is his self-assurance. I might even say, smug arrogance.'

'You have a low opinion of my whole sex, I dare say.'

'I have had the opportunity to observe feckless husbands and idle sons, although most of my fellow islanders work very hard and are devout, good men. Of male English aristocrats my experience has not been, shall we say, encouraging.'

The others had fallen silent, puzzling over this sparring

match, although Alessa was hardly aware of their presence—Chance's brown eyes seemed to fill her sight.

'Your father must be an exception, surely?'

'I loved Papa dearly and I consider him a hero and a patriot of whom I shall always be proud, but as a husband and a father—and doubtless as a son—he could be atrocious. He was reckless, selfish and opinionated.'

There was a sharp intake of breath from the girls at this ruthless dissection of her father. 'And Grandpapa was not very nice to you either, was he, Alexandra?' Frances ventured shyly.

'I must not criticise your—*our*—grandpapa; I did not know him. There may have been faults on both sides.'

'And do you know any other English aristocrats, then?' Maria enquired.

'One sees them all the time, visiting Corfu. They are easy to observe as they now own the island.'

'As the French and the Venetians before them,' Chance observed.

'Indeed. We are an island doomed to be occupied. But the French and Venetians did not bring cricket, of course.'

That reduced the whole group to laughter, breaking the tension and causing Lady Trevick to stroll over, observing, 'You are very merry.'

'Miss Meredith is trying to convince us that the introduction of cricket to Corfu is a benefit of English occupation,' the Count explained.

'You are a connoisseur of the game, Alexandra?'

'I have watched it played on the Spianadha. I have no idea of the rules, of course—it seems very complicated.'

'By no means,' Chance began. 'Let me explain.'

'Oh, no!' The Count threw up his hands in mock self-defence. 'I call upon you ladies to protect me! I see the evangelical light in Blakeney's eye—he intends to teach me how to play cricket.'

The laughter and denials bought Lady Blackstone to the table, observing in her cool voice that they all seemed much livelier since Alexandra had arrived. This had the effect of bringing the gentlemen to their feet and making the young ladies sit up and stop giggling. Alessa wondered if her aunt was always this severe or if it was her own, unsatisfactory, presence.

She glanced across and found Chance watching her, his face unreadable, as he made polite conversation with Lady Trevick about making up a cricketing picnic when they were all back in Corfu Town.

'I am sure Sir Thomas will be able to call up an eleven and they can challenge the officers of the garrison, and any ships that are in port. Would you join the High Commission side, Lord Blakeney?'

'But of course, ma'am, I would be honoured.'

'Perhaps you could teach the Count to play while we are here,' Alessa suggested mischievously. 'The beach is firm, flat sand.'

'I am sure you would play *wonderfully,* Count,' Helena said breathlessly.

The Count looked at her, his dark eyes a little narrowed. 'You think so, Miss Helena?'

Helena nodded vigorously.

'Then it is a pity we do not have the proper bats. Or is it rackets?'

'I brought all the cricket equipment with me, along with the battledores and shuttlecocks and the croquet set.' Lady Trevick smiled, obviously happy that her guests would be entertained. The Count directed an ironic bow of defeat in Chance's direction.

'I owe you vengeance for that, Miss Meredith,' he murmured in Alessa's ear. 'How am I going to take my revenge?'

Alessa stared into the clever, dark eyes and read suggestions, promises and lurking danger in them. A little quiver went through her—for all his affability, this was a man to treat with very great caution.

Chapter Thirteen

Alessa's view of the Count was confirmed by the next day's events. At breakfast Lady Blackstone announced her intention to stroll along the causeway that linked the mainland to the steep rocky promontory. Once across, one could climb the steep track to where the monastery stood watch over the village and the bay.

'It is a cooler day today,' she observed, 'and I should welcome a walk. Perhaps I will go to the very top. Who will join me?'

The entire party, it seemed, wished to share the experience, including Mr Harrison, released from his labours by the Lord High Commissioner, who was paying a visit to the troops in charge of building the road across the island.

Alessa, feeling as though she had been inactive for a week, not a day, was delighted by the idea. 'It is a very beautiful walk,' she observed, 'although quite steep if you intend to go right to the top.'

'We could take a mule or two,' Chance suggested. 'Then, if any of the ladies becomes fatigued, they can ride, and we can carry some refreshments with us.'

'We need not take much, the monks will offer food and drink, and the garden is a very lovely place to eat.'

'They will allow women in?' Lady Blackstone appeared surprised.

'Oh, yes, although we must all take a scarf to cover our heads and make sure that we have long sleeves and modest necklines. And in the church, women must not go through the iconostasis—the screen behind the altar,' she warned.

'One forgets that you have lived here for so long and know all these things,' Helena commented brightly. 'Are you Greek Orthodox?'

'Helena!' her mother reproved sharply. *As if she had asked me something quite scandalous*, Alessa thought. Conforming to the Church of England was obviously going to be important, although both the children were Orthodox, and she was most certainly not going to change that, whatever her new family thought. Surely there must be a Greek Orthodox church in London?

'I am an Anglican,' she said, much to the obvious relief of the older women. Presumably an even greater worry was that she had been brought up by her mother as a Roman Catholic. 'To have attended anything other than the Orthodox church would have marked us out for attention during the French occupation.'

That appeared to be an acceptable excuse. The Count, who was sitting next to Alessa enquired, low-voiced, so as not to attract attention, 'So, you are not truly a devotee of the Saint?'

'Saint Spyridhon? But of course I am.' Alessa smiled at him. 'All Corfiots are, and I consider myself one, just as much as I am English. I expect you have an occasional word with him yourself, Count, when the gales are blowing and the seas are high. But you sound as though you have seen me in church.'

'The day I met my good friend Benedict, you were there in Ayios Spyridhon, in the shadows.'

'What sharp eyes you have, Count.'

'For beauty, always.'

That made her blush and he laughed, drawing a sharp glance, not from her aunt, but from Chance, sandwiched neatly between Helena and Maria. And worryingly she was aware of the Count's gaze following hers. She heard a low chuckle from the Albanian and saw Chance's eyes narrow. Now Zagrede knew Chance was watching her and Chance knew the Count… *Oh, bother all men!*

Alessa changed back into her Greek clothes for the walk, not relishing the thought of climbing to the top of the rock in stays and someone else's borrowed gown. Now, if she wanted to scramble off the track in pursuit of plants, she could do so with a clear conscience.

Lady Blackstone raised an eyebrow at the sight of not just the wide black skirts, but also an empty basket lined with white cloths, but Lady Trevick was enthusiastic. 'Such a useful skill for a lady, to be able to manage her own stillroom,' she pronounced. The other woman did not comment and Alessa was left with the impression that her aunt felt slightly outranked by her hostess and would take care to conform to her opinions.

The Count fell in beside her as they started to cross the causeway, and gallantly relieved her of the basket. 'I have heard of you and your skills, *Kyria* Alessa,' he confided. His use of her Greek name made her feel more comfortable with him. 'You cured one of my men of his bad shoulder last year with a mixture of manipulation and ointments.'

'Oh, yes, I am glad my treatment worked.' She glanced back to where her aunt was strolling beside Lady Trevick. 'I would be grateful if you did not mention that I do more than make medicines and salves. I do not think my aunt would approve of my touching patients.'

'You laying hands on Albanian seamen will be our secret.'

The Count chuckled, and she wondered dubiously if she was leaving herself open to some sort of blackmail. But then Chance knew too, and so did Mr Harrison, so it was hardly a deep dark secret. It was only the Count who might say something out of pure mischief.

'Tell me about your ship,' she asked, turning the conversation away from herself. 'What cargo do you bring, or are you taking it on?'

'Both. I have brought furs and skins and I am taking oil. We produce very fine furs. Do you enjoy hunting, *Kyria* Alessa? My country is famed for it, both in the mountains and the lakes.'

'I have never tried. I do not think I would care to kill something, except for food.'

'A pity; you have sharp eyes and a steady nerve, you would be a good shot.'

'Oh, I can shoot.' Alessa laughed. 'My father taught me, only he showed me how to shoot men, not animals.'

'How bloodthirsty! The French, I hope.'

'Of course. Not that I ever had to do so, but Papa felt I should know how to defend myself.'

For some reason she glanced back. In the lead, they had just reached the point where the track bent back and began to climb the monastery rock, and they had a good view of the others behind and slightly below them. Chance had stopped and was shielding his eyes to stare up at them, his face hard to read at the distance.

'My good friend Benedict is wondering what I am saying to make you laugh,' the Count observed with a chuckle. 'It is very tempting to see if I can make him really jealous.'

'Whatever do you mean?' Alessa had a sinking feeling she knew—Zagrede's sharp eyes seemed to miss nothing. 'I hardly know him.'

'You saved his life, so I hear. And when you do not think he is looking, you watch him, and when he thinks you are not looking, he watches you. It is obvious he desires you—which is quite natural. He is a man, after all, and you are a beautiful woman. And now you are so well chaperoned by your new aunt, what can he do about it? Why, nothing at all. It is very amusing.'

'It may be amusing to you,' Alessa snapped, too startled to be diplomatic, 'but you are making a story up out of nothing. It is complete nonsense and I would be most embarrassed if you repeated it to anyone else.'

'Oh, ho! A raw nerve. But of course, a sensible girl like you would never give her virtue to some passing English aristocrat, however attractive she finds him. After all, however well bred the lady, no Earl is going to want to marry someone whose past, even if it is spotless, is so unconventional. I admire your discretion and your restraint—I imagine Benedict can exert considerable charm. No, no…' he held up his hands as Alessa turned indignantly to confront him '…it is our little secret. We are beginning to have several, are we not?'

He was a rogue and a tease, and possibly something much more dangerous, but he was also very charming, even if alarmingly frank. Alessa eyed the Count, eyes narrowed, and made herself stand up to him. She would worry about his insinuations about Chance later. 'You *think* you have two secrets of mine, I know I have none of yours. I hardly think that is a fair exchange.'

'What can I confess?' he wondered aloud. 'I know, I will open my heart and perhaps you will help me. I am looking for an English wife.'

'Goodness.' Alessa turned to look at him and began to walk backwards uphill, the better to study his face. 'Do you mean it?'

'But of course. And here I am, surrounded by four lovely

young Englishwomen of good family—and what do I learn? Two of them are about to be whisked off to Venice before I have the chance to fix my affections with either.'

'Lady Trevick is taking her daughters to Venice?' Over the Count's shoulder she could see Chance, walking at her cousin's side, but looking up the hill at the leading pair. She skipped round to walk beside the Count again; the sight of Chance, after Zagrede's insinuations, made her uncomfortable.

'But, no, Lady Blackstone is taking her daughter and you with her when she travels on to join her husband in Venice.' He must have realised he had given her a shock, for he added, 'You did not know?'

'No, I did not.' Now, what did that mean? She had no objection to visiting Venice, it sounded fascinating, but it took her no nearer establishing herself and the children in England, nor to claiming her small inheritance. And by how long would it lengthen the journey? She did not want the children unsettled and without a fixed home for any longer than she could help it. And it made her the pensioner of her aunt for an even greater period.

'You will love Venice, and I will visit you there.'

Alessa pulled herself together. She must speak to her aunt when they were back at the villa and discover the truth of the matter, but meanwhile to brood on it was rude. 'I am sure I will. I have read so much about it. Do you visit the city often?'

'But of course, I trade there, as I do through all of the Adriatic and the Ionian islands. I will call upon you and Miss Blackstone and I will bring you silks and pearls and you will both fall in love with me.'

He was impossible. Alessa laughed, linking her arm through his as the track suddenly steepened. 'You have not fixed your affections, then, Count?'

'But no, although I suspect that in the case of one young

lady it is already a lost cause.' He gave her a very speaking look and Alessa found she was blushing.

'Oh, look, fennel in flower. I must pick some. I have none fresh.'

'It grows everywhere.' The Count held out his hand to steady her as she scrambled up the bank.

'Yes, I know, but it is a very good variety here—see how large the flower heads are,' she improvised. She picked one and held it out and the Count cupped her hand to look at the floret just as Chance and Frances caught up with them.

'Are you all right?' Chance demanded, looking furious.

'Of course.' Alessa returned his glare with a haughty look of her own, then caught the Count's eye. She could read the message he was sending as plainly as though he had spoke aloud: *jealous.* 'Of course,' she repeated with a smile that hid gritted teeth. 'I am very used to this terrain, my lord.'

Could Zagrede be correct? Was Chance truly jealous because he lusted after her or was the Count wrong and he entertained some deeper feeling, despite her shady past? Surely neither was correct—this was dog-in-the-manger behaviour, two virile men sparing over the womenfolk.

Instead of irritating her—which of course it should, as an independent woman—she realised she found it rather endearing. 'Something is amusing you, Miss Meredith?' Chance enquired politely. He had edged closer to the side of the track so that she had an equal choice of whose hand to take if she wanted to be helped down.

'For some reason something reminded me of Demetri,' she observed, reaching out to take Frances's hand instead and jumping down beside her. 'I cannot imagine why.' She tossed the bunch of fennel heads into the basket with a smile of thanks to the Count and linked her arm through her cousin's. 'He is my young ward,' she explained to Zagrede.

She had half-expected Chance to catch her meaning, and the darkling look he shot her told he that shaft had gone home, but she had not expected the Count to take her up. 'Oh, ho!' he chuckled, turning away. 'The lady has a sharp tongue, my friend, let us walk on and nurse our wounds in private.'

Alessa let them get well ahead before strolling on with Frances, who appeared to notice nothing amiss with the by-play. It was dawning on Alessa that her cousin was both very young and very sheltered.

'He is so handsome.' Frances sighed.

'The Count? I agree, such a romantic figure,' Alessa teased, straight-faced, knowing her cousin meant Chance. She had no real worries about the state of Frances's heart; this was calf-love, she was certain. In a way, her own lack of concern at the girl's wide-eyed adoration was proof of it. She really loved the man, and she felt not a twinge of anxiety about Frances's admiration for him.

Whereas you should be concerned about how he feels about you, she told herself and this time a stab of fear found the pit of her stomach. He might be bristling at the Count, but he seemed not to be a man in love, nor even attracted, just one feeling defensive because he had seen a woman first. *What do I want? What can I hope for? How could I have let myself be so carried away as to let him kiss me the second time?*

The first time, that encounter in the sea, was so outrageous as to be beyond explanation or defence. The only thing to do about it was to ignore it and hope Chance would do the same. But if he was bent on seduction, could she resist him? Oh, the wretched Count! She had thought she was ready to try to set things right between herself and Chance; now she had no idea *how* she felt, let alone what his intentions were.

But walking up a steep track while making polite conversation under the observant eyes of a number of people was not the right place to be agonising about the state of one's heart. Alessa turned to her cousin with a smile and tackled the other worry that was nagging at her.

'Is your papa at home in England while you are on your travels?'

'Oh, no, Papa is in Venice on some diplomatic business, to do with trade, I believe. He is with the Foreign Office.'

'I am impressed; he must be both highly knowledgeable and very skilful,' Alessa flattered. 'But I had no idea the Foreign Office had anything to do with trade. I am very ignorant about the government, I'm afraid.'

'It is all to do with piracy.' Frances lowered her voice. 'I am not supposed to say anything, but as you are family, I am sure it is all right to tell you.'

'Piracy? Of course, these seas are notorious for it.' Alessa pondered as they climbed, the sea sparkling blue below them and the fragrant pines and herb-covered rough ground rising on their right hand. 'I suppose the British will use their naval power in the area to suppress it, now they have control of the Ionian islands.'

'How clever you are.' Frances sighed. 'I really do not understand all this business about alliances and what happens in Venice, and the Papal States now Napoleon is gone, and all the other things that seem to occupy Papa. Still...' she seemed to cheer up '...I am sure we will have a lovely time in Venice—after all, you and I do not have to worry about this boring diplomatic stuff.'

Alessa thought it fascinating, and would have liked to know more, but she did not want to encourage her cousin to be indiscreet. And there was a perfectly innocuous question that was far more important to have answered. 'How long do you expect to stay in Venice?' she asked casually, stooping to pick thyme.

'Oh, until Papa's mission is complete—about two more months, I think—and then we will all travel back together. Still, we will have plenty to occupy us. Mama will be holding lots of parties, I expect, and I believe the shopping is excellent.'

Two months in Venice. The only way to look at it was as an adventure; she could only hope the children would take to travel. Strange that her aunt had not mentioned their destination yet.

Alessa looked back over her shoulder. The two older women were walking side by side, heads together in deep conversation. Helena had apparently found the ascent tiring and was perched on one of the two donkeys that a groom was leading and Maria was climbing steadily, and in apparent silence, next to Mr Harrison. As Alessa watched, she tripped and he put out a hand to steady her.

The smile she gave him was warm and sweet and she made no attempt to free her arm, letting him hold it protectively as they walked. *Ah, ha!* So that is Maria's secret. Now, what will Sir Thomas make of his secretary falling in love with his niece? And what will Lady Trevick make if it? Perhaps she already knew, although it seemed unlikely, if Maria was so secretive with her own sister.

Alessa was still preoccupied when they came to the flat area outside the monastery gates. Chance was lying on his back under an olive tree, his straw hat tipped down over his face. The Count had cast off his jacket and was leaning against the sloping trunk of the tree, looking out over the bay. As the girls reached the terrace he straightened up, nudging Chance with his toe. 'The first of the intrepid ladies has reached us. And what are you dreaming about with that smile on your lips, *Kyria* Alessa?'

The question took her unawares and she answered without thought. 'Love.'

Chance sat up abruptly, his hat falling off.

'You are in love? Of course you are.' The Count's eyes were sparkling with mischief. 'But who is the fortunate man?'

'I did not say I was in love,' Alessa corrected with a smile. 'I was thinking about it in the abstract.'

'How can love be abstract?' Chance stood up, stooping to retrieve his hat and clapping it on his head. Bending had made him flushed, which seemed odd for such a fit man.

'Divine love,' Miss Blackstone observed solemnly. 'And disinterested love of one's fellow man, those could be abstract.'

'Well, by all means, let us collect ourselves in a suitably reverential frame of mind if we are to enter the monastery,' Chance said, somewhat tartly, but Frances merely gazed at him wide-eyed, and nodded agreement.

The Count put on his coat again and Alessa untied the shawl she had been wearing as a sash and threw it over her head and shoulders, topping it off with her straw hat. 'I will go and ask for admission to the church and gardens.'

When she got back, a young lay brother at her side, the rest of the party had reached the gate. The groom lifted down the provisions and tied the donkeys in the shade while the ladies fussed with shawls and hats, then the group made their way up the steps and into the monastery.

The lay brother led them through a maze of paths, up and down steps and then into the first of the terraces of the gardens, overlooking the sea. With a shy gesture he invited them to sit and hurried off.

'But how beautiful!' Lady Blackstone was shaken out her usual calm by the vista of sparkling blue sea and craggy cliffs and islands. 'What an exquisite place.'

The others began to explore, exclaiming as they found view after view, and endlessly tempting nooks and benches from which to admire them. Alessa, who had visited several times, turned to help the groom set out the food they had brought and was soon joined by the lay brother, a servant at his side, with jugs of water, a pitcher of wine and a big bowl of glossy olives.

'Should we pay? What would be appropriate? I do not want to cause offence.' Chance came across as the lay brother took himself off with a smile.

'An offering would be appreciated; you can leave something with the porter at the gate when we leave. And in the church, put money in the box for candles. Even if you do not choose to light one, they will do so for our safe return home.'

She called to the others and the group clustered round the picnic, helping themselves and then finding a comfortable spot to eat. Alessa took her repast and went to perch on the edge of the well-head, which allowed a view, not of the sea, but of the complex tiled roofs of the monastery buildings. The scrape of leather on the flags made her glance up, half-expecting the Count, bent on more teasing, but it was Chance, plate in one hand, beaker in the other.

'May I join you, Alessa?'

'Of course.' Everyone else was out of earshot, choosing to eat with a sea view. Alessa braced herself for whatever Chance had to say. They had not been alone together since their falling-out on the terrace and she had no idea what to expect from him. If the Count were correct, only a proposition of a shameful sort.

'Will you light a candle for your safe return home?' he asked, setting down his plate next to hers and seating himself on the broad stone well-top.

'I expect so, although my aunt will probably regard it as superstition.'

'Safe return home to where, though?'

Wherever you are. The words were so vivid in her mind that for one awful moment she thought she had spoken them aloud. Chance was staring at her—*had* she said something?

Chapter Fourteen

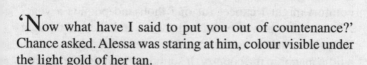

'Now what have I said to put you out of countenance?' Chance asked. Alessa was staring at him, colour visible under the light gold of her tan.

'Nothing! I mean, you have made me think about returning to England, and I truly do not know if it is for the best. Corfu has been home for so long. What if I do not like England? What if my family does not like me? And then there are the children to consider. Part of me thinks this is the best way to give them opportunities, and part of me thinks I am wrenching them away from everything they know.'

'Children are adaptable,' Chance said bracingly. 'And it is up to you to make the decisions, not for them to dictate to you, their guardian. And you will soon settle with your family.'

'I do not know whether I would want to live with them permanently.' She was looking dubious.

'But of course you must—unmarried ladies do not live independently.'

'I am not a conventional unmarried lady, am I?' She sent him a sideways look and he wondered if she was testing to see just how far she could go.

'No, you are not, and to be comfortable in England I would suggest you become as conventional as possible, as soon as possible. Surely you want to make your come-out in society?'

'And find myself a nice conventional husband? Hmm.' She wrinkled her nose endearingly.

No, that was not what he wanted for her. He wanted her to fall in love with him and remain, in private at least, his very unconventional Alessa. But how could he say any of that, here in a monastery garden, surrounded by other people?

'Would one want me, though? My past is dubious, after all.' She did not seem to expect an answer to her own question, for she changed the subject abruptly. 'Tell me, what degree of comfort might I expect for one thousand pounds a year?' Alessa took a bite of bread and cheese and chewed thoughtfully for a minute. 'My aunt says I have about that much, and a little manor in the country. It sounds a great deal of money.'

'A respectable competence,' Chance agreed. 'Not a fortune, but you can maintain a small staff and dress well. You could keep your own modest carriage as well.'

'And a good school for Demetri? And a governess for Dora?'

'Why, yes, if you feel it best for them.'

'I do.' Chance found she was regarding him severely over the rim of her glass. 'Please do not suggest to my aunt that there is any other solution, because if they cannot come with me, I am not going.'

'Really, I have nothing to say in the matter,' Chance protested.

'Oh, yes, you have, if you choose. Status is very important to her, and I think she feels sometimes that she has married beneath her. She defers to your opinion, and to Lady Trevick's—have you not noticed?'

'I would expect her to defer to male opinion,' Chance began.

'Why? Now you are being stuffy again, just as you were

on the terrace the other day, and I do not want to argue with you again.'

'Stuffy? That was not what you said at the time, if I recall.'

'Arrogant, then, if you must have it.' Alessa scowled at him and Chance realised he was scowling back. Then suddenly her expression lightened and she smiled. Something inside him stammered and he realised it was his heart. 'Oh, no, we must not quarrel. I will say sorry if you will.' Chance found he could not resist the sparkle in her eyes. Then she looked away hastily and he was stricken with the fear that the sparkle had been tears, not humour. When she turned back, she was blinking a little in the sunlight.

'Of course. I am sorry if I was—' her brows drew together '—*am* arrogant. And I am sorry for what happened in the bay.'

'And I am sorry I jumped to conclusions about your motives and because I was just as much to blame as you for what happened in the bay, and at the villa, and I should not have been cross about it.'

'I take full responsibility for that,' he protested, determined to do this apology properly.

'Now that *is* arrogant.' A chill had come over her. Why? A moment ago he thought they could be friends again. 'I am not a sheltered little miss like my cousin,' she observed. 'Men take these things less seriously than women.' Alessa popped an olive between her lips and bit into it slowly with even white teeth.

Something turned hot and tense inside Chance's chest and he hurriedly looked away across the garden to where Zagrede was lounging in the shade next to Frances and Helena. There was something familiar about that shrub…

'Should I warn the Count about lying in that particular place?'

Alessa looked across and gave a gurgle of laughter that turned the heat to molten desire. He turned, and knew from the way the amused smile froze and faltered that she had seen his feelings in his eyes. To hell with waiting until they were back in England and she had found her feet. She thought he was not taking her seriously, she had just said so. That must be put right. He took her hand, feeling it tremble for a moment before she regained her calm.

'Alessa, there is something I need to say to you. This not the place, but when we leave, contrive to walk at the back, with me.' Could he trust what Voltar had said so surprisingly on those last few hundred yards up to the monastery? *Trust your instincts, my friend, hazard a little, surprise yourself*, he had concluded, his habitually mocking tone making light of serious advice.

She looked away, then down at her hand clasped in his. The little shiver ran through it again. 'Why?'

'Because I have a proposition to make to you, and I would like a little privacy to make it in.'

'No.' She said it quietly, but with a vehemence that shook him. 'After what was said on the terrace yesterday, I can only assume you are mocking me. I made a grave mistake in allowing myself to…to yield to temptation to the extent that I did. I deeply regret it. But there is nothing else, nothing, that can be between us.'

Confused, he shook his head. 'I thought from what the Count said that you might consider—'

'Never! He has no business meddling, and he is quite wrong. I would never accept.'

Before he could stop her, Alessa wrenched her hand free and jumped down. Her face was pale beneath the soft golden glow the sun had given her, and her teeth were shut hard on her lower lip. She swept over to where the two older women were sitting, their backs to the courtyard, looking out over the sweep of sea.

'Would anyone like anything more to eat, or shall we visit the church?' she called, her voice light and cheerful.

She can turn down an offer of marriage, and sound so carefree? Damn it, how could I be so wrong? She did not even hesitate. Chance watched Alessa blithely rounding up the little party. *How could I have misjudged her so?*

How could he! How could I have misjudged Chance so? I never truly thought he would have cynically set out to make me his mistress. But the Count was right. Damn the man for interfering—hadn't I been definite enough that I would not consider such a thing? 'Do mind your head under this arch, Aunt Honoria.' *He must have thought I was protesting for form's sake. The Count certainly has divined the truth of my feelings for Chance.* 'Here on the right, Frances, isn't that a wonderful icon of St George and the dragon? Such rich colours.' *I was right that he was dangerous, and so wrong to give him even a hint of encouragement.* 'Ladies, we must stay here, although the men may pass through the iconostasis.'

Alessa told herself that she made an excellent guide to the little church, and was pleased to see a generous number of coins fall into the collecting box by the candles. Lady Blackstone looked scandalised when both her niece and the Count took candles and lit them, then Lady Trevick followed suit, exclaiming, 'How very pretty they look; I really cannot see the harm.'

Although Lady Blackstone did not go so far as to light one herself, she did not protest when Frances added hers, turning instead to lay her hand on Chance's arm 'I see you do not follow the local custom, my lord. Perhaps you could assist me out—it is so very gloomy in here and the incense makes my head ache.'

Alessa heard her voice, low but penetrating as the two ducked out through the door into the sunshine. 'I must say I prefer the reverent simplicity of an English country church. But you do not light a candle?'

'I do not think I am in a suitable frame of mind,' Chance returned.

Alessa looked around, her lips tightly compressed against a word that would be highly improper in such a setting, and found Voltar Zagrede regarding her quizzically. 'How could you?' she hissed at him, taking him firmly by the arm and pulling him out of the church. Her aunt and Chance were talking over by the well, so she dragged the Count to the other end of the courtyard and behind a spreading tree.

'My dear Alessa,' he purred, 'I am flattered—'

'No, you are not,' she snapped. 'How could you give Chance the idea that I would accept a *carte blanche* from him?'

He shrugged. 'But that was not my intention. I thought to indulge in a little matchmaking.'

'How, exactly?'

'I told him I thought you were very much attracted. Perhaps I gave him the wrong idea, exaggerated the extent of your passion, perhaps. But I will go and explain, make it right.'

'You will do no such thing! I have already put right any misapprehension the Earl might be harbouring about my willingness to agree to what he wants, and I would be obliged if you do nothing, absolutely nothing, to interfere again.' She knew she was being both rude and abrupt, but as the man seemed impervious to hints, and was a stranger to tact, only a bludgeon would do.

'My dear, you have my pledge. Not a word will I utter.' Zagrede lifted her hand and pressed it to her lips before she realised his intention. 'I am your most devoted slave.'

A gasp behind them made Alessa turn, her hand still trapped in the Count's. The three young women had emerged from the church and were all staring at her: Frances and Maria with expressions of delighted shock, Helena with a look of wounded betrayal. And to put the cap upon it, her aunt and Chance turned from their conversation at the well to see what the small stir was about.

Alessa snatched her hand free and stepped back, only to find herself virtually standing on Lady Trevick's toes. Her ladyship smiled serenely, tucked Alessa's hand under her elbow and strolled off towards the terrace edge. 'Do come and tell me what the striking building I can see over there is, Alexandra dear.'

She pointed vaguely along the coast, lowering her voice and adding, 'Do not be too discomposed. The man is an incorrigible flirt and I am certain you have not had the experience to either expect such advances, or know how to deal with them.'

'I am sorry, Lady Trevick. Your daughters and my cousin saw…'

'And it will be a salutary lesson to them not to trust gentlemen to hold the line if opportunity presents. You are not to reproach yourself, I am sure you did nothing to encourage him.'

'Thank you, ma'am. My aunt looks *so* displeased.'

'I will have a word with her. Frances is very young; I expect it makes her mama more protective than necessary.' She strolled round to join Lady Blackstone and Chance, freed her arm from Alessa's and linked it with the other matron's. 'Such a rogue,' she murmured with a smile. 'Poor Alexandra is so flustered at his effrontery. I declare I will have to go and flirt with him myself—now *that* would teach him a lesson.'

How cleverly done, Alessa thought admiringly. *She has made Aunt Honoria feel unsophisticated for wanting to scold me.* Then she looked at Chance and saw he had absolutely no qualms about looking unsophisticated, nor about wanting to scold.

'How could you be so imprudent?' he demanded.

'As to do what? To stand a little aside, in an open place surrounded by others—two of whom are chaperons—with a gentleman who is a guest of the Lord High Commissioner? In what way, exactly, is that imprudent?'

'To trust a rogue like Zagrede, of course! Do you tell me you are so innocent you did not expect such a thing?'

'Of course I am not. I know exactly how *gentlemen* may be relied upon to seize any opportunity to flirt, or much worse. But, as our conversation was not in the slightest way flirtatious, I must confess to being taken aback that he chose such a moment. But then, he is naturally a very flamboyant character, is he not?'

'He is a damned mountebank,' Chance said furiously. 'I have a mind to call him out.'

'For kissing my hand in a public place? Now if he had taken advantage of me, assaulted me while I was on a lonely beach, say, or dragged me into a deserted room—why, then, I agree, there could be grounds for outrage.'

'You were hardly reluctant,' Chance retorted furiously.

'And I am not exactly averse to the Count's caresses, within reason and in a place where he cannot overstep the mark.' Alessa smiled sweetly and swept off to where the three girls were perched under the shade of the Chaste Tree that Zagrede had been lying beneath earlier, trying to look as if they were not speculating wildly on what was afoot.

'Wretched man,' Alessa said composedly as she joined them. 'He will be up to his tricks with each of us, make no doubt, just to see if he can make each of us jealous.'

Helena gave a stifled sob and her sister hissed, 'I told you Alexandra would not try to fix her interest with him, knowing how you feel. But I was right, you see—he is an arrant flirt.'

'I am afraid so,' Alessa said sadly. 'And I was talking to him about a most serious matter, one that caused me a little emotional distress, and he presumed upon that to…to take my hand and force a kiss upon it.'

'Wretch,' Frances said stoutly. 'Will Lady Trevick ask him to leave, do you think?'

'She does not take it seriously,' Alessa confided. 'I fear we are all a little sheltered, and doubtless such things are commonplace in high society during the Season. No doubt she considers it a useful lesson to us to be on our guard.'

'Are all men such flirts?' Frances demanded. 'I am sure Lord Blakeney would not be.'

Alessa did not feel that she could go so far as to acquit Chance of dangerously predatory tendencies. As it was, she had massaged the truth to try and press home the warning to the other girls that the Count was not to be trusted.

'No, not all men are like that,' Maria said softly, her eyes cast down to her folded hands. 'There are some true gentlemen.'

A glance at the other two girls confirmed Alessa's opinion that neither had any idea that Maria was in love with Mr Harrison. Of course, they simply thought him too old to possibly be a candidate for such affection. She controlled her smile, happy, despite her own muddled misery, that someone had found true love.

The walk downhill towards the villa was very different than the ascent that morning. Lady Trevick led the way, leaning on the Count's arm, engaging him in conversation in a way that was a positive education in sophisticated flirtation. Lady Blackstone followed, accepting Chance's arm over the rough parts of the track, not revealing in any way what she thought of her hostess's tactics. The younger women followed behind, each of them subdued by her own particular preoccupation, with Mr Harrison silently ready to offer his assistance, should it be required.

When they finally reached the villa Lady Trevick shepherded her own daughters and Frances off to their rooms to rest before dinner. The men vanished, whether to make up their differences in the billiard room, or to their own chambers to wash and rest, Alessa had no idea. Calling up her resolution, she followed her aunt into the sitting room the ladies had claimed as their own retreat.

'Aunt Honoria.'

'Yes?' Lady Blackstone regarded her with her usual cool reserve.

'Tomorrow I have asked Mrs Street to bring the children down to see me. I would like you to meet them.'

'If you feel that is best, Alexandra.'

'I do. If we are all to be travelling together, and perhaps living together while I find my bearings in England, I think it important that they meet you and Cousin Frances as soon as possible. This will be a big change for them.'

'Indeed, it would be.' *Surely that should be* will *be?*

'Aunt, I understand that Lord Blackstone is in Venice on a mission.'

'That is correct.'

'And would we be travelling to Venice before returning to England?'

'But of course. We would be there now, but I felt it my duty to investigate the possibility that my brother's child might be on this island.'

Her duty. Alessa tried to imagine her own feelings if a niece or nephew were cast adrift, alone on a foreign island. It seemed the cold English climate entered the blood if one lived there long enough.

'I see. I had not perfectly understood. Perhaps it would be better if I made my own way directly to England?'

'Certainly not! That would give rise to the most unfortunate comment. Naturally you will come with me to Venice and we will return together when Lord Blackstone's mission is accomplished.'

'But, ma'am—'

'I will not brook any alteration to that plan. It would be most improper of you to travel alone and would cast the family in a most unfortunate light.'

'Yes, ma'am,' Alessa agreed meekly. *I must get to England, claim Papa's inheritance and then establish myself independently as soon as I decently may—I cannot bear to be part of such oppressive respectability.*

She dropped her eyes as her aunt nodded magisterially. Why had Chance intervened in her life? Only a few days ago life had seemed so simple. Hard, but simple. There were people she loved, a living to earn, skills to perfect.

Now she had a new family she must learn to like. A whole new society to navigate and survive in, for the children's sake. And a new love to forget. If that were possible in a lifetime.

Chapter Fifteen

Chance leaned on the balustrade of the terrace and watched grimly as Alessa ran out of the front door to meet Kate Street and the two children. He had to look twice to recognise Mrs Street with her hair braided up severely under a vast bonnet and her figure laced tightly into a plain, high-necked gown. She would never look like a lady, but at least she had achieved the appearance of a respectable upper servant, and that ought to satisfy Lady Blackstone.

The children ran to meet Alessa, who bent, arms wide, to catch them both to her. Chance felt a constriction in his throat as she stood for a long moment, the children clasped tight, her face buried in their hair. *God, she loves them so much.* Was that why she did not have any to spare for him? He was still baffled by her vehement rejection, and so apparently was Zagrede, who apologised lavishly for misleading his friend.

'But I asked her directly, as we walked up the hill—how could I be so mistaken?' he lamented.

'You were flirting with her soon enough,' Chance had said frostily.

The Count shrugged. 'I try to charm some answers out of

her. That gets me nowhere. The lovely Alessa is at outs with the two of us, my friend.'

Now Chance stood and watched the small group approaching the front door. Alessa had one child on each side, their hands clasped in hers, and was nodding vigorously as they both spoke at once. They came to a halt just underneath where he was and her voice reached him clearly.

'You look very smart and neat. Now remember, you must call Lady Blackstone *my lady*. Only speak when you are spoken to, and do not chatter. Lady Blackstone is not used to having young people in the house, so you must make a good impression upon her. Can you do that?'

All Chance could see of Dora was her head nodding energetically, curls bouncing out at the side from under her sun hat. Demetri was nodding too. 'Should I bow?' he demanded.

'That would be very nice. Now, time to go in.' She turned and pulled a wry face at Kate over her shoulder. Chance shifted slightly and a small pebble fell off the stonework under his hand, falling just in front of the boy. He looked up, his brown face lighting up with his smile as he recognised Chance.

'See, Alessa! It is my lord.' He waved energetically and Chance waved back.

Alessa cast him a single harassed glance and shooed the children in through the front door. 'Shh!'

Chance stared down at the empty space, so suddenly silent and still, and shivered. When he looked up, the sun had vanished behind a cloud.

Alessa marshalled her little band in the hall and practised her calm smile on the butler. 'Is Lady Blackstone in the front parlour, Wilkins?'

'Yes, Miss Meredith. I will announce you.'

That was more formal than Alessa had been expecting, but she followed him through the door. 'Miss Meredith and… party, my lady.'

'Aunt, here are the children and my companion, Mrs Street, just as I promised.'

Lady Blackstone stood up gracefully and extended a hand to Kate. 'Mrs Street. I gather I have you to thank for the chaperonage of my niece.'

Kaye bobbed a respectable curtsy. 'I'm pleased to meet your ladyship. I've done my best to stand by Alessa—Miss Meredith, I should say, but it's been no hardship, so quiet and hardworking that she is.'

'Hmm. And these are the children.'

'Yes, Aunt. This is Dora.' Dora wobbled into a curtsy. 'And Demetri.' The boy's bow was much more successful.

'*Kalíméra, Kyria,*' they chorused, then, 'Good day, my lady.'

'Ah. They speak English, then.'

'Certainly Aunt. Dora speaks English, Italian—and Greek, of course. Demetri has a flair for languages. He also speaks French.'

'Indeed.' There was a long silence. 'Please sit down.'

Alessa established the children side by side on a sofa facing Lady Blackstone. She wanted her to see how attractive and well behaved they were. They stared wide-eyed at their hostess; she in turn regarded them warily, as though two wild animals had come to perch on the over-stuffed upholstery.

'Do you go to school?' she asked Demetri.

'Yes, my lady. I go to Dr Stephanopolis. He is a very learned man and he teaches boys. I learn languages and reading and writing and mathematics and geography and—'

'And you?' Lady Blackstone cut through the enthusiastic list and looked enquiringly at Dora.

'I go to the nuns, *Kyria*…my lady. And I learn my letters and sewing and—'

'Nuns?' Her ladyship's dark brows arched.

'Greek Orthodox nuns, Aunt.' For some reason her aunt seemed prepared to countenance the Greek Orthodox church while she recoiled from any suggestion of Roman Catholicism. Alessa was aware of the prejudices in England about religion, but, raised in a colourful and tolerant hodge-podge of faiths, she found it deeply unattractive.

The children were beginning to fidget. They had been brought up to be respectful to adults, but at the same time they were used to being listened to. 'Tell Lady Blackstone how you have been helping while I have been away.' She wanted to demonstrate what good, obedient children they were, and she was rewarded by their bright smiles at the implied praise.

'I have been looking after the ladies,' Demetri said importantly. 'And the animals, and watering the garden.'

'And I have been helping Kate with the cooking and visiting old Agatha,' Dora added with her sweet smile.

Bless them, how could anyone fail to adore them?

'You may go out on to the terrace,' Lady Blackstone announced. 'I will ask Wilkins to have lemonade and biscuits brought out for you before you return home. Good day, Mrs Street.'

It was dismissal. Bewildered, Alessa stared at her aunt, but Kate was on her feet, her lips tight together. 'Come along, children, say goodbye to her ladyship.'

They were out of the door before Alessa could move. 'But, Aunt, did you not want to make the better acquaintance of the children? After all, if we are all to travel together…'

'I hardly think it fair to drag them off to England, do you, my dear? Ask yourself, what would become of them? They are nicely spoken and respectful, I will say that for them, and it does you credit—but they are *foreign*. And superior upper servants are two a penny in London. Much better for them to stay here where their languages will be of some use.'

'*Servants?* I intend sending Demetri to a good English school and finding a governess for Dora. I can afford it, can I not? And then they may do as they please when they grow up. But neither of them is going to be a servant, not if I can help it.'

'My dear girl, surely you must see how impossible it would be? Think how it would look.'

'How what would look?' Alessa demanded.

'You reappearing with two children in tow. People would leap to the conclusion that they are yours, of course.'

'Then I will disabuse them of their idiotic and intolerant ideas!'

'Alexandra!' Her aunt took a deep breath and appeared to compose herself afresh. 'Alexandra, it is going to be difficult enough to establish your character and to gloss over your life these past years, without you turning up with two Greek brats at your skirt-tails.'

'They are not brats!'

'They are most certainly not well-bred English children. They are Greek peasants.'

'They are honest, intelligent, loving, loyal children and they are mine and I love them. If you will not allow them to accompany us to England, then I am staying here.'

Lady Blackstone went white. 'Impossible.'

'Why?' Alessa was beyond deferring to her aunt now. 'You were willing enough when we first met for me to stay here and for you to arrange to have my inheritance sent to me.'

'That was before anyone else knew about you, foolish girl. Think of the scandal if I leave you here now. The Lord High Commissioner knows about you, Lady Trevick knows about you, that mountebank of a Count knows about you, the Earl knows—why, all of island society will know about you soon, if they do not already. I cannot possibly leave the grand-daughter and niece of the Earls of Hambledon on a Greek island to earn her own living—it would be an outrage.'

'I am afraid you do not have a choice, Aunt.' Alessa drew herself up and met the older woman's furious glare with hard-won composure. 'Either you take us all, or we all stay.'

'How dare you make me an ultimatum, you ungrateful chit!'

'Aunt, I will quite happily return to my former life, with the addition of the inheritance from my father, to which I am entitled. I make no demands upon you or the family in England, I have no intention of boasting of my connections all around the island. In a few weeks there will be no gossip—people will find more important things to chat about.'

'Here they may well do,' Lady Blackstone retorted. 'But when the news reaches London it will do the family great harm. Frances's come-out might be compromised.'

'Then take us all,' Alessa said again, clasping her hands to stop them shaking. 'I will not change my mind. Now, if you will excuse me, I must go and tell the children when I will see them again.'

She was hoping her aunt would call her back, but she found herself out on the terrace with only the sound of a sharp, ex-asperated sigh following her. There was no sign of the children. Puzzled, she walked to the balustrade and looked around, then she heard the sound of Dora's voice raised in an excited shriek and saw them down on the beach.

Everyone was paddling, shoes and stockings off, trouser legs rolled up and skirts hoisted. Kate, her bonnet in her hand, was standing ankle-deep, fanning herself with the broad brim, Demetri was skimming stones and calling to Chance to admire the number of skips he was achieving and Chance was swinging Dora out over the incoming wavelets with his hands under her arms. She was laughing with delight and Alessa felt tears start in her eyes.

With the exception of old Agatha, everyone in the world she loved was on that beach, laughing and playing, and behind her the representative of her real family was making decisions based on nothing but prejudice and a concern for what other people would think.

Angrily she dashed the back of her hand over her eyes and ran down the exterior stone staircase at the side of the house. By the time she reached the beach she had regained her composure and was able to find a smile for Kate. Chance, Dora clutching his hand, was pursuing Demetri along the beach, waving a clump of slimy seaweed.

'Look at him!' Kate mopped her face and stuck the bonnet back on her head. 'Nothing but a big boy himself. He's wonderful with those children, you know.'

'I can see.' Chance had caught up with Demetri and they were now having a mock swordfight with pieces of driftwood, cheered on by Dora.

'He took one look at our faces when we came out and took them straight down here, telling the footman to bring along the tray.' Kate grinned and nodded towards an expressionless footman setting out lemonade and biscuits on a flat-topped rock. 'Told me he thought it would be a good idea to take their minds off that starched-bum of an old besom.'

'He never said that!' *What a wonderful description…*

'No, but it was what he meant, and she is too, isn't she?'

'Absolutely,' Alessa said with a sigh. 'My aunt wants the children to stay here. She thinks that even though they are a credit to me, they remain Greek peasant brats and the best they can hope for in England is a future as upper servants.'

'What? Load of nonsense! That boy's going to end up

an ambassador, and Dora's that sweet and pretty she'll marry a duke.'

They stood and studied the future star of the diplomatic service and future duchess as they chased a peer of the realm though the shallows, screaming at the tops of their voices.

'What are you going to do, then?'

'I told her that we all go or none of us goes.'

'Bet that pleased her.' Kate studied the trio romping in the surf. 'Do you think he has any idea how hard it is to get salt-water stains out of wool cloth?'

'None at all. What man would? As for my aunt, she is afraid people will think they are my illegitimate children if I take them, and that she will be accused of abandoning me if she does not bring me back.'

Kate's response was unladylike. Chance stripped off his coat and cravat and rolled up his shirtsleeves, the better to grapple with Demetri, who was scaring Dora by pretending to have a crab in his hand. 'Blimey. Do you think he'll take any more off?' Kate asked hopefully. 'That is a very beautiful man.'

'That,' retorted Alessa tartly, largely to disguise the fact that she was admiring the breadth of Chance's shoulders and the muscles in his forearms, 'is a man who asked me to be his mistress.'

'He never did!' Kate's tanned, freckled face was a picture of speculation. 'What did you say?'

'*No*, of course. The Count warned me what would happen, and he was quite right.'

'Why doesn't he marry you? Your granddaddy was an earl too; he can't say you aren't well bred enough for him.'

'He is planning to go home and marry some little chit on the Marriage Mart. He might want me, but in England I'll be thought to be on the shelf, and my aunt made it quite clear that everyone will regard my past as shady. He'll be looking for some eighteen-year-old virgin with pink skin who giggles.'

'You're a virgin. You are, aren't you? All right, don't glower at me like that. So, you aren't a spring chicken any more, and you've been out in the sun a bit, but you've got looks and a brain. He'll come round.'

'I don't want him to come round.'

'Liar.'

'Shh! They are coming back.' Chance had swung Dora up on to his shoulders, and he and Demetri was trudging back through the shallows, panting and wet.

'Look at you!' Alessa scolded the children the minute they came within hearing. If she ignored the state they were in, they would assume something was wrong. 'Come and sit down quietly and drink some lemonade, you are over-excited.'

'Yes, ma'am,' Chance said meekly, earning himself a sharp look and the retort that his lordship was old enough to take care of himself.

Although her instinct was to keep them close, Alessa shooed the children off home with Kate once they had demolished the pile of fruit biscuits and most of the lemonade. Thanks to Chance, the memory of the stern-faced Lady Blackstone seemed to have vanished, but she did not want to run the risk of another encounter that day.

After she had kissed them goodbye she came back and sat down beside Chance on the shingle, their backs against a sea-worn tree trunk that had been tossed up by last winter's storms. 'Thank you,' she said simply. 'That was kind.'

'To play with them? They are delightful; I enjoyed myself.'

'I could see.' Alessa found they were sharing smiles and hastily stared out to sea. She felt easy and relaxed with him:

it must be the reaction of finding someone who liked the children after her aunt's frosty reception. 'I thought you said you were not used to children.'

'I was a small boy once; I do remember what was fun.' He reached for a handful of fine gritty sand, letting it run through his fingers until only the little shells were left. 'The interview with your aunt did not go well, then? Mrs Street did not say anything when they came out, but I could tell something was wrong.'

Alessa recounted the conversation, as closely as she could recall it. Repeating it again, she found it made her more, not less, angry. 'I shall stay here,' she concluded. 'I have made up my mind now.'

'No. Come back to England, bring the children. I will be back too; I will make sure that any rumours that start are soon put right. My mother and sisters know all the Society hostesses and will vouch for you. Before you know where you are, you will be regarded as a romantic and intriguing figure and will be invited everywhere.'

Alessa gave an unladylike snort. 'Indeed? I suppose I had better pack my Corfiot costume, the better to appear exotic.'

'Why not? I would not suggest you wear the *toute ensemble*, but some embroidery, a sash—those will be much admired.'

'You give fashion advice?' Alessa watched him slantwise from beneath her lashes. It seemed he had taken her refusal of an illicit relationship to heart if he was suggesting ways she could become respectable.

'I have sisters. Remember?' Chance said darkly. 'A man would have to be blind and deaf to live in a houseful of women and not become an expert on every detail of fashion. "Chance, please may I have an advance on my allowance? Hemlines have gone up—or down or sideways—and I haven't a thing to wear,"' he mimicked with a grin. 'Or every bonnet in the house has to be retrimmed because *no one* would dream of being seen in bright green ribbons this week. Or their lives would be blighted because dawn blush is the shade for silk stockings and they are all looking complete frights in soft rose.'

'You are obviously hard done by,' Alessa agreed, privately thinking that his attitude to his sisters was attractively affectionate. It did not stop him being an unprincipled rake as far as other women were concerned, of course.

'We are getting off the point,' Chance said, cutting across her thoughts. 'You will be fine once you get to England, we just need to make sure you do all get there together. Your aunt is going by way of Venice—did you know?'

'The Count told me.'

'Did he, indeed? What a lot that man knows.' Chance threw the handful of shells away down the beach. 'I believe Venice is a strange and lovely city. I hope we can explore it together.'

'You are going there?'

'It is my next stop. Then I was going to travel back to England overland. We will discover Venice together, with the children as chaperons.'

'If I can persuade my aunt to let me take them.' Venice with Chance. Gondolas, masked balls, canals and shadows, exotic spices and silks. Temptation and risk.

'The problems of taking them outweigh the potential scandal of leaving you here and people finding out,' Chance said shrewdly. 'She will treat them frostily, I am afraid; perhaps the best we can hope for is that she will ignore them. They are children used to affection and openness. Do you think it may affect them?'

'I will explain to them that she is to be pitied because her heart is cold. They understand Anna in the next courtyard, who is not right in her mind, and are quiet and kind around her. They can learn that great ladies are also afflicted in some way they must be tolerant of.'

'Your judgement cuts like a knife,' Chance said.

'She called my children *peasant brats*,' Alessa said. 'I am sure the priest would say it was my duty to forgive her. He would also be shocked that she would think that way. Frances will be nice to them, I am sure,' she added in an effort to be fair.

'Yes, a sweet child, that.'

Just the sort of well-bred, very young lady you are looking for. Alessa stuffed that thought firmly away and brought out the more immediate one, the worry she could talk about. 'I am still not certain my aunt will let me take them.'

'Alessa.' Chance swivelled round until he was facing her. Now she could no longer ignore the impact of his closeness, the effect on her senses. He smelt of the sea, there was a hint of fresh sweat from his exertions, intriguingly male, and he was warm, large, close and overwhelming.

'Yes?'

'I promise it will be all right. I promise you will go to England, and the children with you.' He took her hand and raised it to his lips. 'See? Sealed with a kiss.'

Chapter Sixteen

The kiss was the most fleeting caress. Barely a touch, in fact, Alessa told herself, retrieving her hand in what she hoped was a dignified manner. Chance's brown eyes were serious.

'You think I am flirting?' he asked in a disconcerting echo of her thoughts. 'I am being quite sincere, Alessa. We should start again and forget sea bathing and questions asked, don't you think? Start again and see what England brings. You will need friends there, as well as your family; I would not like to think I had cut you off from that because I let myself—'

'Alessa!'

'I am sure she went down here…'

It was the Trevick sisters and her cousin, laughing as they picked their way cautiously over the shingle to the firmer sand. 'Oh, look, there she is, and the Earl. Hello!' Helena waved gaily and Alessa waved back.

'Miss Helena appears to have recovered from her wounded heart,' Chance observed wryly. 'And she seems to bear you no grudge for revealing her hero's feet of clay.'

'You realised she fancied herself in love with him?' Alessa

regarded Chance with surprise. Now was no time to puzzle over what he had been about to say just then.

'As I was just saying—I have sisters and I recognise the signs of calflove. The real thing, for some strange reason, is much harder to detect.'

'Ah, so you have not observed the one real case of love in our little party?' Up on the terrace she could see Mr Harrison leaning on the balustrade and watching the girls as they made their way across the beach.

'No! Who?' Chance demanded, just as the three reached them.

'I am not telling,' Alessa murmured, then raised her voice to call, 'Come and join us, the stones are quite dry. I am keeping his lordship company while he recovers from his exertions.'

'Really? What have you been doing?' Helena asked cheerfully. Frances, perched a little way off on the end of the tree trunk, gazed soulfully at Chance who had got to his feet at their approach and now dropped back down besides Alessa.

'No, surely you don't mean…' She followed his gaze, smiled brightly at Frances and hissed back.

'Of course not. Calf-love.'

'Did you say calf-love?' Maria made herself comfortable next to Alessa, tucking her skirts neatly around her ankles, safe from the fretful breeze.

'Calves' foot jelly,' Alessa improvised. 'I was recommending it for its strengthening properties.'

'Really?' Maria glanced from Frances to Chance, caught Alessa's eye and stifled a smile. 'What have you been exerting yourself for that you are in need of such restoration, my lord?'

'Playing with Miss Meredith's delightful wards. They have made me feel my age, I must confess.'

'Well, if you will insist on playing horses for Dora and duelling with Demetri, what do you expect?' Alessa teased.

Where had all the antagonism and tension gone? Was it simply that Chance had ceased to flirt with her, so she could relax? And to relax was what she wanted to do, very badly. To lean into the broad shoulder next to hers and rest her head on the crumpled white linen of his shirt. Alessa sat up straight.

'I wish we could have met the children,' Frances said, apparently beginning to recover a little from the impact of finding Chance in a state of exciting undress. 'They look charming.'

'Are they very excited at the thought of coming to England?' Maria asked.

'Yes, and a little daunted,' Alessa confessed.

'Then it is certain they are coming with us?' Frances frowned. 'I would love it if they were—I always wished for a little brother and sister—but Mama said they were not.'

'There are arrangements to be made,' Chance said diplomatically before Alessa could reply. 'I expect you are looking forward to Venice, Miss Blackstone? I am travelling there next.'

Oh, Chance, that was a slip, Alessa chuckled to herself as Frances beamed at this wonderful news. She found she was looking at Chance's bare feet with their long, elegant bones, his toes curling in the sand. The unconscious sensuality with which he was flexing them in the warm, fine grains made her heart beat harder and her mood of light amusement fled to be replaced with one of vague dread.

'Excuse me, my lord. Miss Trevick, Lady Trevick sends to say that luncheon is served.' The footman eyed Chance's state of dress. 'Shall I tell your lordship's valet that you will require him immediately?'

'Lord, yes. Fetch my coat and shoes from over there, would you?' Chance got to his feet with a rueful glance down at himself. 'Ladies, if you will excuse me!' He set off up the beach as fast as the pebbles would allow in bare feet, then took to his heels as soon as he reached the road.

'I swear all men are small boys at heart,' Alessa remarked, as the girls shook out their skirts and prepared to follow the hurrying footman with more decorum. 'I do hope Lady Trevick is not a stickler for punctuality!'

Chance arrived at the dining-room door in the wake of Lady Trevick, who was gracious enough to pretend to ignore his somewhat slapdash neckcloth and hastily combed hair. Lady Blackstone was already at the table, looking her usual cool self. Chance brooded on his best tactics—to make some remark straight out about the children, or not? Best perhaps not to mention them at once, or she might suspect that Alessa had been discussing her opposition to them.

Alessa caught his eye as she entered the room and smiled. Whatever had caused that antagonism had gone, it seemed. He was still puzzled by it until the thought came to him that the intensity of their lovemaking had shocked her. She was so mature, compared to the other girls, so independent, that he thought of her still as the young widow he had first mistaken her for. But she was not. She was inexperienced, although not sheltered, and they had found each other in a way that was shockingly sudden. No slow courtship, no gradual awakening. It was no wonder she had reacted strongly to him.

Chance realised he had been asked twice by Miss Trevick to pass the artichokes and pulled himself together. Absent-mindedness was not going to help matters. He needed time with Alessa, time to court her properly and build up her trust.

'A courier has arrived with the post, my lady.' Wilkins was at Lady Trevick's side. 'I have placed the business correspondence for Sir Thomas in the study, but as everyone is gathered together I wondered if you wished the rest brought in after the meal, ma'am?'

'Why, yes, I think so, Wilkins, thank you.' She smiled around the table. 'It is several days since we received anything; I am sure everyone is as eager as I to see what news there is of the outside world.'

As the staff began to clear, the butler placed a large salver by Lady Trevick's side and she began to distribute letters. 'Three for you, Lord Blakeney. A pile for you, Count. Lady Blackstone, Miss Blackstone.' She carried on passing the packages out. Alessa watched her aunt carefully slit one seal with her knife and scan the contents thoroughly before passing it to Frances, who seemed to find nothing amiss in having her correspondence so thoroughly perused.

She realised that Lady Trevick was giving a far more cursory scrutiny to her daughters' post, twitting them gently about the number of party invitations they were missing by being out of town. Would Lady Blackstone expect to read her niece's correspondence? They were due a battle royal if she did. Then Alessa realised that there was no one to write to her, so the question was hardly likely to arise. Even so, it added to her unease about her aunt's controlling ways.

'Oh!'

'Is something amiss, Lady Blackstone?' Her hostess put down her own letter. 'Not bad news from Venice, I trust?'

'No, not at all, but I am afraid that Frances and I must break up the party and return to Corfu Town shortly. This letter has come on board the ship that will take us to join my husband. ' She turned the page. 'They must make some slight repairs, it seems, and take in supplies, so the departure is not imminent, but we should make our way back and prepare.'

Her green eyes sought out Alessa. 'You, too, Alexandra.'

'Of course, Aunt.' As she spoke, Alessa realised she had definitely made up her mind. She would go to England and she would take the children, even if she had to smuggle them on board in her trunk.

Mr Harrison put down the note that had constituted his only mail. 'Sir Thomas writes that an urgent dispatch reached him by the same ship, and he is returning directly to Corfu Town, rather than to us here. He asks me to see to his office being transferred back, and I am to join him immediately.'

'Oh, dear,' Lady Trevick said wryly. 'It appears that no sooner have we arrived than I must be packing and returning. I am sorry, gentleman, but it seems our little holiday is at an end, unless perhaps you would care to keep the villa on? I can certainly arrange for staff to remain here.'

'Thank you, ma'am, but as it is my intention to travel on to Venice, I will return with the rest of the party and see if I can take passage on this ship.' Chance kept his eyes firmly on his hostess as he spoke, but Alessa was aware of her aunt's own gaze flickering to Frances and a small smile curving her lips. *So, she thinks she can catch him for Frances?* Alessa smiled inwardly, then caught herself up. *And why not? If not her, then another pretty young lady with a sheltered background and no skeletons in her cupboard.*

'Count? Do you care to stay on alone and explore the coastline in your skiff?'

They all looked at the Count of Kurateni, who for once was not relaxed and smiling, listening to all the conversations and lightly teasing the girls. He was staring at the letter in his hand, his face dark. Alessa, sitting next to him, cast a rapid glance at it, and saw it was covered in a sprawling black hand in a language quite unfamiliar. *Albanian*, she thought. He folded it, running his nail along the crease in a gesture that seemed to speak of anger barely contained, then glanced up, his black eyes narrowed, and realised that they were all looking at him.

'Ha! My fool of a captain. He makes a muddle with a simple thing, makes it worse by overreacting, then expects me to sort it out for him. I must return.'

And I do not envy the captain, Alessa thought. The anger was radiating off the Albanian like the heat from a fire. Whatever the captain's error, she suspected it was far worse than the Count was making out. Perhaps he stood to lose a lot of money. She saw Chance watching him too and raised her eyebrows. He answered her with a wry grimace, the corners of his mouth turning down in a fleeting imitation of the Count's scowl.

Lady Trevick was organising their departures, Wilkins at her side. 'I imagine you will be leaving immediately, Mr Harrison, and taking the papers in the gig?'

'Yes, ma'am. I will take two outriders, if I may. I believe that will leave sufficient grooms and outriders for the remaining carriages.'

'Two outriders, with the army units already working on the road? Is that necessary?' Alessa saw Mr Harrison's quick warning glance and the way he laid his hand meaningfully over the letter from the Lord High Commissioner. 'But of course,' Lady Trevick said smoothly, 'one cannot be too careful with government dispatch boxes.'

'I will ride,' Chance said, 'providing there is room for my valises with your luggage coach, ma'am. I have a fancy to explore off the main road a little.' He was staring at Alessa, his expression bland, but she thought she knew the message he was sending. He intended to escort her and the children back and had no intention of letting Lady Blackstone know it.

'I will sail,' the Count announced curtly. He stood, and bowed to Lady Trevick, something of the lazy charm coming back into his voice. 'I will require a period of solitude to recover from the disappointment of having to leave so many lovely ladies.'

'When do you expect to be back in the town, Alexandra?' Alessa stopped wondering about the Count and focused on her aunt's question.

'Tomorrow evening, ma'am. I shall need two or three days to settle my affairs and pack.'

'Well, the clothes we have ordered for you should be ready before we sail.'

'Yes, indeed. I imagine Miss Trevick will be glad to have her property returned to her.' Still no mention of the children. Alessa realised her aunt was avoiding any confrontation in front of witnesses. She could precipitate matters by bringing the subject up now. But no, Lady Trevick was pushing back her chair and everyone was rising to their feet in a babble of plans and conversation.

'You and Frances will be able to attend at least two parties with us when we are back,' Maria announced. 'What a good thing your aunt has ordered you an evening gown.'

'Yes, indeed.' Alessa tried to smile and look pleased, but her mind was already whirling with plans. 'Will you excuse me, I really must go up to my cottage and begin packing.'

The next morning Alessa let Kate drive the cart with the luggage piled in the back. Dora sat up beside her and Demetri was thrilled by permission to take the second mule. Alessa rode ahead in silence, her vision clouded with unshed tears.

It had been so much harder than she had imagined, to leave the cottage where she had lived with her father, and harder still to take leave of Agatha. The old woman might not be here when she returned, they both knew that, although neither spoke of it. Alessa gave her the papers for her cottage and had seen the priest before she left the village. He would make sure that a suitable family moved in, one who would look after their neighbour as she got frailer.

'Don't fuss, girl,' Agatha had said briskly. 'This is the best thing for the children, and you know it.'

Even so, she rode through fields of wild flowers, the little gladioli waving purple in the breeze and her mule's feet picking their way amidst the sheets of cyclamen and orchids, until the sound of hoofbeats made her focus on the here and now and look round.

It was Chance, his grin as he exchanged greetings with Demetri turning to concern as he saw her woebegone face.

'What is it? That old besom again?'

'No, it is hard leaving the cottage and Agatha, that is all.'

'It is no small thing.' He reached down from the saddle and touched her shoulder fleetingly. 'You love the old lady. Did she want you to go?'

'Mmm,' Alessa mumbled, not wanting to talk in case she started crying again and upset the children. They had no idea they might have parted from their surrogate grandmother for the last time.

'We will talk of other things.' Chance was brisk. 'Tell me what all these flowers are.'

'All of them?' She managed a watery smile. 'Have you a month?' Even so, she began to point things out to him and as the little party made their way at the pace of the cart along the dusty track she felt her heart lift. Was Chance aware of what he was doing? Whether he knew or not, he was letting her imprint the loveliness of the island in her memory so that she would be able to conjure it up, fresh, hot and fragrant, whenever she needed it.

They stopped to eat and rest the mules at mid-day by one of the old Venetian wells that were scattered amidst the groves throughout the island. Kate, replete with bread and cheese, tipped her hat over her nose and began to snore softly in the back of the cart and the children, after rushing around playing hide and seek for ten frantic minutes, suddenly went quiet and curled up to sleep in the soft grass under an olive.

Alessa was feeling drowsy herself. Chance was sitting close by, his shoulder as tempting to rest her head on as it had been on the beach the day before. She set herself to make lists in her head instead.

'Alessa?' He spoke softly; none of the sleepers stirred. She was conscious of butterflies in her stomach. 'What do you think the Count is up to?'

'Oh. I have no idea, but surely it cannot be anything too disreputable. After all, he tells me he is looking for a well-bred English wife. That argues that whatever his business, it is open to scrutiny, does it not?'

'He told you that, too, did he? If he's after one of the Trevick girls, he is due for a disappointment—their mama has sized him up very tidily!'

'Well, Helena is disillusioned with him because he kissed my hand, and I did what I could to reinforce that feeling. And Maria—' She stopped on the edge of an indiscretion.

'Is in love with Mr Harrison. I kept my eyes open after your hint yesterday. Go to sleep, Alessa. I'll watch out for the animals.'

To her own amazement, she did sleep, waking an hour later to find Kate packing the cart again and the ludicrous sight of Dora, Demetri and Chance, all kneeling with their noses virtually on the same spot on the ground, their sterns pointing skywards.

'What can you be doing?' She strolled over, stretching.

'Trapdoor spiders,' Chance explained, straightening up. 'Demetri has been showing me how they hunt. That boy has the makings of a scientist.'

'Kate thinks he will become an ambassador.' Alessa untethered her mule and swung up into the saddle before Chance could help her.

'Good God,' he said, regarding the grubby child with awe. 'Had she been drinking?'

Chapter Seventeen

The warm glow from the journey lasted Alessa all night and through the next morning, despite the horrors of deciding what to pack, finding valises and boxes to put it into and re-membering all the tasks to be carried out.

Finally she sat down wearily while the children ran off, bearing letters and money to pay the final bills for the landlord, Demetri's teacher and the nuns. Kate put her head round the door. 'All finished? Lord love us, what's that?'

'Papa's pistol. I wasn't sure what to do with it.' With a shrug Alessa closed the polished walnut box on the deadly object and pushed it into the leather satchel that was the nearest thing she had to a reticule. Aunt Honoria was going to have a fit when she saw her niece's inelegant baggage. Possibly she should go shopping for a few such pretty trifles, but that could wait until Venice.

Not that she knew how she could pay for such things. Her small savings were already dwindling, what with having to pay all her bills at once and buy new clothes and shoes for the children. She supposed she would have to ask her aunt to advance her some money, but she recoiled from anything that put her deeper into Lady Blackstone's debt. Or she could borrow from Chance, which of course no respectable young woman would dream of doing. But then, as her aunt kept warning her, she was not respectable.

'Stop frowning,' Kate ordered. 'Now, Fred's here—what of this needs to go downstairs for the children, and what are you taking to the Residency?'

Alessa had decided to leave the children with Kate until they sailed. With any luck, until the last minute, her aunt would think she had given in to her. In any case, if there was to be any unpleasantness about their travelling, the further the children were from it, the better.

It seemed very strange to be living in the Residency, after the many times when she had come here for the laundry or to physic one of the staff. But everyone was tactful and after half a day Alessa stopped worrying that one of the servants would let something slip in front of her aunt.

There was no sign of the Lord High Commissioner or his secretary, only a subdued bustle amongst the clerical staff and several arrivals of groups of naval officers for meetings.

For the ladies, the first day back was filled with fittings for Alessa and shopping expeditions for last-minute items. However disapproving her aunt might be about the children and her niece's lifestyle, she was sweetness and light in the shops. 'My dear, consider it a present,' she kept saying, pressing trifles such as fans, shawls and the necessary reticule into Alessa's hands, and laughing off any suggestion that Alessa repaid her.

'How generous your aunt is,' Helena whispered after they had emerged from the milliners in the Liston. 'I wish mine were as kind.'

'Indeed, yes,' Alessa responded, wondering uncharitably

if all this generosity was intended to give a good impression to the Trevicks. Depressed, she decided it probably was.

The next morning the young ladies were invited by the wife of the colonel of the garrison to a picnic on the hill south of the town, where a sweeping view of the Bay of Garitsa might be had. It was Alessa's first social gathering and she dressed in her fashionable new promenade dress with trepidation. It did not seem to her, with its complicated skirts, that it would be much use for walking, but she soon realised that the gentle, gossipy strolls amidst the olive trees while the view was admired was considered quite vigorous exercise.

She instinctively moved to join the young matrons sitting on their rugs and sipping lemonade, until Maria caught her arm. 'We girls are supposed to giggle together over here,' she said with a shrug. 'They'll be talking about men and childbirth and lovers—all the things we are not supposed to know about.'

They sat and shaded their eyes to admire the bulk of the Paleó Frourio—the Old Fort—as it jutted out into the bay, the little Venetian harbour nestling on the southern side.

'I wonder which is your ship,' Maria mused.

'I know that, I asked Mr Harrison yesterday,' Frances interjected. 'It is the far side, in the big harbour, you can just see the top masts.'

'That one is the Count's.' Alessa pointed to a smaller, rakish vessel in the Venetian harbour. It looked sleek and fast amid the British naval vessels with their high sides and banks of gun ports. Forming a backdrop to the whole scene were the looming mountains of Albania, so close across the narrow neck of sea.

Surprisingly, Alessa found she enjoyed the picnic, although it seemed criminally lazy to lounge around chattering of nothing when they could at least have been taking some exercise, or gathering herbs. Her hands, devoid of mending, or a shirt to stitch, felt restless.

At last, after the ladies had napped in the shade and taken yet more refreshments, they climbed into their carriages and drove back down the hill and along the coast road back into town.

As they reached the start of the Spianadha, a horseman drew up alongside the Residency coach.

'Lord Blakeney! Is anything wrong?'

'No, nothing at all, Miss Trevick; I did not intend to alarm you.' Chance replaced the hat he had doffed and handed Frances a note. 'Your mama asked me to deliver this, that is all. I do not believe she requires an answer.

'Now, if you will excuse me, I have very rashly promised the Captain of Marines to join his side for a game of cricket this afternoon and I must change. Goodbye.' The look he gave Alessa was serious—there was something in his eyes she could not read. Then he touched the brim of his hat and cantered off, leaving Frances studying the note, a rather conscious look on her face. *Oh, dear, she is still fancying herself in love with him*, Alessa thought.

'Mama asks that we go out to the ship, Alexandra,' Frances said brightly, folding the note into a tight square and stuffing it into her reticule. 'Something to do with cabins and where the luggage needs to be stowed.'

'Oh.' It seemed odd, but the afternoon was hot, and the thought of the cooler breeze out in the bay was tempting. 'Does she want us both to go?'

'I think so. The note is rather hurried.'

'We will drop you off,' Maria announced, calling up instructions to the driver.

When Alessa and Frances climbed down, the farewells her cousin made to the Trevick sisters struck Alessa as somewhat excessive, given that they would all be seeing each other in a few hours. But then, she concluded, as a respectful seaman helped her into a rowing boat, Frances did seem prone to strong emotions. She hoped she would have a cabin large enough to have the children in with her; goodness knows what sort of sailor Dora would prove to be. She smiled fondly as the long oars propelled them out into the harbour—Demetri would enjoy it, whatever the weather.

Chance accepted the bat from Captain Michaels and walked out onto the grass of the Spianadha, wondering what on earth had possessed him to accept an invitation to play cricket when it was a year since he had handled a bat, the ground seemed hard as iron and all the players were a completely unknown quantity.

There was also a large crowd of spectators, including a number of ladies in their open-topped carriages, parasols deployed. He recognised the Residency landau, although there only seemed to be two pretty sunhats on show; perhaps the missing young ladies had found the excitements of the picnic too much and were resting. He repressed the fantasy that Alessa was one of those remaining, and would sit admiring the athletic prowess with which he accumulated runs. More likely he would be out first ball.

He nodded to his batting partner and took his position, squinting into the sun as the bowler, a man built like a whippet and with a similar turn of speed, began his run. The ball flashed down, Chance hit it squarely for a respectable two and prepared to receive again.

As he shifted his stance, movement from the edge of the great green space made him glance away from the bowler. A horse was being ridden, at the gallop, straight through the crowd and on to the pitch. Ladies scattered, screaming, dogs

barked, men shouted and the ball went right under Chance's
slack guard and took out the stumps.

'Out!'

He could see now that the big bay, a thoroughbred hunter,
was being ridden bareback on a halter by a boy. Demetri. The
horse skidded snorting to a standstill halfway down the
crease, digging up divots of earth with its hooves.

'Now see here!' The lieutenant who was umpiring strode
up, but Chance was already lifting the boy down.

'What is it? What is wrong?' *Alessa.* His heart seemed to stop.

Demetri was crying, great angry gulping sobs. He took a
flailing swing at Chance, catching him painfully on the elbow.
'Traitor! Swine! Liar!' His English failed him and he continued
to storm in Greek and Italian, still kicking and hitting at Chance.

'The lad's gone mad, get a doctor,' someone suggested in
the midst of the hubbub. 'And catch that damn horse and get
it off the pitch!'

Chance dropped to his knees and wrapped both arms round
the furious child. 'Demetri, stop it. What is wrong? I can't
help until you tell me what is wrong.'

'She's gone. She's gone without us and she said you
promised we could go too.' He broke off to gulp down air and
scrub at his eyes with the handkerchief Chance produced. 'I
went to say goodbye to the cook at the Residency, 'cos she's
my friend, and she said they are all leaving this afternoon,
Alessa's aunt and her cousin and Alessa. And I said they
couldn't be, 'cos Dora and me'd be going too, but then the
coachman came in and he said you'd brought the message and
the young ladies went to the ship.'

'But that's impossible. Demetri, it is all a mistake; perhaps
they have just gone to look at the ship.'

'No!' The boy stamped his foot. 'No! They said all the
luggage went on board this morning, and I made Cook

take me up to Alessa's room and it's all gone. And her aunt told Lady Trevick she's had a message and they had to leave and go to Venice in a hurry. But she would never have left us, never.' His face crumpled and he began to sob, all his anger draining away, leaving only despair. 'I thought you were our friend, but you told her to go to the ship without us.'

'No, I didn't know. Demetri, we've both been tricked.' Chance felt cold, whether from fear for Alessa, or anger, he did not trouble to analyse. 'Do you know which ship it is?'

The lad nodded, scrubbing his sleeve across his face. 'I went and had a look yesterday,' he muttered.

'Come on, then.' Chance swung up on to the horse, which had been caught and was standing placidly in the midst of the expostulating cricketers. 'Sorry, Michaels, this is an emergency—pass me the boy, will you?'

The Captain tossed up Demetri and Chance drove his heels into the animal's sides, dragging its head round towards the Old Fort. Fortunately it seemed an obedient beast, despite the uproar and the lack of bit or saddle. 'That way…' Demetri pointed to the left, and they clattered across the roadway and on to the waterfront. 'It's still there, see! Make her come back!'

'Right.' Chance took a deep breath and tried to think. 'I'll find someone with a rowing boat and I'll get out there and bring her back. See, the sails are still furled up, we've got time.'

'Promise, you must promise!'

'I promise.' He seized the boy by the shoulders and looked him straight in the eye. 'I swear on my honour that I will bring her back home. Now, let's find a boat.' There wasn't one, nothing tied up to the waterfront and nothing within hailing distance either.

'There's the harbour the other side,' Demetri started to say, as Chance was trying to work out if he could ride into the fort and out along its seaward side close enough to hail the ship. They must have some form of small boats in the fort.

'Come on—'

'Look!' Demetri pointed. The merchant ship was lying perhaps two hundred yards out from the shore and the outbreak of shouting carried clear across the water. As they watched, a slim figure in fluttering white appeared on the rail near the prow, clung to the rigging for a moment, then dived.

'Oh, my God. Alessa.' For a moment Chance stopped breathing, then she surfaced and struck out for the shore of the fort. *She can swim like a fish*, he reminded himself desperately as he stripped off his coat and yanked at his shoes. *But she's fully dressed in all those damn frills and petticoats.* 'Demetri, find a boat, anything that will float. Tell them I'll pay them whatever they want, in gold.' He boosted the boy up on to the horse, thrust the rope into his hand and sent it off with a clap on the rump before turning and diving into the water.

The temptation was to flail through the water, risking exhaustion. Chance forced himself into a strong, steady stroke, ignoring the drag of his water sodden clothes. Down at this level he could not see Alessa, so he checked his bearings against the ship and struck out for a line halfway between that and the fort. They were lowering a boat from the ship, swaying down on ropes. The men were already in it, oars hoisted upright to clear the sides. They would be an experienced crew, good strong rowers. Chance redoubled his efforts.

Through the water in his ears, and the roaring of his blood, he heard shouting, stopped, trod water and looked. The boat had reached Alessa and the men were hauling her, struggling furiously, out of the water. At least she was conscious and *could* struggle. Doggedly Chance adjusted his line and began to swim for the ship, still a hundred yards away. There was more shouting, a rumbling sound. He risked breaking stroke again and saw they were hauling up the anchor. The sails were crashing down from the cross-staves—they were making ready to put to sea.

His legs and arms felt as though they were held together by hot wires now, and the breath was rasping painfully in his throat. Where the hell was Demetri and the boat? It was too late. As he trod water again to correct his angle he saw the rowing boat had reached the ship, a sailor was climbing the rope ladder, something white draped over his shoulder. Already, as they began to haul up the boat, the ship was gathering way, slipping out of harbour towards Vidos Island.

Defeated, Chance hung in the water, straining to catch some glimpse of Alessa, but they must have hustled her below.

'Hey! Catch hold!' An oar splashed behind him and he turned, taking a wave in the face. As Chance spat out salt water he could make out Voltar Zagrede's familiar face, a rope in his hands as he leaned over the bows of a boat rowed by two stalwart sailors. 'You think you can swim to Venice, Benedict, my foolish friend? Eh?'

Chance caught the rope and was unceremoniously hauled over the side, to collapse gasping like a landed fish on the bottom boards. The Count snapped something at the rowers and they began to turn the boat.

'They've got Alessa, tricked her on board without the children,' he managed to croak.

'I know, the boy told me. You want to get her back?' The Count tossed him a piece of canvas. 'Here, wrap that round your shoulders.'

'Of course I want to get her back, damn it!'

'Right. We take my ship. It is faster than that thing she's on—fat-bottomed trader.' He spat over the side and made a remark in Albanian to the rowers, who cackled.

'You'll do that?' Chance began to shiver and dragged the canvas tighter.

'But of course. It is not a nice thing to do, to trick a young lady like that. And it will be amusing, to have something to chase.' His smile was feline as they bumped against the harbour wall.

Demetri was pacing frantically up and down, his grubby cheeks tracked with tears, his face twisted with distress.

'Right, now then.' The Count clambered ashore and caught Demetri by the shoulders. 'You, boy, go back to the good woman who looks after you and tell her what has happened: your Alessa has been kidnapped and we go to rescue her. No! Do not use that face with me—who looks after your sister if you come with us? You, my friend, you go and get dry clothes, a valise, your weapons, and come back to the Venetian harbour as soon as may be. And then we hunt.' And this time the smile was not that of a cat—all Chance could think of were wolves.

Chance managed to get Demetri back to Kate, despite his protests. 'The bastards,' she swore, all pretence at gentility cast aside. 'Don't you worry none, my lord, I'll look after the children until you get her back. And stop all this nonsense and give her a damn good kissing when you get her,' she yelled at him as he ran, dripping still, down the stairs.

The stable yard at the Residency was in a state of recrimination and confusion when he arrived back and slid off the horse. 'My lord! Where did you find the animal? It is his Excellency's best hunter—that wretched boy stole it, but I have the word out for him to be apprehended.' The head groom was almost beside himself.

'The boy only borrowed it in order to reach me in an emergency. See to it he is not punished. Have someone ready to drive me down to the harbour in a gig in fifteen minutes.'

Leaving the grooms gaping after him, Chance entered the Residency at a run, taking the stairs two at a time. On the landing he almost knocked Lady Trevick off her feet. She gave a small scream, then stepped back to look at him as he stood there dripping on her polished floorboards. 'Lord Blakeney! What has happened? Has there been a boating accident?'

'Did you know Lady Blackstone has sailed, taking Alessa with her, Lady Trevick?' he demanded.

'Why, yes. I was so sorry not to be able to say goodbye properly to Miss Meredith. Apparently Lady Blackstone's husband is most anxious for her early return and the repairs to the ship…'

'She tricked Alessa aboard and has sailed without the children because she did not want to take them, and Alessa refused to leave without them.'

'What! But why would she not take them? From what I have seen of them, they are delightful children.'

'She is afraid of scandal,' Chance said grimly. 'She thinks people will believe them to be Alessa's own offspring.'

'What nonsense!' Lady Trevick shook her head in exasperation. 'I will give her scandal, foolish woman! Anyone can see the ages do not work out, and neither child bears the slightest resemblance to Alessa. I will write to my sister in London—Honoria Blackstone will find the true story has reached home long before she does.'

'Alessa would not wish her family to be exposed to ill will,' Chance cautioned.

'Of course not. I will say nothing of Honoria's idiocy, simply that Alessa has so bravely brought up two charming orphans. Such a pretty story. In fact, her whole tale is so romantic, do you not think?'

'It is turning into a positively Gothick novel,' Chance said with a grim smile. 'Ma'am, I have no idea when I will get back, and I must change now.' He was conscious of the spreading pool of water around his feet and the clammy clothes clinging to him.

'It is no matter when you return. Just make sure you bring her with you when you do…' she paused as he padded wetly into his room '…and give her a kiss—with my love, of course.'

Chapter Eighteen

The Count's ship was ready when Chance reached it. He tossed a valise on to the deck as he came up the gangplank, his other hand full of his box of pistols and his sword. Zagrede paused long enough to clap him on the shoulder, then began shouting orders. Within minutes they were slipping out of the harbour and rounding the point of the Old Fort.

'You are very much in command,' Chance commented, watching the Count giving orders to the helmsman. 'Do you not have a sailing master?'

'Oh, yes. A good man. But when I hunt, I like to lead.' He gestured to a seaman and snapped an order. 'This man will show you your cabin.'

Chance ducked below, surprised at the comfort, almost elegance, of the fittings. The ship was panelled in fine woods, brass gleamed. The cabin he was shown to had a fine coverlet on the bunk and gimballed lights over a fixed desk. He changed rapidly into the clothes he had worn on the long voyage through the Mediterranean, and which he had used when his leg was injured. He left his feet bare to grip on the deck and picked up his sword consideringly.

No, too melodramatic, for heaven's sake. They would simply overhaul the merchantman, explain that the lady was being taken against her will and remove Alessa in a civilised manner. This was hardly the Spanish Main. He grinned in self-mockery at the thought of swinging on to the deck with a boarding party, cutlass between his teeth, then tossed the sword back on the bunk and made his way back up the companionway to the deck.

'Ah, you have the clothes for a voyage, my friend.'

'I brought these with me for comfort at sea on the journey here—I did not expect to find myself so close to the action.' Some instinct led him to change the subject. Chance stared ahead, straining for a sight of white sails, but could see nothing but fishing boats. 'The coasts are very close together up ahead.' The looming bulk of Albania seemed almost to touch the island. The channel was a mile, if that, across.

'Yes, indeed. It is most convenient.'

To Chance's eye they seemed to be heading, not for the gap, but for the Albanian coast.

Within the hour he was proved right. Without orders from Zagrede the ship glided into a deep inlet, the mainsails came down and it was steered smoothly into a hidden harbour.

Cabins and workshops stretched along the dockside, other ships, all smaller than the one they were on, but all with the same lean, predatory lines, were tied alongside, the whole place was a bustle of activity.

'One of my ports,' the Count explained casually as they tied up.

'But why are we stopping? Do you need to take on provisions?'

'No, we need to change the ship, my friend. Now, we are traders no longer.'

Chance looked around again. There was nothing bigger, surely nothing faster. Men began to climb the rigging, the white sails were lashed up, then freed and lowered to the deck. In their place the seamen began to haul up a grey set. Along the sides men were hammering and freeing long planks of wood. Leaning over, Chance could see that, in effect, they were removing false sides. Revealed were the sinister black eyes of gun ports.

Zagrede snapped his fingers and a man began to haul up a flag. It snapped free and open in the wind and Chance looked up at a snarling silver wolf's head on a black ground.

He stared at the Count in dawning comprehension. 'You are a pirate. This is a pirate ship.'

'But of course. my friend. Welcome aboard the *Ghost*.'

Alessa landed in an undignified, panting heap of sodden clothes and sprawled there on the deck, struggling to recover her breath. Gradually the shaking in her limbs subsided and she raised her head and stared around. Someone had thrown a cloak over her. Above, the sails snapped in the wind as the ship heeled to get on to course. She was at sea. They were sailing and the children were left behind on the island without the slightest idea what had happened to her.

She tried to stand and someone took her arm, steadying her. 'Oh, poor Alexandra, are you all right now?'

Frances. 'No, I am not all right.' It was hard to speak without screaming in rage and frustration. With an effort Alessa kept her voice low and steady as she looked at her cousin's pretty, anxious face. 'I have been kidnapped and the children are still on Corfu.'

'Oh, no, you have not been kidnapped. It is all for your own good. Mama warned me you would be upset at first,' Frances said soothingly, as though speaking to someone simple-minded. 'She said the children did not want to come and made themselves ill crying when she tried to persuade them.'

'Your mother has said but a dozen words to them,' Alessa retorted. 'And none of them were to encourage them to come with us. Take me to the captain.'

'No, dear.' It was Lady Blackstone, smiling grimly, a neatly dressed man at her side. 'You see, Dr Cobb, quite distracted, poor child. I have hopes of a recovery if we can get her to rest quietly. What the cause of the problem is, I have no idea—perhaps there was instability on her mother's side. When we return to London I shall call in the leading specialists in hysterical maladies. No expense will be spared for my poor niece'

Alessa stared around her. They were well out of harbour now, too far to swim; in any case, there was no hope of that if they saw her jump. Resisting now would only get her confined under lock and key, perhaps even physically restrained, for her aunt appeared to have convinced the doctor that she was mentally unstable.

She put up a trembling hand to her face. 'I don't know what happened,' she murmured. 'Did I fall in? I want to lie down.'

'Of course you do,' the doctor said soothingly 'Now, this nice man will carry you to your cabin.' Alessa found herself scooped up by a seaman. 'Miss Blackstone, would you accompany me? I am sure your cousin would want your support.'

Finally, undressed and washed by Frances, reluctantly assisted by Lady Blackstone's bracket-faced maid, Alessa was tucked up in bed. The doctor reappeared to urge her to take a paregoric drink of his own invention and finally, mercifully, she was left in peace.

Who knew what had happened? Presumably Lady Trevick had been given some tale to convince her that all was well, or Aunt Honoria would be creating the very scandal she sought to avert. Kate and the children would have no idea what had occurred. When they became worried at not hearing, they would go to the Residency—and find she had left them without a word.

They would be so hurt. Alessa tried to imagine it, biting her lip to keep back the tears. Demetri would pretend to be brave, but inside he would feel betrayed, lost and bewildered. And little Dora, who had been abandoned once already—would she ever recover?

But they were with Kate, and Kate would know something was wrong, that Alessa would never leave like that without a word. Kate would reassure them she had not gone willingly and she would look after them like a mother cat with kittens until Alessa managed to get back to them.

Who else knew? The memory swept back like a black cloud. Chance knew. Chance had handed over the note to Frances, who, looking back now, had obviously known all about the plan to sail. And as he had left he had looked at her so strangely, had said *goodbye*. He had known. He had lied to her, tricked her, after all he had promised. She had been betrayed by the man she loved. For respectability. For convention.

Alessa turned over, seized the pillow from behind her head and punched it with all her might. Right from the beginning Chance had supported her return to England and her family. He had found excuses for her aunt's attitude and behaviour and had pressed on her the importance of conforming to English society.

She lay on the bunk, almost oblivious to the motion of the ship and the discomfort of her bruised, aching body. *I am going to escape, I am going to get back here to the children, we will make our own way to England and cause my aunt the greatest possible embarrassment. And then I am going to make Benedict Casper Chancellor, Earl of Blakeney, wish he had never been born.*

'Are you insane? Do you hope to get away with this?' Chance strode furiously along the deck of the *Ghost* as the Count made his dispositions. Men were coming on board with guns slung over their shoulders, a strange mix of antiques with immensely long barrels and the latest modern rifles. All had a sword and a long knife thrust through their belts; all looked as though they knew exactly what they were about.

'Away with what?' Zagrede grinned as he stopped aside to allow several baskets of bread to be carried below.

'With kidnapping an English Earl, for a start, let alone whatever else you are intending.'

'My dear Benedict, you are not being kidnapped! What an idea. You came on board willingly, in broad daylight under the eyes of the sentries on the fort. No, you will be carried on precisely the journey you wished to take—the pursuit of the merchant ship *Plymouth Sound*.'

They were casting off now, the strange grey sails were lowered, shouted orders floated up from below decks and there was the rumble of gun carriages. 'There is no need to fire on her, for God's sake.' Chance seized the Count's arm. 'Outrun her, hail her. I will go aboard and explain to the captain that Alessa has been taken against her will—that is all that is required.'

'It is all *you* require.' The Count squinted up at the set of the sails as the *Ghost* slid out of the inlet. 'I want that ship, and all the ladies on it.'

'Have you got a death wish?' Chance demanded, dodging to keep beside Zagrede as he strode through the mass of seamen to look at the rigging. 'Those ladies are the kin of a senior British diplomat, they are under the protection of the

Lord High Commissioner. When news of this gets out there will be hell to pay. How do you expect to continue your business in British-controlled ports after this?'

The Count dropped his eyes from the sails, apparently satisfied with what he could see. 'Stop this display of outrage,' he said genially, dropping one hand on to Chance's shoulder. Chance shrugged it off. 'My—what is the word?—*legitimate* trade is of little consequence to my wealth, and is of less now the British are filling the sea with their merchant ships. My freebooting brings in the money, and that improves with the number of your ships—they are rich pickings, my friend. And so many of them!

'But now I have a fight on my hands. This Lord Blackstone in Venice is out to sweep pirates off the surface of the Ionian Sea. My agents tell me that a naval cutter is due into Corfu in days, with orders that would make life very difficult indeed for me and my compatriots. Already the British are stirring; all this fuss at the Residency is but the beginning. Time to cut my losses and leave, I think.'

'They know who you are?'

'Not yet. They will when that cutter gets here.' A man appeared with a tray with bread and wine and olives and set it down on a hatch cover. 'Here, eat and stop trying to think of ways a single man armed with a sword and two pistols can take this ship.'

Chance regarded his infuriating captor. He was quite correct—ideas, all of them wildly impractical, had been rushing through his brain. But so far he was on deck, not restrained and having a civil conversation; better to keep it that way than for any of the alternatives he could imagine. He tore off some bread, dipped it in the olive oil and chewed.

'What do you want with the women?' He had no fear for

himself, but the thought of Alessa in the power of this crew made his blood run cold.

'Lady Blackstone and her pretty daughter? Now, they are quite safe with me, for they are valuable hostages. I shall have to put them somewhere so that I do not have to listen to that woman's sharp tongue, but they will be very comfortable.'

'And if the British do not do what you expect? If Lord Blackstone and Sir Thomas do their duty, at whatever the cost to the women?'

'Then I move the ladies further inland and all communication from them ceases. I am not a murderer of innocent women, Benedict, but neither do I surrender. They will come in handy eventually.'

'And Alessa?' He had to force himself not to run his tongue around his dry lips.

'Oh, I think I will marry her.' Chance was on his feet, the wine bottle in his hand before two seamen had him by the arms. '*Marry,* I said, not rape.' The Count said something to the men and they let go, stepping back warily. 'She thinks you only want her as a mistress, my trusting friend.' He grinned. 'You really should not believe everything another man tells you, not when a lovely woman is involved. And who knows what that man is saying to the lady? She knows that her background is smudged enough for things to be difficult for her in England. When she comes to believe that marrying me will make life easier for her aunt and cousin, she will agree.'

'Blackmail her into it? And you do not call that rape?' Chance felt his fingers cramping around the bottle and made himself relax. He poured wine and set the bottle down.

'I call it seduction, my friend, and I will be most ashamed of myself if the lady does not thoroughly enjoy it.' He twitched the glass out of Chance's hand and raised it in a mocking toast before draining it. 'And it is no good looking at me with murder in your eyes, my dear Benedict: you would be dead before you could reach me.'

'As I doubtless will be by the end of this voyage.'

'But why should you think that? I have no wish to harm you—I like you. You will find yourself dropped off on some remote island when it is no longer convenient to carry you with us. If you try anything foolish, I will have you locked in your cabin. If it is *very* foolish, in chains. You understand?'

'Oh, yes.' Chance stretched his lips into a parody of the Count's insouciant smile. 'I understand.'

He filled the other glass and drank, his eyes roaming over what he could see. *How many men?* Impossible to tell at the moment, when many were below and he could not yet differentiate between one moustachioed face and another. He studied the rigging and the set of the sails. *Could I sail her? Yes, with a skeleton crew who knew what they were doing.*

Weapons. I need something to give me an edge. His sword and pistols were in the cabin where he had left them. 'I need my hat,' he said, getting to his feet. 'Is there a problem with my going below decks?'

'None in the world, dear friend. But they have gone, you know. Such a nice pair of pistols.'

'Indeed they are,' Chance said civilly, trying not to grind his teeth, 'but I still require a hat.'

He went down to the cabin, unmolested by any of the crew he passed on the way. The pistols had indeed gone—so had the sword, his penknife and his razors. Everything else was neatly stowed.

Chance shut the door quietly, stood in the middle of the cabin and allowed himself the luxury of losing his temper for a solid minute of vicious swearing. Then he sat down at the writing ledge and tried to think logically and calmly. And failed.

All he could do was to try to fight the cold panic that

seemed to paralyse his guts and his brain whenever he thought about Alessa. Now she would be frantic about the children; that was bad enough. Soon she would find herself in the clutches of a crew of eastern Mediterranean pirates, and in the bed of Voltar Zagrede.

Would he take her by force? Chance found the quill he had unconsciously picked up broken in two. No, probably not. If nothing else, the Count would think the less of himself if his vaunted powers of seduction failed him. But would she give in to him? Possibly, if she thought she must do so to help her relatives, or if she thought she had no future in England, or Corfu, after being so thoroughly compromised. And she liked the man. Damn it, so did he. He just wanted him at the end of a rifle barrel, with the trigger under his own finger.

To be fair, the Count would probably send for the children if she asked him to, and he would look after them all well. Demetri would love learning to be a pirate, the little wretch.

But the lad was never going to get the opportunity to try it, not if he had anything to do with it. Chance set out to explore and find out just what the limits on his freedom were.

Almost complete, as it turned out. He was blocked only twice—once in front of what he guessed must be the armoury and magazine and once at the door to Zagrede's own cabin. He returned on deck to find the Count standing besides the helmsman, studying a chart that had been weighted down on the nearest hatch cover.

'Good ship, eh?' He glanced up as Chance approached. 'You have a look round?'

'Yes, thank you. How am I going to shave myself?'

'My man will do it. He has a steady hand, so long as you do not distract him.'

Suddenly curious about something that had been niggling

at the back of his mind, Chance demanded, 'Where did you learn your English?'

'Harrow,' the Count responded with a flash of amusement. 'Somehow they failed to make me a complete English gentleman.'

Harrow! This was rapidly becoming like a bad dream. Chance looked down at the chart, then up at the coastline. Corfu had vanished into the haze, but the bulk of Albania still loomed on the starboard bow.

'When?' he asked abruptly.

The Count glanced up, not making the error of thinking that Chance was referring to the promised shave. 'Tomorrow, when we are into the Adriatic. Soon we will be at the heel of Italy. I would like to be beyond it and have a little more sea room before I strike.'

'You hunt alone?' Chance looked up at the heights.

'Yes, this time. You are right to look up; if I lead a wolf pack, then we use fires to signal where the quarry is.' He released the weight that held the chart and it rolled up, the sudden noise rasping Chance's raw nerves. 'Relax, my friend, enjoy the peace. Tomorrow we fight.'

'How could you do such a wicked thing?' Alessa faced her aunt across the cabin. 'The children will be terrified.'

'Nonsense. Peasant children have no sensibility; besides, they have that Street woman to look after them.' Her aunt was looking at her as though Alessa was being utterly unreasonable. *She really does not understand*, Alessa thought, shocked into seeing the truth. *It does not fit her image of how things should be, of how she feels, so she fails to see the pain she is causing.*

'When we get to England I will tell everyone what you did,' she threatened. That should do it, surely. Scandal was what she most feared.

'What have I done? Removed you from poverty? Reunited you with your family? People will understand if you are vapourish. They will sympathise when I tell them that, all alone, you comforted yourself by doing good works with orphans and became hysterical when you had to be parted from them.' She smiled serenely. 'If you do not have the brats clinging to your petticoats, then I am sure one nasty little rumour will not circulate.'

'People will believe me,' Alessa said doggedly.

'Alexandra, listen to me. Two years ago the daughter of Lord Portington had an affair with his valet and got herself with child. He put her in an asylum. Society thinks he did the correct thing. It will be very distressing to have to take such drastic action, but people will applaud my efforts to at least ensure you are looked after in England, you poor, distracted child.

'And if you stop this nonsense…why, then you can live a good life, as a respectable, conformable lady. It is your choice.' She shut the door softly behind her, leaving Alessa staring at the panels, her blood chilled in her veins.

Chapter Nineteen

It was mid-day before Zagrede allowed the *Ghost* to begin to overhaul the *Plymouth Sound*. Chance shaded his eyes as the merchantman, still a distant shape, began to lose way.

'They are slowing down.'

'Perhaps the damage that was mended so quickly was not mended very well and someone on board knows how to weaken it again,' the Count said airily. 'We have them soon. And you, my friend—will you give me your word you will do nothing to intervene?'

'Like hell I will.' *She is over there, so close.*

'Then I will have you tied up and locked in your cabin,' said the Count equably.

Chance wrestled with the choices. 'I will give you my parole until you capture the other ship,' he said eventually. 'Or, if you do not succeed, until dusk tonight.'

'And then?'

'*Then* you can try to lock me in my cabin.' He was answered by a crack of laughter as the Count strode off.

'There is another ship behind us,' Frances called. She was leaning on the rail, holding on to the brim of her wide sun hat.

The young lieutenant, with whom she had been flirting mildly, stared back at the sleek shape drawing up on the starboard side. On deck the men who were working on the splintered spar glanced up, then went back to their task.

Alessa came over to join them, grateful for the distraction from her churning thoughts. 'What is it?'

'A coastal vessel of some sort, ma'am. Not British. A trader, I have no doubt, curious for a look at us. If we were not hampered by that dashed spar splintering, we would soon show him a clean pair of heels.'

'How odd those grey sails are,' Frances commented. 'You can hardly see them against the sea. She shivered. 'Like a ghost ship, so quiet and fast.'

The young man smiled, patronisingly. 'There are all sorts out here, ma'am, no need to be alarmed.'

'Is there not? There is something so…' Alessa stared as the other ship altered course, slicing though the water between them. With a thud that carried across the narrowing gap, the gun ports fell open and the black muzzles ran out.

'Hell, pirates!' The lieutenant seized them both by the arm, dragging them urgently towards the companionway. 'Get below, stay there.'

The merchantman was in uproar, orders being shouted, the wheel spinning, the rumble of guns being run out. Alessa pushed Frances unceremoniously down the companionway and pulled the two slanting hatch doors almost closed. Through the small gap that remained she could just see the deck. Below there was screaming, the sound of someone having hysterics and the slam of doors. Keys turned. She would stay out here, come what may, not huddle in a tiny cabin like a rat in a trap.

The chaos on deck was settling down to something more purposeful now, and Alessa felt her confidence returning. The damaged spar was cleared out of the way, hands ran to run up more sail, a gun was trundled across the deck and men were loading it in a disciplined manner.

The roar of the cannon when it came was so sudden that Alessa almost lost her footing and tumbled back. There was a strange screeching sound, cracking, and the entire mainsail began to collapse on to the deck.

'Chain shot!' she heard an officer shout. 'They got the top mast, cut this free.' But the ship was wallowing now, sails flapping, and with a grinding crunch their attacker was alongside.

Alessa slammed the door shut and swung down the bar. *Much good that will do*, she thought grimly. *I need a weapon.*

And then the recollection of sitting on the chair looking at her father's pistol and pushing it into the leather satchel came to her. *Where is it?* She scrambled down the companionway and ran to her cabin, wrenched open the door and began to dig through the pile of luggage for which, up to now, she had spared only a cursory thought. There, at the bottom, was the satchel, and in it the reassuring bulk of the box containing the pistol.

She loaded it slowly, forcing herself to take care, ignoring the racket on deck overhead and the shrieks from the cabins further along. The last thing she needed now was a misfire.

When the pistol was loaded Alessa stood for a moment, just looking at it. Could she fire it? She knew she was a good shot against a static target. But could she fire on a man? *Yes*, she told herself firmly. Yes, if it was that or rape. Yes, if by shooting from a hiding place she could aid the ship's defenders.

No one had tried to come down below yet. The action was all still on deck. Cautiously Alessa eased her way up the companionway and reached the barred door just as everything went silent. Her heart was thudding, her mouth dry, as she took hold of the bar and began to lift it up. The quiet was terrifying, far worse than the shooting and shouts had been. She lifted the bar with hands that shook, and cracked open the door.

Ranged before her, their backs to her, was the boarding party, their clothes an exotic mixture of east and west. They were barefoot, their baggy trousers and wide sashes splashing ragged colour against the white-scrubbed deck and the heaped wreckage. Knives and curved swords were grasped by some, others held long-barrelled guns. Through the gaps between them she could see the ship's crew, disarmed and scowling.

The man in the centre was talking, the wind whipping his words away from her, towards the captives. For a moment she thought she recognised his voice, then realised it must be the accent; these would be Albanian pirates—no wonder she had mistaken the man for the Count of Kurateni.

Alessa eased back the doors and stepped over the sill on to the deck—if she could surprise them, hold their leader for even a minute or two, the crew might be able to rush them.

'Stand still! I have a gun on your leader's back! Put down your weapons or I will fire.'

No one moved. The boarders, with a discipline she had not expected, faced forward still, their weapons steady. The broad shoulders in front of her moved: she might have mistaken it for a laugh under other circumstances. Then the man turned round.

'My dear Alessa, I am glad to see you unharmed.'

'Count!' The muzzle of the pistol drooped and she jerked it back to point squarely at his chest. 'Stop this at once, or I will shoot.'

'But, no, of course you would not! Shoot me in cold blood? I do not believe it, my sweet.' It was the same mocking, charming, dangerous man as before, only now she had not the slightest inclination to flirt with him.

Alessa lifted her other hand to steady her aim. 'I am a good shot: I can hardly miss you at this range.' Indeed, she was so close she could see the steady rise and fall of his chest under the flamboyantly draped shirt.

'Shoot a friend?'

'Shoot a pirate, you mean. I will count to five. One…two…'

The Count reached out a hand and drew a man forward, a tall man who had been concealed behind the wall of Zagrede's crew.

'Three… Chance!' Zagrede moved like a snake. As the pistol jerked in her hand with the shock he was on her, twisting her wrist, sending the weapon flying across the deck.

'My apologies, my dear, but if you will play rough games—' His fist caught her neatly on the point of her chin, the world spun.

Stars, you really do see stars…Chance… The deck came up and met her and everything went dark.

Chance doubled his fist and lunged for Zagrede, only to find himself grappled hard from behind. He bucked, stamped and kicked, but three men were too much, even in his present killing rage.

'You bastard…'

'My dear Benedict, if she had shot me, my men would have killed her. I hit her for her own protection. And speaking of protection—we have the ship, so I believe your parole has expired.' The Count spoke in rapid Albanian and his captors began to drag Chance towards the rail. He fought desperately. How far were they from land? Could he hope to swim, or would they put a bullet in him before he hit the water? The merchant ship's crew took a step forward and a single gunshot jerked them to a halt. As he was dragged to the rail Chance twisted his head and bit one of the hands holding his shoulder hard, to the bone.

The blow on the back of his head came out of nowhere; he was unconscious before he hit the deck.

Alessa came to herself slowly and she lay, eyes closed, listening, waiting while she regained her senses. Her head and neck ached, but it was not disabling. Nothing else hurt. She was lying on something soft, which was swaying. No, the cabin was swaying, she was still on board.

Cautiously she opened her eyes on to a completely unfamiliar, luxurious cabin. She was not on the same ship, she realised. By the way it moved, this was smaller. She was on the pirate vessel.

It was then, as she attempted to sit up on the bed, that she realised her hands were tied. Someone had used silk scarves or sashes, for the fabric was soft against her skin until she tried to jerk at it. Each wrist was secured separately and the bonds went to the posts at the head. There was enough length to them to let her sit up, to move her arms up and down, but get off the bed she could not.

She could see the Count's hand in this. Tied up and a prisoner, certainly, but secured with silk, on a comfortable bed, and able to move and make herself comfortable. This care was sinister: what was he keeping her for? She would have been happier to find herself in the bilges.

The door opening brought her as upright as she could manage. He was not going to see her trembling, whatever he had come for. And whatever it was, there was one question she must have an answer for first, and before anything.

Voltar Zagrede lounged into the cabin, his dark eyes amused, the wide sensual mouth twisted into an appreciative smile. 'My dear Alessa, how very lovely you look like that.' He moved to sit on the edge of the bed and swerved elegantly as she kicked out at him. 'I much regret having to hit you, but really, my dear, what *do* you think would have happened to you if you had shot me? I would not have been able to forgive myself.'

'It would have been worth it,' she snapped. 'And you would not have to worry about it: I would have killed you.'

His dark brows shot up as he whistled in admiration. 'So fierce! I was right about you. Magnificent.'

'Oh never mind about that. What have you done with Chance? What was he doing here?'

'My good friend Benedict has been with us from the start of this chase. We followed you out of harbour, changed our appearance a trifle, took on more men and we have been on your track ever since.'

'But how did Chance come to be with you? He cannot have known this is a pirate ship, that you are a pirate.'

'Of course he knew what I am. He is not what he seems, any more than I am.' The Count took advantage of her concentration on Chance to approach the bed again. His hand slid down her hair to her shoulder. 'You are too trusting, Alessa; that must change if you are to marry me—my wife must be ever on the alert.'

'Marry you?' She stared at him, but there seemed to be no sign of lunacy. The Count smiled calmly back at her with the same quizzical charm she had come to expect from him. 'This is some sort of joke, I assume? I have to tell you, my sense of humour is not what it used to be.'

'No joke.' He wandered down the bed and began to stroke her ankle. Alessa kicked at him and he withdrew his hand, smiling. 'I have your aunt and your cousin—they will be hostages against the actions of Lord Blackstone and Sir Thomas in suppressing piracy. Or at least, attempting to do so. Everyone tries, no one succeeds, but it is tiresome while it lasts.'

'I am of no value as a hostage,' she pointed out.

'No. Your value to me lies elsewhere.'

'As a wife?' she queried sarcastically. 'I have heard rape given many euphemisms, but that is a new one.'

'Now you insult me.' Alessa stared into the impudent black eyes. He *is insulted?* 'I need a wife, I need sons. You are well bred, you are courageous, you are beautiful and you are a virgin. I desire you.'

'Well, I do not desire you,' Alessa said firmly.

'But you will, my sweet, you will.' The Count stood watching her and the mocking light in his eyes became hot. She swallowed, determined not to show any fear. 'You are a valuable exercise in self-discipline for me, Alessa. Now, rest. I am busy just at the moment, but I will return in an hour or so. There is water there, just within reach of your right hand. Sleep, and dream of fine castles, rich silks, a passionate husband and tall sons.'

Alessa tried to relax as he suggested, but it was a ridiculous ambition to sleep when her mind was in such turmoil. What the Count had said about the fate of her relatives and his plans for herself were the least of her worries. She believed him, rogue that he was; none of them was going to be physically mistreated, although she doubted her aunt would credit it.

No, what was gnawing at her was what the Count had said about Chance. *Of course he knew what I am. He is not what he seems…* What did he mean? Not an honest man? Not an earl? Could Chance be a confidence trickster, a fraud? Why not? Where better to prey on rich, unsuspecting people than a remote island in the Mediterranean? None of them knew the Earl of Blakeney by sight—he could be a short, fat red-head with gout for all they knew, and probably was, comfortably at home in London, unaware that his name was being used by a sharp, loose among the trusting marks, far from home.

She shut her eyes, trying to find some repose, but the memories chased themselves across the darkness. *I cannot believe it of him,* yet presumably gullible people were saying that every day as they discovered the skilled deceptions that were practised upon them. *I cannot afford to be gullible, I cannot afford to let love conquer commonsense. Frances and my aunt and the children all depend upon me now.*

The click of the door latch cut across her thoughts. Alessa froze, her eyes still shut, listening. The door opened, closed. Someone was inside the room. She braced herself to scream if it was one of the crew, and brought her head round sharply on the pillow. But the man leaning a negligent shoulder against the door jamb, his hands behind his back, was no randy sailor.

'Chance!' He stayed so still that for a moment she thought she was imagining him. 'Chance?'

'Are you all right?' He sounded concerned; there was something in the steady voice she could almost believe was anger, but he made no move towards her.

'All right?' Alessa wriggled until she was sitting upright. She grabbed the rails to which the silk bonds fettered her to the bed and glared at him. 'Do I look all right? I have been betrayed by a man I thought was my friend, kidnapped by my aunt, and then again by your friend Zagrede. I have been hit on the chin, tied to this bed, entertained by a madman with a proposal of marriage—and now you stroll in to amuse yourself by mocking me. No, Lord Blakeney, or whatever your real name is, I am *not* all right.'

Chance shifted his stance against the door frame. 'What do you mean, *whatever my real name is?*'

'Well, as I assume the real Lord Blakeney is not cruising

the Adriatic in the company of pirates, you are presumably some sharp travelling under his name. Or perhaps you are nothing but a pirate with an English education.'

Chance's eyes were fixed on her face, his own dark with whatever emotion he was experiencing—Alessa doubted that it was remorse.

'The Count went to Harrow,' he remarked.

'Did you meet there?' She tried to match his conversational tone and merely achieved sarcasm.

'No. I went to Eton. For heaven's sake, Alessa, I am not a sharp, I am not a pirate, I am Blakeney and exactly who I told you I was. I came on this ship to follow you, for no other purpose.'

'Oh? And I suppose the Count gave you the run of it, did he? And you stood by while he boarded an English ship by force and took three Englishwomen hostage? I had not thought you a coward.'

That brought the colour up under the skin drawn taut over his cheekbones. Whatever he was about, Chance did not appear to be enjoying the situation, that was one comfort, and things felt so desperate, any comfort was welcome.

'There was nothing I could do to stop them. If I had tried to, I would have been dragged below and locked up. I gave my parole until the ship was taken; I thought at least then I had some hope of stopping bloodshed, of looking after you.'

'Indeed? And why should I believe you would care? You have already betrayed me, broken your word to me, abandoned those children—' Her voice broke, and with it her temper. Better to shout than to weep, better to hurl all the bitter, hateful things she had been thinking about him than to let him gloat over her foolish trust for him.

'You promised me you would make sure they sailed with me, and you have betrayed that promise. Have you any idea how they must feel? I shouldn't imagine you have. You tricked me with that message to go to the ship, you connived with my aunt and my cousin—you are a liar and a traitor and a coward with no conscience…'

She could feel her voice beginning to shake and controlled it with an effort. 'And now you lounge there, amusing yourself seeing me in this predicament and you do nothing, *nothing* to help make this better.' The tears were welling up in her eyes now; Alessa bit down savagely on her lip to halt them. 'I hate you, and I thought I…. I hate you.' She yanked at the restraining ties, bruising her skin. 'If I was free, I would like to kill you.'

There was silence in the cabin. Above their heads feet thudded on the deck, the faint sound of shouted orders reached them. The square porthole threw light across the middle of the room, touching Chance's bare feet. He pushed away from the door frame, his hands still behind him, and stepped towards her.

'There is nothing to be said to that, except that it is not true. None of it is true.' Now she could see his face clearly Alessa saw he was white under the tan. 'I was tricked too. I delivered that message in all innocence, and when I found out, I followed you, not knowing what Zagrede is. The children know what has happened, they are with Kate. I am no friend of the Count's, and he knows it.'

'The Count told me that you were not what you seemed. He warned me you wanted only to make me your mistress,' she shot at him.

'Do you believe what you are told by a man like that, or do you believe what you know in your heart and can see with your own eyes, Alessa?'

As he spoke Chance turned so she could see his hands, not clasped casually behind his back as she had imagined, but lashed together. His wrists and hands were bloody: he had struggled to free himself until he had cut the flesh raw, she realised, her stomach swooping into a sickening lurch.

'How did you get in here?' Alessa's voice was hardly a whisper.

'I picked the lock to my cabin, which was easier than I imagined it could be, with a hair pin and my hands behind me.' Her face must have shown the question she was about to ask. Chance smiled faintly. 'My good friend Zagrede appears to make a habit of entertaining ladies—my cabin has a dresser scattered with pins.'

'How did you find out what happened?' How could she have believed the Count rather than the man she loved? Had she been alone so long that she had forgotten how to trust, and expected to be betrayed? Perhaps she simply did not believe she could find, and hold, a friend like Chance.

'Demetri told me—he stole a horse from the Residency stables to do it and rode right into the middle of the cricket match to storm at me that you had gone, with all your luggage, and I was responsible. The ship was still in harbour. I was trying to find a boat to get out to you when I saw you jump into the sea.'

'Demetri saw?'

'Yes. I sent him for help and tried to swim out to you, but they had you before I could get there. The Count fished me out like a drowned rat and offered to give chase. I was surprised, to put it mildly, when he slipped into a hidden harbour and transformed this ship into what you see now.'

'And the children?' She could not get the anxiety out of her mind.

'With Kate and quite safe. I promised them I will get you back.' His smile was gentle. 'And I will.'

Chapter Twenty

❧◦❧◦❧◦◦

'I did not trust you.' Alessa made herself meet Chance's eyes squarely. Strangely she felt worse inside now than she had at any time since she realised she had been tricked aboard the *Plymouth Sound*. Everything she felt for Chance seemed to be wrapped around her heart so that she could hardly breathe. 'I insulted and abused you—can you forgive me?'

He sat beside her on the bed, awkward because of his bound hands. 'You have been alone for a very long time and life has not been very kind. Why should you trust me? I certainly cannot blame you for what you believed.' He hesitated and his smile was rueful. 'But it hurt.'

'Hurt!' She snatched up the word, taking it literally. 'You are hurt and I am lying here, doing nothing! Turn around, put your hands close to my right one and I will untie you.'

But one-handed, twisted round against the restraint on her other wrist, she could do nothing with the viciously thin twine. She knew she must be hurting him, although he only betrayed it with a sharp intake of breath when her nail dug into his raw wrist.

'Hopeless—try to see if you can free me.'

But Chance's efforts were as futile. 'Silk, I see,' he commented wryly, as he struggled with the hard, tight knot. 'Your pirate admirer treats you well. No, I give up; we need a knife.' He sank down on the bed next to her again. 'You say he has proposed marriage?'

'Oh, yes.' Alessa allowed her head to rest back against the wall for a moment, wishing she dare rest it on Chance's shoulder. He seemed to have forgiven her. She clung to that hope, but dared not risk rejection.

The struggle to free them both had left her shoulders aching. At first the position had not seemed too uncomfortable; now she longed to be able to lower her arms and bring her hands together. And Chance must be in an even worse state. 'I think he must be mad if he believes he can get away with kidnapping three English ladies. My uncle and Sir Thomas will have the entire fleet after him.'

'The fleet will have a hard time catching him in the midst of the Albanian mountains. Alessa…' Chance turned his head to look into her eyes. He was so close she could see the individual whiskers of the stubble on his unshaven face. 'Has he touched you?'

'Other than hit me on the chin? No, I understand what you mean. Nothing untoward has occurred; he appears to think he is irresistible and has only to wait for me to fall into his arms.'

Chance gave a snort of laughter. 'I know, he informed me so himself when I promised him that if he tried to rape you I would kill him. However, Zagrede maintains that, such are his powers of seduction, you will succumb. He appeared to find my indignation amusing.'

'Succumb? I will do no such thing,' Alessa said indignantly. 'Why, you would have more chance of seducing me with one hand tied behind your back than he has.'

There was silence. Chance's pupils widened and Alessa heard his breathing hitch. 'I have *both* hands tied behind my back.'

'Chance, you can't—' She got no further before his mouth crushed down on hers by the simple expedient of him leaning forward and allowing his momentum to carry them both down on to the pillows. He shifted his weight, unable to balance by using his elbows. Instinct made Alessa part her legs so that he was cradled between her thighs. The unfamiliar, masculine weight created a tense tingling sensation at the base of her belly that she had never felt before, any more than she had felt the full length of male arousal pressed hot and hard against her secret softness.

She moaned a little, half in fear of her own response, half in anxiety that she might not please him. Her wrists strained inwards against the bonds, but she could not touch his head or stroke his hair as she longed to. Then the heat of his mouth claimed all her attention. He was angling his lips over hers, seeking to find a position where he could control the kiss without being able to use his hands. Alessa felt the tip of his tongue teasing at the join between her lips and parted for him, shuddering in delight as Chance traced the sensitive flesh for a tantalising moment before plunging in, ravishing her mouth with the heat and the thrust of his tongue.

She might be inexperienced, but Alessa understood only too well what this invasion mimicked, and her body understood as well. Without conscious thought she arched up against him, pressing against the impossible, terrifying size of him.

'Oh, God, sweetheart, I want you so much,' she could hear the whisper, husky against her inflamed skin as he shifted, licking and nibbling his way down her throat to her shoulder, down to the swell of her breasts.

'I want you too, Chance.'

He said nothing, only murmured something against her

skin as his mouth swept lower and his lips and teeth began to tug and worry at the edge of her light lawn gown. Then he found the drawstring that gathered the neckline, nipped the end of the ribbon in his teeth and pulled. The bow came free and he teased at the fabric until it fell away, exposing the fine line of her camisole.

'It…ties…the same way,' she gasped, struggling against the overwhelming urge to rock her pelvis against him.

Chance was growling softly with either frustration at her clothing, or desire, she had no way of knowing. And then the chemise was free and he was suddenly still, gazing at the white curves of her naked breasts.

'You are so beautiful. Before, in the sea, on the beach, there was so much sensation, I did not look closely enough at you. So lovely, so perfect.' He dipped his head and began to shower tiny kisses on to the soft flesh. Alessa could feel her breasts become fuller, heavier. Everything seemed to throb and yearn, every part of her body wanted him to touch it.

The sudden shock as he took her nipple into his mouth and sucked hard until it peaked sent her bucking against him, her indrawn breath rasping her throat. The act seemed to send a dart of sensation deep into her belly, deep between her thighs as she twisted and strained against him.

She moaned, her head twisting on the pillow as Chance switched his attentions to the other breast, teasing that nipple into aching arousal in turn. Something was building inside her, tense, demanding, unfamiliar. Desperately she gasped, 'Chance, *please*. I don't understand…but I want *something*, I don't…'

'Hush, sweetheart, I know.' His voice was soothing and she quietened, despite the anguish as his mouth left her breast and his weight slid off her. Too weighted down with sensation and strangeness to move, she lay limply, arms outstretched, passive to whatever he chose to do to her next. This was Chance, she trusted him, she loved him—nothing else mattered.

The sudden cool air on her legs brought her out of her trance. He was drawing the hems of skirt and petticoat up with his teeth. Bemused, Alessa craned her neck to try and see what he was doing, then fell back with a gasp as she felt his kiss on the inside of her thigh.

'Chance, what are you doing?' There was no answer as the trail of kisses moved higher. He pushed her gently, the feel of his hair on her skin unexpectedly soft. The message was unmistakable—quivering with mingled excitement and shyness, Alessa parted her thighs. *What is he doing, surely he cannot mean to kiss me* there?

But he did, and not just kiss. Alessa stifled a cry as the flick of his tongue parted her, sought out the core of those overwhelming sensual demands that were clamouring at her now. She could hear panting, and realised it was coming from her own throat; she knew she should stop him, stop this outrageous, immodest... 'Chance, no...oh, *yes, yes!*'

If he even heard her incoherent pleas she had no idea; it seemed nothing was going to stop the skilled assault on her very core. She knew she was wantonly lifting herself into the sweet torture of his mouth, yearning towards whatever was twisting every nerve into screaming arousal. It would kill her—she could not be this tense, this consumed with sensation, and live.

Then, as though understanding she could bear no more, his demanding tongue ceased. For a moment she seemed to hang there, suspended in a whirlpool of desire, then his lips fastened on the aching centre of it, suckled ruthlessly, and the world broke apart.

Alessa broke with it, every part of her limp and quivering, her head empty of everything but a silent shout of love and completion. How long she lay there, abandoned to the impact of it all, she had no idea. Gradually she became aware of warmth next to her cheek, of the scratch of stubble, of breath stirring her hair.

'I want to hold you,' Chance murmured.

'I want you to,' she confessed, her eyes still tight shut. 'Chance, that was like nothing I ever imagined.'

'I wanted to pleasure you,' he informed her huskily.

'You succeeded,' Alessa responded with a shaky laugh. Somehow she managed to open her eyes and found herself looking into the dark depths of his, only inches away. 'Chance, you made love to me—but what about you?'

He straightened up and sat back on his heels beside the bunk. 'I may be able to pleasure my lady with both hands tied behind my back, but not being a contortionist I cannot remove my trousers or undo the fall in this state.'

My lady. Alessa recalled the awe-inspiring sensation of his body pressed against her. 'Isn't it rather uncomfortable?' she ventured, struggling to sit up. Unexpected, intimate parts of her body rippled with the aftershocks of her passion and she felt weaker than she had after they had dragged her out of the harbour.

'Very,' he confessed ruefully. 'But unrequited desire is probably the least of my problems right at the moment.' He swept a tender glance down from her face—which she could feel was glowing—down the length of her body. 'Hell!'

'What?' That was hardly the reaction she was expecting. Then she followed his gaze. 'Oh, my heavens!'

Her breasts were exposed, the drawstrings of both chemise and gown tangled and knotted, her skirts were round her waist and her hair was all over her face.

The next ten minutes, if they had not know the likely consequences of Chance being discovered, would have been as hysterical as any stage farce. Chance shook the tangled ribbons like a terrier with a rat in its teeth until he had untangled them, then wrestled with making the first part of the knot without hitting Alessa on the chin with his head. He did not always succeed, but after the first few blows, all of which seemed to find precisely the point where Zagrede had struck her, she gave up yelping in pain and concentrated on keeping still.

Finally Chance managed to slip one chemise ribbon through the other and lifted it towards her mouth. 'You hold this,' he mumbled, 'I'll pull.' Their lips met and Alessa froze, fighting the need to simply press her mouth to his and drown in his kiss. The brown eyes so close to hers sparkled with mischief. 'No,' he said, as firmly as a man with a mouthful of soggy ribbon could, and she caught it between her own teeth, waited until he found the other end, and tugged.

Chance managed to pull up the edges of her gown and they repeated the operation all over again, by which time Alessa was fighting giggles. Chance surfaced from the eleventh attempt to tie off the knot. 'What is funny now?'

'Your nose tickles my, er, cleavage.'

'Hmm…' He shot her a provocative glance. 'Well, let me tell you, Miss Meredith, that this is an agonisingly arousing enterprise for a man. In fact, I imagine the patrons of high-class bordellos would pay a fancy price for this experience.' With a final tug he managed the knot and sat back. 'There, I defy anyone to manage a bow.'

Alessa squinted down at the result. 'The ribbons are a bit wet and mangled.'

'Do you want me to ring for a maid and a flat iron?'

'I doubt they have any heating at this time of day.' Alessa felt the smile waver on her face. 'Chance, are we going to get out of this?'

'Yes.' He said it flatly. 'Yes, we are. And we'll get your

wretched aunt and your silly little cousin out as well. Now, one thing at a time—you still look as though you've been comprehensively rogered.'

'Chance! What a frightful expression.'

'Must be the association with pirates,' he said vaguely, getting to his feet in one smooth motion. 'Can you kick your skirts down? Good. I don't know what we are going to do about your hair, or those trailing ribbons.'

'I have been struggling,' Alessa announced with sudden inspiration.

'Oh, good girl,' he approved with a grin.

'It doesn't explain the chewed ribbons though,' Alessa worried.

'If the man can take his eyes off your bosom long enough to notice, then there is something wrong with him. Everything has ended up several inches lower than when we started, you know.'

'Oh my goodness! Chance, tug it up, quickly.'

'No time.' He was standing, his ear against the door panels. 'Someone's coming.'

'Hide!'

She watched in anguish as Chance spun round on his heel, searching the cabin for cover. There was a door in the panelling across the room; he took one stride towards it and the handle of the main door began to turn. In one fluid movement he dropped to the floor and rolled under the bunk. Alessa kicked frantically at the rumpled bedding on which she was lying and one edge fell to the floor. It was the best she could do. The door opened.

Chance pressed himself back against the wall, ignoring the pain in his wrists in his effort to keep as flat as possible. Above him he could hear Alessa thrashing around on the bed. He licked dry lips and set himself to breathe evenly and softly.

'My dear Alessa, what *are* you doing?' It was, as he had expected, Zagrede, his voice amused as he strolled across the floor to stand beside the bed. 'Why, you look a positive hoyden.' His voice dropped a tone. 'Delicious.'

'I was trying to get free.' Alessa's voice sounded as though she was speaking between gritted teeth.

'But why, my sweet?' The Count sat on the edge of the bed, making it dip perilously low. 'You know you cannot escape.'

'I wish to relieve myself,' Alessa announced in tones of freezing dignity. 'Have you no recollection of how long I have been tied up here?'

'Oh.'

Chance bit his lip in an effort to suppress a snort of laughter. The Count had obviously not thought of that, and his attempts at smooth seduction were hardly suited to a lady who was demanding to use the privy.

'But of course, I will untie you at once.'

'And send me a maid with a chamber pot,' Alessa demanded. 'I have no desire to be dragged through this ship to whatever squalid arrangements your crew uses.' Oh, well done, if she is hoping to distract Zagrede from thoughts of seduction, she could hardly do better.

'No need for that.' Chance rolled over slightly and squinted from under the bed. The Count was walking towards the other door. He threw it open and announced, 'You see, your own private facilities, my dear.'

'Then will you kindly untie me so I can use them?'

'Of course.' There was a pause, sounds of rustling, a thump and a grunt. 'What did you do that for?' Zagrede stood up, sounding indignant.

'To stop you gazing at my bosom,' Alessa retorted frigidly. 'Will you kindly help me up?'

Chance watched her feet as she approached the door and

threw it open, exposing the entire space, no larger than a cupboard, to view. 'It will do, I suppose, but there is no soap and no towel.'

'I will send for some.'

'Please do so. I am sure my aunt has something suitable in her baggage—I have no wish to use whatever Albanian goat's-fat concoction you have on board.'

There was a moment's hesitation, then the Count strode to the cabin door and opened it. 'I will lock this door behind me, the porthole is screwed shut, and, believe me, I will reopen the door with some caution, so please do not trouble yourself to stand behind it, waiting to hit me with the ewer.'

'I am flattered that you think me capable of such daring,' Alessa countered. 'Now, will you please go away and give me some privacy!'

The Count was hardly out of the door before Chance was rolling out from under the bed. He dived into the privy cupboard and Alessa pulled the door shut.

'Quickly, turn around and let me untie your hands.' He turned as best he could in the tight space and felt her kneel down behind him. The urge to pull her into his arms and kiss her until she fainted was instantly suppressed by the pain as she began to worry at the knots. Doggedly Chance fixed his eyes on the view from the porthole—an expanse of sea with no sign of land or other ships—and endured. Alone, he would have sworn ripely to relieve his feelings: now he knew he would rather die than show weakness in front of her.

The relief as the knots gave was replaced with lancing pain as the circulation began to flow again. He twisted round, hauled Alessa unceremoniously to her feet, and stifled his groans against her mouth.

'Stop it,' she hissed. 'He will be back in a moment.' He

watched in admiration as she struggled with the knots they had so recently tied and pulled off her gown.

The outer door opened, there was the sound of approaching footsteps and Alessa opened the door just far enough to put out one bare arm. 'The soap and towel, if you please, Count.'

'My dear, allow me to assist you.'

'I have absolutely no need for any assistance, thank you.' Chance held his breath as she withdrew her arm sharply, a linen towel and a tablet of soap clenched in her fist. She banged the door shut and Chance breathed again at the sound of an indulgent chuckle from the other side.

'I shall return in fifteen minutes.'

They waited, squashed together until the outer door closed. Alessa peered out suspiciously. 'He really has gone. Now, out you go.'

'Why?' Chance poured water into the tiny basin, plunged his hands into it with a whistle of discomfort, then dragged a handkerchief from his pocket and tore it in two. He began to wrap one half around each wrist, and offered the loose ends to Alessa to knot.

'Because I meant what I said to Zagrede. I want to use the privy.'

Chance found himself firmly pushed out and the door closed again. He had some sympathy with the Count's ambitions—this woman would make a fit consort for a pirate. He was already convinced she would make a startlingly unusual countess. And if he had anything to do with it, she was going to preside over rolling English acres and his Palladian mansion, Freshwater, not some craggy castle and miles of mountainside.

He went to stand with his ear to the door jamb, listening for returning feet, and whiled away the time remembering the sensations of caressing Alessa, of bringing her to a shuddering climax. Her first, he was certain, and it was with him. He felt a wave of tenderness that he did not recognise from any previous encounters with women. It was a need to protect and to shelter, he realised. It was love.

'You can come back now.'

He slid into the narrow space, delighting in the way she fitted against him. She smelled deliciously of some floral scent, her hair was braided into a thick plait that had his fingers itching to untie it and muss it up again, and her gown was chastely tied high on her bosom again.

But whatever his thoughts were for passing the next few minutes, Alessa's were resolutely practical. 'See, the top of the privy hinges down. If you crouch on that when I come out I can open the door quite wide and it will seem to be empty in here.'

It worked. Alessa stalked out of the privy cupboard as the Count came back into the cabin, stood for a moment with one hand on the open door to allow the Count an apparently comprehensive view of the interior and shut it behind her. 'I poured the dirty water down the privy,' she announced. 'You do not see fit to allow me a maid, and I most certainly do not want one of your crew in here.'

Now his hands were free and he knew Alessa was unharmed. Things were significantly more promising than they had seemed a few hours ago. There remained only the trifling problem of taking this ship, preventing pursuit and getting the women safely to land. The crew of the merchantman would have to take their chances until the navy caught up with them.

Chance settled back in his hiding place and began to plot, a part of his attention on the spirited conversation between Zagrede and Alessa, who was objecting to everything from his intention to lock her door to the menu he was offering for her dinner. He grinned: any man who wanted to marry that termagant was besotted—or in love.

He let himself be distracted by the thought for a moment, a pleasant interlude rudely interrupted by the cabin door crashing open to admit someone shouting in agitated Albanian.

'What is it?' Alessa demanded. 'Is it the navy?'

'No.' The Count sounded grimly amused. 'My good friend Benedict has decided to go for a stroll. I am afraid I must lock you in, my dear, and put a guard on your door. This, at least, is the one place on the *Ghost* where we know he is not.' There was the sound of the door opening, then the Count must have turned back. 'I understand that Caribbean pirates make their captives walk the plank. In the case of our mutual friend, that is beginning to sound like an interesting option.'

Chapter Twenty-One

〰〰〰〰〰

As the lock on one door clicked shut the latch of the other opened and Alessa found herself held hard against Chance's chest. It felt wonderful. 'I could stand like this for hours,' she confessed, wrapping her arms around as much of him as she could reach and burrowing harder against the solid wall of muscle. 'You make me feel so safe,' she whispered.

A weight on the top of her head must be his cheek resting against her hair. Alessa closed her eyes. He was so tender with her—surely it meant he felt more than sexual desire?

'That is flattering, and I agree this is a deeply pleasurable way to spend the afternoon, but we have a ship to capture and holding you like this makes it very hard to think.' Chance was whispering too, as aware of the guard outside as she. He took her hand and guided her towards the head of the bed, as far away from the door as possible.

'*We*,' she murmured. 'You will let me help?'

'Do I have much choice? I could emulate *my dear friend Voltar*—I really am going to have to knock his teeth in if he calls me Benedict one more time—and tie you to the bed, but I wouldn't want to live with the consequences afterwards.'

'We don't have any weapons,' Alessa lamented. 'He took my pistol.'

'Mine, too, and my sword. I should have taken a leaf out of your book and carried a knife in my boot.'

There was a moment of dawning comprehension as they stared at each other, then Alessa threw herself on her bags, which had been piled in one corner, and began to search. 'Someone has been through them already,' she hissed. Feet thudded past as men ran along the passageway, shouting at each other.

Chance joined her. 'Probably searching for bodkins and embroidery scissors as befits a young lady of breeding, not boots full of knives. Here.' He dragged out the worn pair of soft leather boots and handed them to her. There, snug in its sheath, was the thin, wicked blade that she had last used to tickle Georgi's fat ribs. How long ago that seemed now.

Alessa gripped it for a moment, then handed it to Chance. With only one weapon, he was best equipped to use it. 'Now what?'

'We wait until they have turned the ship upside down and convinced themselves I have gone over the side. Then they will have to search the *Plymouth Sound*, thinking I must have swum over and be preparing to free the crew. With any luck they will take some of the men off here to do it. Zagrede has already had to split his men—some to guard the crew, some to man the other ship and the rest to sail this and guard his hostages. If he takes more off, then we have some hopes of taking this one.'

'But how can we sail it? And he will give chase.'

'I can sail it if I have, say, five crew, but I can't do that and man the guns for a running fight. So we will just have to make certain he cannot follow.'

Where he thought he was going to find five willing crew

members, besides herself, and how he expected to sail something of this size, Alessa had no idea. She could sail a small skiff—so could Chance, she recalled from that day in the bay. He was an intelligent, observant man, so he would have watched the way the ships he had sailed on were handled, but that was a far cry handling this craft. In naval terms she supposed it would be considered a cutter.

'We are coming about,' he whispered. The sounds of activity below deck were gone, everything was happening above their heads. 'They have given up here. Damn it, I wish I could see... Ah!' He was kneeling on the bed, craning to look through the porthole. 'I can see the *Plymouth* and I think—yes, they are lowering a boat.' Alessa stood, heart in her mouth. Would enough go? 'Twelve. Good. Now we act.' He caught her to him roughly, bent his head and took her mouth with a possessive arrogance that made her blood sing. 'Stay behind me, do as I tell you.' He tipped up her chin. 'Don't get hurt, you are very precious to me.'

Chance jerked his head towards the door, then went to stand behind it, the knife reversed in his fist in the same way she had used on Big Petro.

'Help! I don't feel well!' Alessa scrabbled feebly at the door panels. 'Oh, please help me.' She stooped and picked up a soft valise, tossing it into a corner. It landed with a soft thud like a body falling. As the door opened she collapsed artistically in the centre of the cabin, arms outflung.

Chance's blow took the man completely unawares as he bent over the limp body and he folded up on top of her with a grunt. 'Ough! Get him off me!'

But Chance was already dragging the man clear and systematically removing weapons. The haul yielded a cutlass, a long knife and a pistol. Chance handed Alessa back her knife, untied the broad scarlet sash from the man's waist, swathed it around his own and stuck in cutlass and pistol. 'Very piratical,' she said admiringly, flicking at the fringed ends.

'When we get up on deck, I want to look as familiar as possible to those watching from the merchantman. We need to find you men's clothes.' Chance edged out into the empty passage and began to search each cabin systematically. Most were empty, but one had a pile of clean, but worn, clothing in it.

'Try those.' Chance leaned a shoulder against the door jamb where he could watch the passageway.

'Close the door, then.' Alessa stopped with her hands on the much-abused ribbons at her neck.

'For heaven's sake, I have seen you naked. Not an hour ago I was kissing—'

'Never mind! This is different.' Quite how, she had no idea, except that now he made her shy, in a delicious, tremulous way that she wanted to explore. And she did not want to feel like that when they were engaged in a life-and-death struggle.

Chance grinned and turned a tactful shoulder on her as she scrambled into the smallest pair of cotton duck trousers, cinched them at the waist with a leather belt and pulled a coarse linen smock-shirt over her head. The weight of her plait swinging over her shoulder reminded her that disguise would be more difficult for her than for Chance. She snatched up a bandana, used it to trap her hair on top of her head and planted a broad-brimmed straw hat on it.

'There, perfect.' As Chance turned to look at her she tossed him another bandana and watched admiringly as he wrapped it around his head. With it tied rakishly on his dark hair, the smile he gave her turned his tanned face from that of a respectable English aristocrat into pure pirate. It was devastatingly attractive.

'You look very, um…masculine, in that outfit,' she mumbled.

'And I do not normally?' He seemed mildly affronted.

'Of course you do, only like that you look dangerous as well. It is very appealing.'

'Hmm. Remind me when we are out of all this that it might be fun to play pirates.' The twinkle in his eyes cut through her shyness and made her heart sing. 'Come on, let's do it for real.'

Everywhere they went below decks was deserted. It seemed that the Count had stripped the *Ghost* to the number necessary to sail it in his desire to search for Chance. 'We need to find the others, I can't work the ship without them. Listen. The inimitable sound of your aunt in full flow.'

The key was in the lock. Chance turned it and opened the door. Lady Blackstone rose to her feet and Alessa could only admire the icy composure of her stance. Behind her Frances huddled on the bed, her arm around the shoulder of the snivelling maid.

'I demand that you take me to the Count immediately,' Lady Blackstone proclaimed. 'This is an outrage— *Blakeney?*'

'And me,' Alessa slipped under Chance's arm and into the room. 'Aunt, are you all unhurt?'

'He would not dare lay a finger on us,' her aunt said vehemently. 'But what on earth are you doing, Alexandra? Why are you both dressed like that?'

'So we can take this ship. There are not many crew on board, it is our only hope, but you all have to help.' She braced herself, waiting for her aunt's protests that this was impossible, that ladies should not do such a thing, that it would cause a scandal. This was, as she could never forget, the woman who had kidnapped her in the name of convention and saving face.

'Of course,' Lady Blackstone said briskly. 'What must we do, Blakeney? Oh, and Dr Cobb is in the next cabin.'

'The one you told I was hysterical and mentally distracted?' Alessa enquired sweetly.

'Yes, that one.' Her aunt fixed her with a steely gaze. 'This is not the time to discuss that now.' The steel seemed to shimmer into something like regret.' I am sorry, Alexandra.'

The doctor, when released, was inclined to fume and bluster until Chance cut through his protests by the simple expedient of thrusting a pistol into his hands. 'Use the butt,' he said curtly. 'I don't want any gunshots to warn the other ship. Now, this is what we are going to do.'

Ten minutes later Chance flattened himself just inside the hatch on to the deck as Frances, a vast handkerchief fluttering in her hand, brushed past him and on to the deck. 'Oh, help,' she wailed. 'Mama is sick! Do help.'

'Come in now,' he hissed, and she scuttled back, throwing him a watery smile before vanishing down the companionway.

There was a sharp order from the bridge, running feet and a man came through the hatch. Chance stuck out a foot, tripped him neatly, bringing him down, and with him the two who were hard on his heels. Three at once was more than he had hoped for.

Below there was the muffled sound of the doctor applying good medical theory to knocking all three out, and Lady Blakeney, in what she doubtless thought was a whisper. 'Stop sniveling, girl, and help me drag them into the cabin. Silk stockings, those will do to tie them up. Tight, now…'

Chance could see the merchantman lying perhaps two hundred yards off. The anchor was down and there was no sign that anyone had noticed anything amiss on the *Ghost*. He eased out of the hatch doors and worked his way round until the bridge deck was above him. There was no one in front of him: the three who were now safely stowed below must have comprised the deck crew, which was a relief. If they could beat gently up and down with three men, plus, he assumed, the steersman and the sailing master, then so could he.

Boldly he stepped away from the cover and walked to the companionway leading up to the bridge, making no attempt at concealment. Behind him he heard a gasp. Alessa.

He climbed the steps, again letting his bare feet slap noisily on the wooden rungs. The steersman was staring straight ahead, his eyes on the sails, the sailing master was leaning on the rail, about to look over, presumably in search of his missing men.

'Buon giorno,' a cheerful voice remarked. *'Parliamo italiano?'*

Alessa, damn it, this is not in the plan! What the hell is she playing at? The bastard will shoot her…

The man, startled, leaned right over, Chance slid up behind him, plucking a belaying pin from the rail as he did so, and hit him neatly over the head. The man folded up and fell with a thud at Alessa's feet. The steersman let go the wheel, then grabbed it again at the sight of the pistol held unwaveringly under his nose.

'Do you speak English?'

'A little words,' the man said warily.

'You can choose. You steer as I say, or I shoot you. Which?'

'Steer.' The man nodded vigorously. 'I steer good.'

'Alessa!'

'Yes, Chance?' She was right behind him.

'If you ever, *ever*, do anything that stupid again I will throw you overboard, is that clear?'

'That will keep me safe.'

'Don't bring logic into this—I am furious with you.'

'Yes, Chance.'

'And don't pretend to be meek, or I'll drop you over anyway.' He turned to the steersman, who had been trying to follow this interchange with furrowed brow.

'You see this lady? She is very angry because of the Count kidnapping her. She has been hurt and insulted. She wants to hurt someone.' Out of the corner of his eye he could see Alessa nodding energetically, a fierce scowl on her face. 'So I am going to give her this pistol.' He handed it over, giving Alessa's cold hand a comforting squeeze as he did so. 'She does not shoot very well, so she will aim for your fat gut, then she cannot miss.

'Hold it steady for now. Doctor!' He jumped down to the deck and strode over to where a cannon sat, long, muzzled and black. 'Let us see how good our aim is.'

'Can you fire one of these?' The doctor hefted up a shot and looked dubious. 'Is it large enough for what we need?'

'I've fired a starting cannon and I've seen a large one exercised at gunnery practise at a fleet review. This is enough for what I want, and they'll notice if I run one of the big ones out below.' Chance picked up the rammer and tried to recall exactly what he had seen that day. The risk was overloading or underloading the charge. And they only had one shot and he did not want to risk holing her below the waterline, not with her innocent crew on board. *Not much to go wrong, then.*

'Right, run her out.' They strained at the ropes and the long black snout poked though the gun port. 'Go up and tell that fat rogue at the wheel that you are the Lord High Commissioner's personal doctor and a man of much power—slowly, he hasn't much English. Tell him that if he does what he is told, you will order me to release him on shore unharmed. If he does not, then we will shoot him, and, if he survives that, hang him.'

'Right.' The doctor squared his shoulders. 'Just so long as you do not expect me to shoot an unarmed man, I will threaten all you like.'

'Give him the impression that I am a dangerous madman, but you can rein me back and save him. When I raise my hand he is to bring her in alongside the merchantman as though we are trying to get within easy hailing distance. Tell him to keep it steady.'

'I understand. And then what are you going to do?'

'Shoot out their rudder.' *There, I said it as if I believed I can do it.* He glanced up to where Alessa was holding the pistol steady on the fat steersman, said a quick prayer and turned. 'Have you managed to get the match alight, Lady Blackstone?'

Her ladyship, somewhat smudged about her aristocratic features with her efforts with a coal from the mess fire and a length of slow match, produced the results and handed it to him with as much elegance as if she were awarding a trophy after a horserace at Epsom. 'Is that as you required?'

'Certainly, thank you, ma'am. Could you now go below with the other ladies? This may get rather heated in a few minutes.'

'Shall I take Alessa?'

'I doubt you can get her to go with you. I will try. Alessa! Give the gun to the doctor and go below.'

'No!'

He shrugged, attempting to conceal his anxiety from Lady Blackstone who produced a wintry smile. 'My niece, should we live through this, is going to lead you a merry dance, my lord, believe me.'

Am I that transparent? Apparently yes, if Kate, Lady Trevick and now her aunt can see it. He raised a hand and signalled to the doctor and the *Ghost* swung its predatory nose towards the anchored merchantman. *But can Alessa see it? Does she want to?*

He narrowed his eyes as he crouched next to the gun's breech, counting off the yards, judging the angle, trying to visualise the ideal point to hit the rudder, trying not to let himself imagine that Zagrede had seen something was wrong, that at any moment the *Plymouth Sound*'s guns would run out and blast them to hell. He adjusted the angle a touch. Too much? Not enough?

There was some interest from the other ship, men were coming to the rail. Glancing up, he saw Alessa give a jaunty wave, just as there was an incomprehensible hail.

'What are they saying?' he shouted up to the wheel.

'What do you, you sons of female dogs?' the steersman yelled back.

One minute…steady, steady… Chance lowered the smouldering match to the touchhole, remembered to jump back away from the recoil and prayed.

The noise knocked him back, choking in the smoke as the gun crashed back on its ropes. He ran along the rail, straining to see.

'Yes!' It was Alessa, dancing a jig on the bridge, the steersman flinching away from the pistol waving under his nose. 'You've got it!'

There was no time to check, he had to trust it was enough. 'Get the hell out of here,' he shouted up to the wheel. 'Anywhere, just get out of range.'

The fat pirate at the wheel was as eager as anyone to get out of range of the guns that were slamming out through the gun ports.

'Lady Blackstone, go up there please and take the pistol from Alessa. And please look as though you are capable of putting a bullet in that man.'

'My dear Blakeney—' her smile sent shivers down his spine '—I am perfectly capable of doing just that.'

'Alessa, doctor, down here. Frances, bring that maid. I need you all on the sheets.'

The first shots crashed out. Chance held his breath, but surprise, unfamiliar guns, and presumably an unsteerable ship, were all acting against the gunners.

Pushing ropes into their hands, shouting orders at the steersman, Chance chivvied and bullied his makeshift crew into hauling as he demanded. The elegant vessel responded to the clumsy handling like a lady, with scarcely a flap of the sails to show her displeasure when he let the wind spill too quickly, or the women got their ropes tangled.

'Can they catch us?' Alessa panted as he stopped by her side to add his strength to the rope she and Frances were hanging on to with grim determination.

'No. Even if they are carrying a spare rudder, it isn't a quick job to fix, and we are going into the first Italian port we come to, not racing them back to Corfu. Leave this rope with me and go below, see if you can find some charts. I'd rather get somewhere friendly before night falls.'

As he spread the curling charts out on the hatch cover, he puzzled over where they were, but too much time had passed below decks for him to have seen the last landfall.

'Which way?' Alessa asked. He had taken them all off the sheets as the crippled merchantman vanished in to the haze and, with the exception of the doctor, who had relieved Lady Blackstone with the steersman, they were sitting wearily on hatch covers, fanning themselves.

'That way.' He pointed.

'How clever of you,' Frances exclaimed. 'I have no idea how you work that out.'

Alessa linked her arm through his and walked him out of earshot. 'You haven't a clue where we are, have you? It's a case of *turn right for Italy,* isn't it?'

'Yes.' He grinned down at her. Something inside him was bubbling up. Relief, happiness. Love. He wanted to tell her, sweep her off her feet and kiss her, here and now. But caution and common sense kept him silent. They were not out of the woods yet. Better to wait until they were safely back in Corfu for the declaration he wanted to make. He wanted all of her attention, he needed to know this was right for her.

'You know how to sail, don't you?' she asked, leaning back against the mast. 'You have sailed something more than a little fishing skiff before.'

Her figure was tantalisingly hinted at under the shapeless lines of the man's clothing she wore. Her throat was exposed where the neck of the shirt was unbuttoned and her slim calves and slender feet were bare. Under that rakish hat and bandana was a mass of springing black hair, just waiting to be released, and her smile as she watched him touched his skin like a caress.

'I own a yawl,' he admitted. 'Not as big as this, but big enough to transfer the skills.'

'Why didn't you say so?' She watched his face, her own puzzled. Then she gave a sudden crow of laughter. 'I know! You didn't want to say in case you couldn't sail this after all. Men are so funny…' She took to her heels as Chance gave a growl and reached for her. Laughing, he pursued her back to the others where she dodged behind Frances, who looked startled as they chased each other round her.

'Lord Blakeney, ' Lady Blackstone uttered with an awful dignity that had them both stumbling to a halt and shuffling their feet in embarrassed silence, 'is that another ship approaching?'

Chanced snatched up the telescope that lay beside the charts. 'Yes, a big one. I think our luck is in.' He swung himself up on to the rail, grabbed hold and began to climb until he could hook an arm through the rigging and get a better sighting. 'A man of war. It can only be British. Doctor! Steer for it.'

He slid down the rigging to the deck and smiled round at his unconventional crew. 'We've done it.'

And Lady Blackstone sat down with a thump on the nearest hatch cover and burst into tears.

Chapter Twenty-Two

'And that was almost the worst thing,' Alessa said feelingly. She wrapped her arms round her knees as she perched on the old bench and willed Kate to understand.

'Because she is always so cool and poised? Yes, I can imagine that was a bit of a shock,' her friend agreed. Kate, as usual, was perched perilously on the parapet of the roof of their house. The children, as reluctant to move far from Alessa as she was to be out of sight of them, played quietly in one corner with the new kitten Dora had been given by the nuns.

'And then Frances, who had been wonderful, burst into tears too, *and* the maid, so when the *Argos* came alongside there were three wailing women, Chance looking like the perfect pirate, a real pirate at the wheel, me in men's clothes and only the doctor to give any appearance of respectability to the entire crew.' She curled up and hugged her knees tighter in an effort to push the hideous embarrassment away.

'Whatever did the captain say?'

'It took ages to convince him we were not escaped lunatics, or a decoy by pirates or a floating orgy. Then he put a skeleton crew on board to sail us back to Corfu and he went after the *Plymouth Sound.*'

'Did they find it?'

'I have no idea,' Alessa said. 'I suppose we'll hear sooner or later.'

'You do sound depressed,' Kate said anxiously. 'I would have thought you'd be thrilled to be rescued and back safely with no one hurt. Wasn't it exciting? Lord Blakeney seems to have been an absolute hero.'

'Oh, yes,' Alessa agreed wearily. 'He was wonderful.'

'What's wrong, then?' Kate shot a glance at the children, but they were totally absorbed. 'The Count didn't…you know…take advantage of you?'

'No. He announced that he was going to marry me, but fortunately his pride in his own masculine charms is such that he expected to seduce me easily once he got me home. He would not stoop to rape.'

'Well, thank goodness for that.' Kate studied her in silence. Alessa dropped her cheek on to her knees and looked out over the town. 'And? You weren't raped, no one was injured, you have got home safely. Why are you drooping about like a wet hen in a thunderstorm? Is it because your aunt wants you to go back and stay with her at the Residency now you are certain the children are all right?'

'No. Not that.' The misery was welling up, hot and tight in her chest. She had thought she could keep it inside and not betray how she felt, but Kate's astringent sympathy was undermining her resolve. 'We have been back for two days and Chance hasn't been here. He hasn't written. *Nothing.*'

'Um, is there any reason—any *urgent* reason—why he should be coming to speak with you?' Kate asked. 'Other than common courtesy, of course.'

'No! Yes. Possibly. Kate, I don't know. I do not understand

what happened. I do not understand how I feel or what it meant to him. I don't know what happens next.'

'Do you want to talk about it?'

'I *think* so, only it is so embarrassing…'

'Lord love you child, nothing you can say is going to shock *me*.' She raised her voice. 'Dora, Demetri! Alessa and I are going down to my apartment. You'd better go and play in the courtyard.'

'Right, now tell me all about it,' she demanded when they were sitting on the couch in front of the fireplace, a glass of wine in their hands.

Alessa took a deep gulp for courage. 'I told you the Count tied me up in a cabin and Chance picked the lock and hid in the privy and then we were able to escape?'

'Yes.'

'Well, we made love. In between him breaking in and hiding in the privy. Only we didn't, you know—I mean, I think I'm still a virgin.'

'Let me get this right.' Kate frowned in concentration. 'You had your hands tied to the bed head and he had his hands tied behind his back and you were only able to untie him after the Count freed you so you could go to the privy?'

'Yes.'

'So his lordship had no clothes on?'

'No! He was fully dressed.'

'Then he has my heartfelt admiration. I think you had better tell me exactly what he *did* do.'

Blushing and stammering, Alessa stumbled through the barest outline. 'I didn't know that people did that sort of thing. I mean, is that normal?'

'Very,' Kate assured her. 'Perfectly normal. You've got a good man there.'

'But I haven't got him, that's the problem,' Alessa blurted

out. 'I love him and I thought perhaps if he had made love to me when he couldn't enjoy it himself it meant he cared for me and wanted to please me.' *To pleasure my lady.* 'But why, then hasn't he come and said anything? He hasn't even offered me a *carte blanche*. Not that I'd accept one,' she added hastily.

'That's a poser, I agree.' Kate chewed her lip thoughtfully. 'I don't know enough about these smart ladies and gentlemen and what's the done thing. But do you think he thinks he needs to have your aunt's blessing? Or at least ask you formally up at the Residency, to make it all respectable, sort of thing? And you did say your aunt has taken to her bed and isn't intending to get up until tomorrow.'

'Oh, yes, that must be it. Chance is very conventional in some ways, you know. Oh, thank you Kate, that is *such* a relief.' Alessa felt an almost physical weight lifting off her heart. He couldn't have made love to her so selflessly, spoken to her so tenderly, if he didn't feel something for her. Tomorrow, when she went to the Residency, then he would say something.

Chance spent the day, as he had the previous one, closeted with Sir Thomas, Mr Harrison and the senior naval officers in port. They traced routes on charts, measured distances and interrogated him for every detail he could recall until his brain ached.

'Yes, definitely modern rifles,' he confirmed when the senior gunnery officer looked up from his lists and queried what Chance could recall of hand weapons. 'All mixed up with flintlocks and some incredible long-muzzled objects that looked antique to me.'

'Right.' Admiral Fortescue ran an eye over his notes. 'And this pirate who was at the wheel when *Argos* picked you up— where is he now?'

'I have no idea,' Chance said firmly. 'I would have had one hell of a job managing without him, and although he was only helping us to save his fat hide, I still owed him a debt, so I let him slip away.'

'Very well.' The admiral looked down his beak of a nose disapprovingly. 'Let us go over the description of the hidden harbour one more time.'

Finally, at about seven o'clock, the meeting broke up. Sir Thomas ushered out the naval men and Chance found himself slumped at the long baize-covered table opposite Mr Harrison.

It occurred to him that the man was looking less than his normal composed and efficient self. He would be tired, of course, they had spent two intensive days in talk and analysis; but even so, he was looking positively haggard. Chance felt a spurt of fellow feeling—he could sympathise with any man in that state, just at the moment.

He did not expect the suggestion to meet with agreement, but he asked casually, 'What do you say we take a bottle of claret down to the billiard room and knock a few balls about?'

The other man looked down blankly at the piles of paper littering the table, raked one hand through his usually neatly ordered hair, and said, 'I'm damned if that doesn't sound a good plan. Just let me get these locked away safely.'

'I'll ring for the wine; see you down there.' Chance strolled down to the billiard room and began to chalk a cue, brooding pleasurably on the prospect of seeing Alessa in the morning.

She had had two days to recover and to be reunited with the children; it would have been insensitive to intrude on that, and unwise considering the touchy state of Lady Blackstone's nerves over the involvement of the young women in that adventure. She had the comfort of knowing that Frances had been with her every moment, but her niece had vanished, only to reappear in his company and in male clothes.

And the doctor knew about it, and the captain of the *Argos* had seen Alessa in male attire. Chance felt confident that neither would gossip, but he could understand her ladyship's anxieties. Everything would go much more smoothly once he explained his intention of a secret betrothal, which could then be made public on their return to England. There could be no suspicion then that he had found it necessary to propose as a result of anything that had happened abroad and Alessa's character could be established in society first.

He was pleasurably recalling those heated moments in the cabin when Harrison arrived, along with the footman and the wine. 'Fine, thank you, leave it.' The secretary seized the bottle and poured himself a large draught, which he swallowed at a gulp before slopping some into Chance's glass.

Chance felt his eyebrows rise. Harrison was a moderate drinker at all times, silent to the point of being self-effacing, and always composed. Now he looked like a man who had experienced a nasty shock.

Chance began to pot balls at random. 'We've had a tough couple of days. I feel my brain's been through a ringer,' he tossed back over his shoulder.

'Sir Thomas is like that, thorough. I'm used to it.' The secretary took another gulp of wine and began to chalk his cue.

'Play for love, or do you want some money on it?' Chance enquired, filling both glasses and pushing one into Harrison's hand. The secretary sank it without apparently noticing he had done so.

'What the hell, money if you like. What's the point of saving my salary if I can't use it how I want?' He sent a red violently across the table to strike the cushion.

'Want to talk about it?' Chance offered, refilling the glasses. 'I'm not given to gossip.'

'Women!' Harrison said wildly. 'What's the point?' He refilled his glass and stared owlishly at Chance. 'All right for you, you're an Earl, I'm just a damned secretary.'

'Is this about Miss Trevick?' Best to cut to the chase. Chance began to wonder if he'd overdone the wine. He had intended to loosen the man up a little; at this rate he was going to be carrying him to bed.

'How do you know?'

'I've got eyes in my head,' Chance retorted. 'What's the matter, have you fallen out?'

'The Lord High Commissioner, my worthy employer, his Majesty's representative in the Eastern Mediterranean, He Who Must Be Obeyed—Sir Thomas is arranging a marriage for her. To a Viscount, if you please.'

'Then she must turn it down.'

'Won't.' Harrison shook his head sadly. 'Good girl, Maria, dutiful. Her mama wants her to make a good match.'

'You are a good match.'

'I'm not. The family is all right, but I'm just a secretary.'

'Well, you will be a great administrator yourself someday. How did Sir Thomas start? The same way as you, I'll be bound.' Chance said bracingly. 'Have you told her you love her?' Harrison nodded morosely. 'Does she love you?' Another nod. 'Right. You go and tell Sir Thomas and she can tell her mother. Neither of them can want her to be unhappy.'

'They'll browbeat her, tell her about duty and family and— oh, hell, I'll just go and shoot myself.'

Chance whisked the bottle out of sight, now seriously worried. 'Don't do that. It makes a mess, it's unfair on the servants and Maria will break her heart and probably go into a decline.'

'Hadn't thought of that.'

'Can't you compromise her?' Chance could hardly believe he was saying this. It must be the effect of being in love.

'Shouldn't think so. No idea how to go about it. I never was much of a rake, and she's too well brought up to go and wander in the garden in the moonlight. What would you do? You seem to understand this romance business.'

Chance potted two more balls to give himself time to think. They dined late at the Residency to make the most of the cool of the evening. 'Do the young ladies still have a rest before dinner as they did at the villa?'

'Yes.' Harrison glanced at the lock. 'I expect Lady Trevick will be waking them up shortly.'

'Excellent. We haven't a moment to lose. Here, drink this.' Chance poured the remainder of the wine into Harrison's glass and pressed it into his hand. 'Now, we'll just undo your neckcloth, and unbutton your waistcoat and pull out your shirt a bit…' He stepped back and eyed the result. The secretary blinked back at him. 'Perfect. Come along, no time to lose. Do you know which is Miss Trevick's bed-chamber? Show me.'

Chance bundled his befuddled companion up the stairs, along the passages to a door where the secretary stopped. 'This one. But what have you done that to my clothes for?'

Chance opened the door. 'In you go, and give the girl a damn good kissing.' He shoved the bemused secretary between the shoulder blades and propelled him into the room.

'What? Henry, darling—'

Chance shut the door and leaned against it. So far, so good. He thought Alessa would approve.

He did not have long to wait. Lady Trevick swept round the corner to rouse her daughters. Chance did his best to look shifty and stood in front of the door. 'Good evening, ma'am.'

He kicked the door panel with a backward flick of his heel and coughed loudly.

'Lord Blakeney, what exactly are you doing here?'

'Er, got lost, ma'am. Looking for Har…I mean to say…'

'Have you been drinking, Lord Blakeney?' Without waiting for an answer, Lady Trevick reached for the door handle and turned it. There was a cry of alarm as the door opened.

'Mama!'

'Mr Harrison!'

'Now isn't that romantic?' Chance observed, following the outraged mother into the room. 'But damned indiscreet of you, old chap.'

'Madam, I love your daughter. I beg the honour of her hand in marriage.'

Was he sufficient witness to ensure success? Chance glanced down the corridor and saw Lady Blackstone emerge from her room. 'Ma'am, I believe Lady Trevick would welcome your support,' he said earnestly, guiding her towards Maria's bedchamber. 'All very unfortunate, but true love, you know how it is.'

He hung around, keeping out of sight until he heard Lady Trevick emerging with Lady Blackstone. 'I shall have to agree to it. She seems to love him very much, and unfortunately Lord Blakeney saw it all.' She looked back into the room. 'Mr Harrison, I think you had better have a word with Sir Thomas. At once.'

Chance leaned back against the wall and closed his eyes with a smile of pure mischief. Harrison would be happy, poor chap, once he had been mauled by Sir Thomas and lectured by his future mother-in-law. And Alessa would be impressed by Chance's romantic and unconventional behaviour.

He strolled off, whistling, to change for dinner. He was

looking forward to tomorrow, to telling Alessa how he felt about her, to watching her face as he told her he loved her. To holding her, warm and vibrant in his arms.

The next morning the children were wide eyed with delight at being collected in the Residency chaise, luggage piled behind and the kitten in a basket on Dora's knee. Alessa had a momentary qualm about Lady Trevick's attitude to cats, but mostly her mind was dizzy with thinking about Chance and how it would be when she saw him again.

She had hardly slept the night before, and when she had her dreams were full of him, romantic in white shirt and pirate sash, or naked, holding her in the water, or making love to her so tenderly, despite the cruel lashings on his wrists or—

'Alessa! We're here!'

Disorientated, she stared around her. The front entrance, of course. They were guests.

She settled the children in their rooms and found they had been allocated one of the local girls to look after them. She understood all about cats, and the appetite of small boys, and carried them off to the kitchen courtyard where Dora could play safely with the yet-unnamed kitten and Demetri could try his charms on his friend the cook.

Alessa changed into one of her fashionable new morning gowns, feeling trussed up round the ribcage and scandalously unclad everywhere else in the floating fabric. She had Peters to look after her again. Their eyes met in the dressing-table mirror and Alessa asked anxiously, 'Do I look all right?'

'You look beautiful,' the maid assured her, tweaking little curls out at Alessa's hairline. 'He will admire you.'

'Who?' Peters merely looked coy. 'Peters, I wish to be suitably dressed to please my aunt.'

'Yes, Miss Meredith. But that doesn't stop a gentleman admiring you, does it?'

For goodness' sake! Does everyone know? Am I that obvious?

Alessa directed what she hoped was a suitably repressive look at the maid and went downstairs to the sitting room used by the young ladies. Frances was there in animated conversation with Maria and Helena and they jumped to their feet and ran over to hug and to kiss her. She had never had female friends of her own age before; their uninhibited pleasure at seeing her touched and startled her.

'We are so glad to see you,' Helena exclaimed. 'Frances has been telling us all about how brave you were.'

'She was wonderful too.'

'And Maria has such good news. Go on, tell Alexandra.'

'I am betrothed to Mr Harrison.' Maria went pink and tears welled up in her eyes. 'It is like a dream and *entirely* due to Lord Blakeney. But you must not tell anyone it was all his idea, because we do not want to cause trouble for him.'

'But what did he do?'

'Incited Henry to compromise me in my bedchamber yesterday evening. Darling Henry was too scrupulous to declare his feelings when Mama and Sir Thomas wished me to marry someone else, but Lord Blakeney was so clever. He made Henry tiddly, then he pushed him into my chamber and waited outside looking suspicious and saying he was looking for Henry when Mama came along. So she burst in—and Henry was *kissing* me.'

'Good heavens,' said Alessa blankly. 'And I thought Lord Blakeney was so conventional.'

'He wasn't on the pirate ship, was he?' Frances pointed out. 'Oh, Maria, Helena, I cannot begin to tell you how *swooningly* handsome he was in those loose trousers and the white shirt with a great scarlet sash with a cutlass stuck through it. And we used to think the Count dashing!'

'Excuse me, ladies. Lady Blackstone wishes Miss Meredith's presence in the morning room.'

'Thank you, Wilkins.' Would Chance be there? Alessa remembered to pick up her skirts properly and followed the butler.

Yes, he was there, the very antithesis of that dashing pirate in rigidly correct pantaloons, Hessian boots and dark blue swallowtail coat. Alessa ventured a small, private smile and was met by an expression of blank politeness. *He has to be careful in front of Aunt Honoria,* she thought uneasily, trying to convince herself that there was nothing to worry about. All the confidence that Kate had instilled yesterday seemed to be seeping away through the soles of her kid slippers.

'Please sit down, Alexandra.'

'Yes, Aunt Honoria. I do hope you are somewhat recovered this morning.'

'Thank you, Alexandra, yes. I have asked Lord Blakeney to join us so we can make arrangements.'

'For the journey to Venice?'

'Of course not—to deal with the fact you are comprehensively compromised, of course.'

'But I'm not!'

'Yes, you are,' Chance said. 'Completely.'

'I am a virgin,' Alessa protested indignantly.

'So I should hope!' Lady Blackstone plied her fan energetically. 'What has that got to do with anything, pray?'

'I don't *have* to do anything, because I am not compromised.' *That can't be it, can it? Chance isn't standing there looking like a thundercloud because he thinks he* has *to marry me?*

'You were alone with the Count of Kurateni. You were alone with me. You were seen on deck in male attire by a post captain of the British navy,' Chance said, sounding every bit as censorious as her aunt.

'Then if anyone compromised me, it was the Count. He

tied me to his bed—' Lady Blackstone moaned audibly '—he can marry me. He wants to, after all.' *Which is more than you obviously do.*

'You are not marrying Zagrede,' Chance glared at her. 'You are marrying me.'

It was so far from the tender declaration she had been dreaming about that Alessa's jaw dropped. 'No, I am not!' she snapped when she recovered herself.

'You will get married quietly here, as soon as possible,' her aunt stated.

'We most certainly will not,' Chance riposted.

'What?' Both women stared at him.

'Why not, may I ask?' Lady Blackstone demanded.

'Yes, why not?' Alessa echoed. Not that she wanted to marry the wretched man who had only proposed because he had *compromised* her.

'We will appear to meet in England once Alessa's status has been established and there is no hint of scandal about her. A hugger-mugger marriage out here would give rise to talk.'

'That is all you care about, isn't it? Propriety, convention, what people will think.' Alessa sprang to her feet and confronted them both. 'I thought you cared about me, my lord. I thought that under that conventional, aristocratic, superior skin there was a romantic heart. Well, I was wrong, and I wouldn't marry you if you begged me and I don't care if you feel your precious honour has been compromised by not marrying me.

'I am sorry, Aunt Honoria. I will come back with you and do my best to behave as you would wish until I can establish myself independently. But marry that man I will not!'

Chapter Twenty-Three

'Hell and damnation.' Chance swore without apology. 'Excuse me, ma'am.' He threw the door open in time to see the skirts of Alessa's gown flipping round the corner and gave chase.

He caught her on the terrace, which was mercifully deserted. 'Alessa!'

'Go away.'

'Alessa, I want to marry you.'

'Of course you do,' she said cordially. 'Not to do so would be such bad form, would it not? Whatever would people say?'

'They would say *what a lucky escape from such a sharp-tongued termagant,*' Chance retorted. 'What do you mean, I don't have a romantic heart? Let me tell you what I did about Harrison and Maria—'

'Oh, I know about that. Well done, I am sure they will be very happy. But that was all right, was it not? He is just a secretary, he isn't a stuffed shirt of an Earl.'

'Alessa, I have every intention of marrying you when we get back to England.'

'Oh, have you? I suppose you think so now, but what if

there is a scandal after all? They'll say I'm just a Greek girl that you had a fling with over here. Englishmen on the Grand Tour are notorious for it. They won't like you bringing your mistress home, and then deciding to marry her.'

It was so close to his own anxieties about marrying her on the island that Chance felt himself flushing. She pounced on it as a sign of guilt.

'Some emotion at last! I walked into the room and you pokered up like a clergyman confronted with a loose woman. I realise that you don't want to marry me, but you might at least have *tried* to look enthusiastic.'

'I was deeply resentful of being summoned by your aunt and being dragooned into making a proposal not of my own choosing,' he fired back before he realised just how damningly that could be interpreted.

'Honesty, finally,' she observed. They stood looking at each other. Chance felt as though he was seeing her for the first time. A tall woman, golden skinned, imperious, her head flung back, weighted by the mass of black hair at her nape. She stared at him out of hostile green eyes, those winged black brows giving her an expression that was almost fierce. She was strong, and independent and unshakeable and he was not going to break her will.

'You will marry me!' he thundered, frustrated beyond reason. She stared back out of those magical eyes and he realised that she was trembling, just a little, and the fullness of her lower lips was caught hard by her teeth and the glitter in her eyes was not anger, but unshed tears. He was bullying her and yet she was standing up to him. He would never break her will—and he knew now he did not want to.

'Alessa.' It was a groan more than a word, and he took her face between gentle palms and kissed her, quite chastely on the lips. There had been quite enough drama.

* * *

He is going to kiss me, at last, he is going to show me what he feels. Alessa put up her hands to Chance's chest, ready to brace herself against the onslaught of those wonderful kisses, the proof of his passion, his love, his need for her. She wanted to sink into them, yield to them, surrender to him.

Then he kissed her like a brother and stepped back. Alessa took a deep breath and pushed down the waves of heat that had risen through her body at the mere anticipation of his embrace.

'I am overwhelmed by your ardour my lord,' she said frigidly. 'I do not want to discuss this matter ever again—I do hope I have finally made myself plain?'

'Perfectly, madam.' The pulse at his throat was throbbing, she could see it, despite the immaculate neckcloth, but he was controlling his anger and, presumably, the feelings of chagrin at being rejected. He would be pleased enough, when he had time to reflect upon it.

Alessa dropped a precise curtsy and swept off the terrace. She was so blinded by emotion that she did not realise where she was until the three girls were clustered round her. 'Well?' Maria demanded. 'When is it to be? Do you think the Earl would mind if we had a double wedding? That would be so romantic.'

'Frances and I could be bridesmaids,' Helena chimed in. 'What did he say when he asked you? Did he go down on one knee?'

'I am not marrying Lord Blakeney. He only asked me out of propriety—my aunt is insisting upon it. He is so afraid of appearing unconventional that he won't even agree to us marrying here. My lord expects me to trail meekly back to England and prove myself acceptable and then he will deign to do the right thing,' she said bitterly.

'The beast,' Frances said, tears of sympathy welling in her big green eyes. 'But you will come back to England with us?'

Alessa nodded. 'Then we will find you a nice Englishman. A romantic, dashing, unconventional one, you wait and see.'

The next week passed in a sort of delirium. Alessa supposed she appeared normal. The children seemed to notice nothing amiss, she was able to take part in meals and excursions and stilted conversations with her aunt about travel plans and at the same time everyone looked as though she were seeing them through glass—and their voices echoed a long way off.

Chance kept well clear of her except for the most formal of encounters and the girls conspired to protect her by swooping down with a poem to discuss, or a piece of gossip to exchange, whenever it seemed likely he would stray near to her. Maria kept tactfully silent about her own wedding plans if Alessa was within earshot.

The news came that the *Plymouth Sound* had been retaken with no one seriously injured, but with all the pirates vanished, taken off by a black-sailed ship that had swooped down and vanished into the night before the *Argos* located them. Alessa, still cherishing a reluctant liking for the Count, felt guilty but glad. Despite the fact that the danger remained, the Admiral assured Sir Thomas that it would be safe for the ladies to set sail again next week when a small convoy, accompanied by a frigate, would make the voyage to Venice and the Adriatic ports.

Alessa told herself that she was happy, although she wished Chance was not sailing with them. Being constantly in his company was an agony she had expected time to dull, but which seemed to renew itself afresh every morning. He seemed quite impervious to either heartache or regret.

Her appetite had dwindled to nothing, she noticed at breakfast the day after the news came about the *Plymouth Sound*.

That would never do; she would make herself ill and would not be able to look after the children. Alessa gave herself a mental shake and made herself eat another sweet roll with her coffee.

Helena was full of a new plan. 'It is such a pity there isn't time to arrange a party before everyone leaves for Venice,' she announced. 'So I think we should have a picnic, with all the trimmings.'

'That sounds very pleasant,' her mother approved. 'But we should not go too far, just an easy drive. Lady Blackstone will not wish to undertake anything to strenuous just before they depart, I am sure.'

'The beach at Anemomylos is nice,' Maria suggested. 'It is only about two miles south of the town,' she explained. 'And the views are very pretty.'

Alessa had to agree with Maria when she saw the place. It was a delightful spot, a long sandy beach with low cliffs behind and a sweeping view over the narrow strait to the mountains beyond. She exerted herself to be bright and cheerful, both out of courtesy to her hostess and because the children had been allowed to come, along with their nursemaid.

'Isn't his lordship here?' Demetri demanded as the small convoy of carriages came to a halt and servants began to carry rugs, hampers and cloths down to the beach.

'Apparently not,' Alessa said lightly. 'I expect he has correspondence to catch up with. I think Mr Harrison might play catch with you if you ask nicely.' The children scampered off and Alessa took her aunt's arm as they walked down to the beach. She had made a point of not looking to see whether Chance was with them, but she had felt his absence like a missing tooth.

The ladies were all settled at last, under the shade of an umbrella pine. 'How enchanting the view is,' Lady Trevick exclaimed. 'I really think the cliffs here would make a perfect location for a summer villa. I must suggest it to Sir Thomas. Paleokastritsa is a delightful resort, but an official summer residence near the town would be useful for entertaining.'

'Just think…' Frances sighed '…over there the Count is still at large, plotting his dastardly deeds.'

'*Dastardly deeds* indeed,' her mother said disapprovingly. 'Have you been reading novels, my girl?'

'Only a few, Mama,' Frances admitted. 'They are very educational—all about foreign parts.'

'You are travelling in foreign parts,' her mother retorted repressively. 'You do not need to read frivolous nonsense about them.'

'No, Mama. Oh, look, isn't that a pretty little sailing boat! It looks just like the one the Count of Kurateni had.'

They all shaded their eyes to stare at the skiff, flirting over the waves northward. There was one man at the tiller, a second in the body of the boat. As they watched, the steersman brought the boat round, the sail flapped and it lost way. The other sailor began to haul in a rowing boat that was being towed astern.

'Fishing,' Mr Harrison observed, coming to drop down besides Maria. 'Phew, that lad has quite winded me! They'll be letting a net out between the two boats and hauling it round. It seems to be a good way of two men managing a large net.'

Sure enough, one man was getting into the rowing boat and beginning to row towards the shore. 'I've watched them before,' Maria said. 'It takes *ages*. Let's walk along the beach and see if we can find any shells. I want to make a shellwork frame for a mirror.'

She reached out a hand to Alessa and pulled her to her feet. 'I'll bring this basket, shall I?' Alessa knew she had to enter into things and not to be seen brooding, if only for her own pride, but it was hard to feign an interest in shellwork just now.

The other girls joined them and they began to stroll along the waterline, stooping every now and again to pick up a choice specimen. The man in the rowing boat was keeping parallel with them, close inshore. Alessa thought vaguely that it must be a big net, she did not recall seeing other boats having to make such a wide sweep.

'Is this too big?' She held up a large shell for Helena's inspection, just as the rower dug in his starboard oar hard and the boat shot up to the beach. He leapt out as the girls stood gaping at him—a fat man who Alessa recognised in the same instant as Frances squealed, 'It's the pirate! The one who steered us when we escaped!'

He was in front of them before they could react, a small circular hand net in his grip. He swung it, entangling Alessa, picked her up, threw her into the rowing boat and was pulling hard for the skiff before the other girls could scream.

Winded, outraged and completely tied up in the net, Alessa was too indignant to be frightened. 'Let me go at once! You are going to be very severely punished for this—Sir Thomas will not let you get away a second time.'

His only answer was a grunt. In a few more hard stokes they were alongside the skiff, its sail filling again. The pirate shipped the oars, let the rowing boat scrape up the side of the bigger boat, picked Alessa up bodily and dumped her on board. Then he backwatered out of the way and the skiff skimmed off, leaving him behind.

Alessa struggled frantically with the net, which had pulled her hat over her eyes, finally freed herself and lay panting on the deck, staring at the tall figure at the tiller. Tight black trousers over long, muscular legs, a shirt with flamboyantly wide sleeves, a wide red sash cinching narrow hips and hair in a bandana topped off by a wide straw hat.

She squinted against the sun-dazzle, trying to make out the face in the shadow cast by the deep brim, but failed. Surely it couldn't be the Count? But who else would have the sheer gall, the extravagant showmanship, to snatch her off the beach in the teeth of the full Residency household? 'Take me back this instant,' she demanded, trying to keep her voice steady. 'You cannot hope to get away with this.'

The only answer she got was a quizzical tilt of the head. 'Lord Blakeney will rescue me,' she declared, suddenly utterly convinced it was true. 'He rescued me before and he will do it again. He is an English gentleman and a match for any cowardly pirate.'

That provoked a sudden grin and a flash of white teeth. 'Don't you dare laugh at me, you wretch!' She got enough breath back to scramble to her feet and marched up the short deck towards the tiller. 'Oh, if only there was a real man here!'

'I am devastated,' said her captor, pushing back the hat to the back of his head. 'One moment you are complimentary about me, the next—'

'*Chance!*' Alessa stared at the tall figure. Had she got heat-stroke? Did a broken heart make you hallucinate? 'Chance— what are you doing?'

'Attempting to prove to you that I do not give a fig for convention or propriety—provided I can have you.'

'But you don't want me.'

'Yes, I do. Don't you remember? Because if you do not, then my technique is a lot worse than I had imagined.'

'Oh, I know you want me *that* way. I expect you want lots of women that way, and I haven't got any basis for comparison, but I am sure your technique, as you call it, is amazing,'

Alessa said crossly, still too shaken by the kidnap to take what he was saying seriously.

'Alessa, I love you.'

'No, you don't, you never said so.'

'You never said you love *me*, but I rather suspect you might not positively dislike me.' He glanced up at the set of the sails and adjusted the tiller to take them further out into the bay.

'Chance, I—'

'No, don't try to tell me anything now. Wait until we land. There is something I want to say to you, and I need to give it my full attention.'

Alessa sank down on to the deck. 'They will be sending a rider to the fort. They will have a navy cutter out after us. Chance, you are in so much trouble—how are we ever going to explain this?'

'No need to explain anything. They will all know by now.'

'*What?* How?'

'I told Harrison. He and Maria are particularly grateful to me at the moment and were more than willing to reciprocate in a romantic gesture.'

I don't believe this…Chance is not *romantic.* 'Where are we going?'

'Vidos Island.' Chance nodded northwards. 'We'll be there soon.'

'But it is deserted.'

'There is a small population of goats, I believe, and a ramshackle cottage where I intend to compromise you completely and comprehensively.'

He sounded as calm as though he was discussing taking a stroll along the seafront, but there was something in the timbre of his voice that shook Alessa out of her confusion and her irritation and into belief. Slowly, not taking her eyes off him, she got to her feet and went to stand at the tiller, laying her hand over his as though to help him steer.

'Very well, let us go to the island.'

Chance reached round and moved her until she was standing in front of him, her back against him, his left arm encircling her waist while he continued to steer with the right.

'That's nice,' he murmured, resting the point of his chin on top of her head. Wordlessly Alessa snuggled back against him, feeling the long body behind her sheltering her, and abandoned herself to whatever happened.

Chapter Twenty-Four

The island was, indeed, populated by goats. They came trotting to investigate when they saw the skiff draw into the shallows and watched with their strange yellow eyes wide as Chance splashed ashore with Alessa in his arms.

'Welcome to our first home together.' He set her on her feet on the beach.

'Chance, I—'

'Wait until we get to the cottage. I am damned if I am going to make a declaration of passionate love watched closely by a herd of goats.' He took her hand and began to climb the narrow path that led around the low cliff. Alessa scrambled after him, with a fleeting sigh of regret for the pretty new gown she had put on that morning. It seemed she was about to be proposed to whilst clad in a garment that was soaked around the hem, had split under one arm while she was struggling out of the net and was regrettably fishy from the bottom of the rowing boat.

Any proper young lady would have the vapours—Alessa was only glad that she was obviously not proper. *Chance will take it off in a minute anyway*, she thought with a ripple of excitement.

Chance half-opened, half-lifted a rickety gate and drew her through into the overgrown remains of a paved terrace in front of a stone cottage. Whoever had once lived here—fisherman, goat farmer or hermit—had an eye for a view, she thought, gazing out through a tangle of gorse and long grass to the sea.

'Out!' Chance shied a pebble at the goats who took to their heels, and shut the gate.

'Now, *Kyria* Alessa, I have you alone at last.' Chance took her hands in his and stood looking down at her. Her heart was doing the oddest things. Alessa felt suddenly shy; it was an effort to hold his gaze.

'What was it you wanted to say?'

'That I love you. That I was not used to young women of independence and experience and I misjudged how I should behave.' He smiled ruefully. 'I tried to dictate what you should do, and to decide, all by myself, what was best for us, when I did not understand you.' He lifted her hands to his lips and kissed her fingertips. 'Can you forgive me?'

'Of course.' She had not tried to understand him, she realised, now she made the effort. 'But can you change? It is how you have been brought up to deal with your womenfolk, is it not? And can I change enough not to scandalise those around us?'

'We will learn together. Perhaps in society we will be more conventional than we will when we are alone. My mama and my sisters believe that I am a paragon. They would not believe it if you told them that I have had mistresses, that I have been known to gamble, that sometimes I wake up in the morning with a thick head from over-indulgence. And I believed that it was very important to keep any worry, any decision of any importance, from them.' He pressed another kiss on to her fingertips, his eyes dark. 'I think now that I was smug, and dictatorial and complaisant.'

'Probably,' Alessa agreed solemnly, sheer joy fizzing inside her. 'But you can change, I will help. But I want to know about these mistresses.'

'No, you do not! And I do not have one now, or ever again, I swear.' He freed one hand and led her by the other to where a slab of stone made a bench by the door of the hut. 'I wanted you as soon as I saw you, although why I was so aroused by an icy green-eyed witch, I have no idea.'

'Witch?'

'All I could think of was that you had bewitched me.'

'And I thought the effect you had on me was witchcraft too.' They fell silent, eyes locked, then Alessa put up a hand and touched his cheek. 'Go on.'

'I realised I was falling in love with you when I went to apologise for what happened at the Liston and you were gone. I could hardly believe it. I knew exactly what I wanted: a well-bred, strictly brought up young lady who I would meet during the Season, who would be vetted by my mama and who I would marry, in the fullness of time, in a fashionable London church.'

'And you thought you were falling in love with a widow, no longer in the first blush of youth, with two children and a mysterious past.' Alessa smiled, 'Poor Chance. I realised I loved you when I got to the cottage at Liapades and I thought I would never see you again. And then, like a miracle, there you were in the sea.'

Chance began to toy with the few pins that remained in her hair until it fell about her shoulders like heavy silk. 'I sailed back to the villa and I decided the thing to do was to ensure you arrived back in England under your aunt's chaperonage. I was concerned that if I married you out here, when I got you back people would dismiss you as a Greek girl I had picked up. I wanted to protect you, marry you in circumstances that would cast no shadow of doubt over you.

'I should have talked it through with you, not decided what was right by myself.'

'So it was for convention?' she asked dubiously.

'Yes. It is a fact—we have to make sacrifices to it, make compromises if we are to live in society. I will not have you looked down on, or allow the old cats to whisper behind your back.'

'But they will now,' Alessa pointed out.

'No, I have a plan. I will take the ship after yours to Venice. I will be invited to the British Residence, meet you there and I will conduct a whirlwind courtship in the full view of the international diplomatic community and every fashionable traveller in the city. We will be married in Venice with as much fuss as possible: far from being a quiet and discreet wedding in a fashionable London church, this will be the talk of gossip columns for weeks.'

'*Oh.*' Alessa had never considered her own wedding, not even in her wildest fantasies about Chance loving her had she tried to imagine it. To marry in Venice was suddenly the most romantic thing she could think of. 'Can we go to the wedding in gondolas?'

'But of course, a fleet of them, including several for the orchestra.' He bent and kissed her very softly. 'That is at least a month away. Alessa, if you want to wait, then I will understand and I will take you back to the Residency now. Or we can stay here tonight.'

Chance watched her face, wondering at the softness in those wide green eyes as she looked at him, wondering why this proud, suspicious, passionate woman had decided to trust him and love him.

'Yes, let us stay here.' Her lashes swept down and he realised just how shy she was of him; yet that trust had not wavered.

'Before you have seen the interior?' he asked, trying to

lighten the atmosphere. It was suddenly hard to breathe, as though his chest was being squeezed.

'Yes, even if the goats have been sleeping in there,' she said, her smile flickering.

But Harrison had been as good as his word, and the Residency staff who had been despatched the day before had swept and garnished the simple interior. There was a clean hearth laid for a fire with more logs beside it. A table and two chairs had plates and glasses, and hampers stood shut against any attack by the local wildlife.

And against the far wall there was a wide wooden bed, heaped with white linen and pillows.

'Will it do, my lady?'

'It will do very well my lord.' She was watching him uncertainly. 'I am feeling very shy, which is ridiculous when you think what has already passed between us.'

'I could always tie you up again, if that would help,' he offered, keeping his face straight.

'Don't you dare!' Alessa grabbed the nearest pillow and held it up defensively. Laughing, Chance seized another and took a playful swipe, to be rewarded by a solid hit in the midriff. He collapsed on to the bed, carrying Alessa with him. The sturdy wooden frame creaked and the rope lacing under the mattress groaned, but he hung on, rolling her on to her back until she lay helpless beneath him, laughing up into his face.

He watched, fascinated by her, as the laughter slowly ebbed away to be replaced by her sensual awareness of him, of his weight as he lay on her, of the feel of his hands which were tangling in her hair.

'Chance.'

'Yes?'

'Love me.'

'Oh, yes.' And he took her mouth like a drowning man takes air.

Alessa had thought she knew Chance's kisses now, but this was different. One part of her mind, the part that could still think coherently, tried to analyse it as his mouth angled over hers. As she opened to him, welcoming the surge of his tongue, she realised what it was: he was claiming her. This was not ownership, but it was the kiss of a man who belonged with the woman he was kissing. Alessa took him into the heat of her mouth and returned the kiss with a claiming of her own.

Mine, she thought as she nipped gently at the curve of his bottom lip and tasted the savour of him. 'Mine,' she tried to say against his mouth as he lifted his lips and began to nuzzle into her hair, down her throat.

'How does this undo?'

The gown and its tiny buttons was distracting him. Impatient, Alessa seized the neckline in both hands and tore. 'Like this.'

His laugh was warm against the curve of her breast as he took over the destruction of the fine muslin and the light linen beneath it. 'I don't know what you are going to wear to get back to Corfu,' he said, between tiny hot licks at the pale skin they had exposed.

'We will have to stay here.' She was impatient now to feel his skin against hers, pulling at the wide-sleeved shirt, tugging it out of the swathed sash.

'I will wrap you in this, like Cleopatra in her carpet,' he said huskily as he freed the knot and unwound the broad length of red silk.

His words were muffled as she dragged the shirt over his head and spread her palms on the hard muscle of his chest. He went very still, hanging over her on his elbows, the weight of his hips heavy and hard against the softness that was cradling them. Alessa did not recall opening her legs, but her body knew what to do.

It understood the meaning of the pressure as he began to move slowly against her. One part of her mind flinched at the size of him, but she could feel her body's own preparations, the hot, moist core that was pulsing in anticipation.

She pressed up with her hands, letting her fingertips tease his nipples amidst the intriguingly springy hair. It was darker than the hair on his head, she noticed; then her attention was riveted by the way her touch caused his nipples to harden, just as hers were doing under the heat of his gaze.

Alessa let her hands slide down, feeling his ribs, strapped with muscle, sensing the effort with which he was controlling his breathing. She reached the waistband of his trousers. 'You can undo them now, your hands are free this time.'

'You do it. Touch me.' He bent his head to take one nipple in his mouth, sucking gently. The sensation lanced through her.

She struggled with the fastenings at the waistband, then, with those free, ventured down to the buttons of the straining placket. Distracted by Chance's tormenting attentions to first one, then the other breast, the whisper of apprehension she had felt vanished like mist on a hot day. She just wanted to touch him, to explore to… *Oh! So hot, so hard and yet the skin is so soft. So big.*

Chance gave a groan that was half-prayer, half-pain, and stood up to tug his trousers off. The sight of his naked body had been haunting her dreams ever since the beach. Now, in the half-shadows and cool dimness of the hut, he seemed both more real and strangely unfamiliar. 'Chance,' she whispered, holding out her arms to him for reassurance.

Then their bodies were twining together, skin to skin, and she looked up into his face, awed by the strength and the tenderness and the sheer heat of desire that flowed from him.

She shifted beneath him, finding the position that felt right, raising her knees as he settled between her thighs and she felt the pressure at the core of her, gentle but inexorable. She swallowed, but raised her hips a little and felt him enter her.

'Sweetheart?'

'Yes. Oh, yes, Chance, love me.' She had expected pain, but there was none, just an incredible sensation of possession, of joining, of fullness as he thrust into her. And then they were locked, she felt his hip bones against hers and drew in a deep, shuddering breath of fulfilment.

'Did I hurt you?' She realised he was not moving, although she could feel the incredible sensation of his body within her as her own muscles caressed him without conscious direction.

'No.' She shook her head. 'Should it have hurt?'

'I believe so.' He laughed softly, dipping his head to kiss her. 'All that riding and walking and physical effort had a benefit.' She tried experimentally controlling those mysterious inner muscles she had just discovered, and he broke off with a gasp. 'Witch!'

'Aren't I supposed to move?' If she tilted her pelvis just so… 'Oh!'

'We both are,' he said with a chuckle that sounded breathless. 'And I don't think I can wait any longer.'

The long, slow rhythm of thrust, withdrawal and thrust took her by surprise, then she began to move with him, tentatively at first, then using what she had learnt to tease and torment in her turn. And the wonderful sensations he had conjured up with his mouth in the cabin of the *Ghost* were building again, the same but different, more intense, more widespread, and she stopped thinking, stopped consciously trying to follow his moves and let her head thrash on the pillow as the relentless thrusting possession drove her up, over, down into a crashing release.

But it did not stop. As she regained her senses Chance was

still with her, still holding her, still surging into the very core of her. Hazily Alessa opened her eyes and saw his brow was dewed with sweat, his eyes dark with a passion that was so intense she gasped, reaching up to pull his head down so she could close her mouth with his.

Wonderfully, her body was still responding to his, the powerful, demanding ache was building again, even as his strokes became harder, less controlled, more urgent. She let go of his hair and dug her fingers into the hard muscled shoulders as though clinging to a spar in a shipwreck.

'Come with me,' he urged hoarsely against her throat, 'Alessa…now…'

And as his entire body tensed in one massive thrust she felt her own respond again, tightening around him, as the spasms carried them both into lightning-shot darkness. She heard a cry, did not know whose throat it came from, and then slipped into the velvet blackness with a sigh.

'Alessa?'

'Mmm?' She kept her eyes shut, letting all her other senses explore. There was a hot weight over her body, the touch of skin against skin, the tingling friction of male hair against her breasts, her thighs. She felt damp and sticky in embarrassingly intimate places and found she did not care. His hand was stroking her hair and her cheek and from the touch of his breath against her lips she knew, when she opened her eyes, she would be looking into his.

She smiled, anticipating the moment, and let her lids flutter up. 'Hello.'

'Hello.' There was just the hint of anxiety in the deep, masculine voice. *He is worried in case I am not satisfied*, she realised with a little shock of power. *All that wonderful masculinity, all that strength and confidence and tender skill and he is uncertain.*

'Chance. That was beyond words.' *There, the flicker of relief, of triumph, of male confidence fully restored.* 'I do love you.' *But was I all right for him?* The sudden lance of unease caught her by surprise. She had been so swept up in him, so focused on following his lead, she had not thought of how she should please him best. 'Was I…did I please you?'

'I had no idea it could be like that,' he said, levering himself up on his elbows and rolling over on to his back with a sigh of deep satisfaction. 'Because it was you, because of your love, *I* will never be the same again. There will never be another first time.' He turned his head on the pillow and smiled at her. 'But we will rediscover each other, over and over again, and it will be different and deeper and better in so many ways. Yet it will never be this first time again. I know now I am not going to break simply because I love you so intensely and you return that with all your strength and your trust and your sweetness. There is a future and it is full of loving you.'

'How did you know how I felt?' Alessa rolled on to her side and wrapped her arms around Chance's torso. 'I could not put it into words, but that is how it is for me.'

They were silent for a while, listening to each other breathe, letting their fingertips trace and explore over damp skin, into hidden curves. 'Chance,' Alessa said after a while.

'Yes? Have you any idea how soft your skin is behind your ear?'

'Chance, when we go back, until we are married, we are going to have to…to *behave,* aren't we? We must if we are going to have this big society wedding and quash all the rumours.'

'No, we are not.' He sat up, swinging his legs over the side of the bed, then standing up and stretching. Alessa watched him, wondering if she was ever going to get used to seeing his masculine beauty, so openly displayed, just for her eyes. 'We will conduct a secret affair. We will go to masked balls and slip away in a gondola, returning at midnight for the unmasking. We will hire a gondola to take us to a deserted island in the lagoon. I will climb the vines to your balcony at one in the morning. And everyone will wonder why your skin glows and your eyes shine and why I am intolerably smug.'

'That sounds wonderful. Do we have to get married at all?' she teased. 'Can't we just continue having a wildly romantic affair?'

'I think we will just have to pretend,' he said, turning with a smile to look down at her. 'I could promise to climb the ivy to your room at least once a week when we are at Freshwater—our country estate. And you can sneak out at night wearing a domino and loo mask and meet a mysterious masked stranger at masquerades when we are in London. But I really think we should get married.' He sat down and ran the palm of his hand lightly over the curve of her belly. 'It would be a good idea to start a family soon, don't you think? I wouldn't like Demetri's nose to be out of joint when he realises that he might be my ward, but he cannot inherit—and it might be if we wait until he's older.'

'You will make them your wards?' Alessa sat up, pulling him down beside her, her hand keeping his palm still pressed to her skin. In the back of her mind had been the worry about the children—surely an earl would not want to adopt Greek peasant children? But it seemed Chance was happily prepared to throw every convention to the wind for her.

'Of course. Now, my love, would you like to sleep? No? Are you hungry?' She shook her head. 'There are no books, no cards—what are we going to do to keep occupied? Go for a walk to visit the goats?'

Alessa let her brow furrow in mock-thought, playing his game. 'That sounds very tempting. But I think I should practise making love some more, don't you? There seems to be so much to learn.'

'I know,' Chance said. 'That is a worry. Perhaps we should sacrifice the walk—'

He was interrupted by a querulous bleat. They both looked round to see a nanny goat standing in the doorway, regarding them with deep disapproval. Chance bent down and hurled a stone in its general direction, hitting the doorframe. The goat bounded off with a rattle of stones and they lay for a moment listening to the retreating sound of the herd stampeding away.

'Chaperons,' Chance said with a disgusted sigh. 'You see, the sooner we get married, the better, my love—' He broke off with a gasp. 'What are you doing!'

'Exploring,' Alessa said happily. 'Darling Chance, what happens if I do this?'

And he rolled over with a growl and showed her.

THE STEEPWOOD

Scandals

Regency drama, intrigue, mischief...
and marriage

VOLUME SIX

The Guardian's Dilemma by Gail Whitiker

In order to save his young stepsister from a fortune-hunter, Oliver Brandon places her in a ladies' academy. However, he realises that the schoolmistress may not be as respectable as she appears...

Lord Exmouth's Intentions by Anne Ashley

Vicar's daughter Robina Perceval has relished her season in Town, but what of Daniel, Lord Exmouth? A widower, with two daughters to raise, it would appear that he's in search of a wife.

On sale 6th April 2007

Available at WHSmith, Tesco, ASDA,
and all good bookshops

A young woman disappears.
A husband is suspected of murder.
Stirring times for all the neighbourhood in

THE STEEPWOOD
Scandals

Volume 5 – March 2007
Counterfeit Earl by Anne Herries
The Captain's Return by Elizabeth Bailey

Volume 6 – April 2007
The Guardian's Dilemma by Gail Whitiker
Lord Exmouth's Intentions by Anne Ashley

Volume 7 – May 2007
Mr Rushford's Honour by Meg Alexander
An Unlikely Suitor by Nicola Cornick

Volume 8 – June 2007
An Inescapable Match by Sylvia Andrew
The Missing Marchioness by Paula Marshall

Victorian London is brought to vibrant life in this mesmeric new novel!

London, 1876

All her life, Olivia Moreland has denied her clairvoyant abilities, working instead to disprove the mediums that flock to London. But when Stephen, Lord St Leger, requests her help in investigating an alleged psychic, she can't ignore the ominous presence she feels within the walls of his ancient estate. Nor can she ignore the intimate connection she feels to Stephen, as if she has somehow known him before…

Available 20th April 2007

MILLS & BOON®

Look out for next month's Super Historical Romance

HIS LORDSHIP'S DESIRE
by Joan Wolf

Napoleon's troops defeated, Wellington's Spanish campaign is over. Now a dedicated English soldier enters a very different kind of war: a battle for the woman he loves…

Alexander Devize, Earl of Standish, is summoned home to his duties. Waiting for him, he believes, is Diana Sherwood, the headstrong beauty with whom he shared one unforgettable night. But she has other intentions…

Diana is a soldier's daughter and will not be a soldier's wife! Alex's wild and reckless passion may haunt her dreams – still, she's determined to find herself a proper, steady gentleman. But she's reckoned without Alex's readiness to risk all in a fight he will not lose!

"The always-awesome Joan Wolf proves she is a master in any format or genre."
— *Romantic Times BOOKreviews*

On sale 4th May 2007

2 FREE

BOOKS AND A SURPRISE GIFT!

We would like to take this opportunity to thank you for reading this Mills & Boon® book by offering you the chance to take TWO more specially selected titles from the Historical Romance™ series absolutely FREE! We're also making this offer to introduce you to the benefits of the Mills & Boon® Reader Service™—

- ★ **FREE home delivery**
- ★ **FREE gifts and competitions**
- ★ **FREE monthly Newsletter**
- ★ **Exclusive Reader Service offers**
- ★ **Books available before they're in the shops**

Accepting these FREE books and gift places you under no obligation to buy, you may cancel at any time, even after receiving your free shipment. Simply complete your details below and return the entire page to the address below. You don't even need a stamp!

YES! Please send me 2 free Historical Romance books and a surprise gift. I understand that unless you hear from me, I will receive 4 superb new titles every month for just £3.69 each, postage and packing free. I am under no obligation to purchase any books and may cancel my subscription at any time. The free books and gift will be mine to keep in any case.

H7ZED

Ms/Mrs/Miss/Mr ....Initials ....
BLOCK CAPITALS PLEASE

Surname ....

Address ....

....

....Postcode...................

Send this whole page to:
UK: FREEPOST CN81, Croydon, CR9 3WZ